Black And Blue
(Lord & Lady Hetheridge, Book #4)

By

Emma Jameson

Once again, this book is dedicated to the fans of Lord & Lady Hetheridge. You'll never know how truly grateful I am.

# CHAPTER 1

Once upon a time, Anthony Hetheridge, ninth baron of Wellegrave and chief superintendent for New Scotland Yard, enjoyed a neat, orderly life. Awakening before dawn most days, he ate breakfast with his subordinates, spent lunch poring over his open cases, and remained on the job until six or seven that evening. Yet he never felt overworked, because his London home, situated in the heart of Mayfair, was an oasis of tranquility. Gracious rooms, a walled garden, a place for everything and everything in its place. His old-fashioned manservant, Harvey, always kept a hot meal waiting. After supper, he read in his study for an hour or so, then retired to bed, content to repeat the cycle the next morning. But somewhere in the vicinity of his sixtieth birthday, Tony's private life began to feel a little, well, *too* private. Tempting fate, he wished for a change. And something wonderful and terrible happened: his wish came true.

"It's not fair!" a small boy shrieked as Tony entered the kitchen, knackered from another long day at the Yard.

"I say." He caught the boy, Henry Wakefield, before he could dart past him into the night. It was only a quarter past six, but pitch dark and bitterly cold as only mid-January could be. "What's all this?"

"I'm leaving!" Henry, pudgy and short for almost nine years old, glared up at Tony, his round face scarlet with rage. "I'm going to Robbie's. His mum said I could sleep over anytime. They like me at Robbie's. They *listen* to me at Robbie's. Here, no one cares! I'll never get Kate's attention unless I kill someone."

"Is that so?" After a day spent tackling phone calls, meetings, and policy revisions—the unglamorous bulk of police work at a chief superintendent's level—Tony could have done with a real murder just then. But it was bad form to say so, at least outside the Yard. "Why don't you sit down? Put me in the picture."

"There's no point. It's hopeless!" Henry twisted in Tony's grip, wild enough to break free. Perhaps their weekly fencing sessions had begun paying dividends of strength and agility. That, or his fury was borne of true desperation, not just another boyish disappointment.

"*Henry.*" The word filled the kitchen, echoing off tiled floors, gleaming countertops, and a multitude of copper pots and pans, relics from his grandmother's day. How long had it been since a child threw a tantrum in Wellegrave House's preternaturally serene kitchen? So long Tony could practically hear bustles creak and walking sticks thud as Edwardian ghosts bestirred themselves to investigate.

Henry stopped halfway to the kitchen door. Slowly, he turned, mouth quavering, hands clenched into fists at his sides. One kind word, and he'd burst into tears.

"It's hardly fair to say I can do no good when you haven't given me a chance," Tony continued, deliberately stern. "Why don't we—"

"Terribly sorry, Lord Hetheridge." Harvey, who never ran if he could walk and never walked if he could glide, burst into the kitchen, panting as if he'd run all the way from Battersea. His face was crimson, forehead glistening. That normally immaculate uniform was splashed with reddish-brown. And his comb-over, usually shellacked in place, had reversed direction, giving the appearance of a man who'd flipped his lid.

"I fear there will be no supper tonight. The soufflé has fallen. The sauce is burnt. And the state of the chicken—" Harvey closed his eyes. "Simply shameful. Forgive me, my lord. We've had more excitement than one servant can manage."

Keeping a firm hand on Henry, Tony eyed Harvey's shirtfront. "Is that blood?"

"Yes."

"Whose?"

"Lady Hetheridge's."

"Good God. Is she quite all right?"

"Yes, my lord. But we may yet need to ring 999 for, er—" Harvey's eyes slid to Henry, and he censored himself. "Our guests."

"I'm going to Robbie's," Henry declared stoutly. He wiped his nose with his sleeve.

"No, you're not." Tony tightened his grip on the boy's shoulder. "You're coming with me. Harvey, where is my wife and our guests?"

"The parlor, sir."

"And where's Ritchie?"

"In his room, playing Legos. I don't believe he's aware of what's happening."

"Thank heaven for small favors," Tony said. "Harvey, why don't you sit down? Have a brandy. Order us all some takeaway—curry will do. Hot for me, mild for Kate and the boys. Now then, Henry." He steered the child out of the kitchen. "Let's get this sorted, shall we?"

For years, Tony had relied on Wellegrave House's stairs. A day or two off from such activity and his arthritic left knee might conclude it had been given a license to pack it in. What would fail next? An elbow? His spine? Tony's view on stiff, aching joints was simple: one who admits the existence of pain stops, and one who stops, dies. Given his status as a newlywed (a term he publicly flinched at but secretly enjoyed), Tony had no intention of stopping anytime in the next forty years. So Wellegrave House's antique lift was more or less off limits to him. But Henry, drawn to all forms of technology, loved it. He particularly enjoyed playing elevator operator, closing the brass gate, working the mechanism, pulling the gate open and announcing the floor. Tonight, however, he walked past the elevator like it didn't exist. Trudging up the stairs beside Tony, he kept his head down and his mouth set.

"Who is it?" Tony asked the boy, though from Harvey's utterance of "our guests," there could be little doubt. His new in-laws, the Wakefields. What else could cause Harvey, an aspiring stage actor before he'd swapped the footlights for domestic service, to pour so much fear and loathing into two little words?

"It's my mum. My gran, too." Henry sighed. "I thought I wanted this. I used to pray every night that Mum would get out of the hospital. I prayed to meet Gran, too. And now I have."

Tony didn't know what to say. Before Henry had come into his life, his experience with children had been virtually nonexistent. Was he meant to offer some platitude? He wasn't in the habit of coddling his subordinates. And heaven knew, his father had never coddled him. In the late Lord Hetheridge's estimation, praise, encouragement, and treats were for his prized Springer Spaniels, not his children.

*Perhaps that's why I've never owned a dog*, Tony thought. *I considered them competitors, not companions.*

A framed portrait on the landing caught his eye—a faded oil of his father enthroned *en familie* in a leather chair, whiskey in hand, favorite bitch and three pups at his feet. Arranged on the wall around it were black-and-white photographs of Hetheridges long dead: aunts and nephews, cousins and uncles, all with the same grim mouth and icy stare. Though Tony passed this landing at least twice a day, time had rendered the portraits invisible. Now, for the first time in ages, he found himself truly seeing the frozen faces that had scrutinized him since boyhood.

*I can't even name half those people. Why in bloody hell have I let them look down on me for so long?*

Henry gained the landing with obvious reluctance, stopping a few meters from the closed parlor door. It was inviting enough— oak stained dark brown with a crystal door knob, identical to every door on that floor. Henry eyed it like a condemned man might eye the gallows.

"I don't know Gran too well. But Mum?" he stammered, fighting to get the words out. "She seems ... you know. Not sick so much as ... um ...."

"Just you wait, you bloody stupid cow! You'll be sorry," a female shrieked from inside the parlor. Tony didn't recognize the voice, but Henry did.

"Mum. Stop!" He flung open the door and rushed inside.

Following, Tony slipped automatically into detective mode. As he absorbed the scene, even the parlor's basic details leapt out. Foam green wallpaper flecked with gold. Shelves packed with leather-bound books. Two brass lamps, a velvet settee, a cold fireplace with a polished fender, and a glass-fronted drinks cabinet. Usually, that cabinet was locked, but tonight it stood open, two bottles of scotch removed. One had migrated to the coffee table; the other lay smashed on the India rug.

Kate looked more tigress than baroness. Her upper lip was cut and crusted with dried blood; her wild blonde hair floated around her face like a mane. By the drinks trolley stood her elder sister, Maura Wakefield, a glass in one hand and an icepack in the other. Her hair, brassier than Kate's, was threaded with white. Deep lines cut along the sides of her mouth. Her nose was twice as red and swollen as Kate's upper lip. As the younger women faced off, their mother watched from the velvet settee. These days she styled herself as Mrs. Louise Wakefield, but her rap sheet listed her as Lolo Carter, Lolo Shumway, and Lolo Dupree. In those old mug shots, bottle-blonde Louise sported hairstyles of the rich and famous: Twiggy, Kylie, Diana, even Baby Spice, back when the Spice Girls were a recording group, not a quiz show answer. But time and hard living had turned her hair white, stacking lines four deep on her brow. For all that, she looked happy, perhaps because of the large scotch in her hand. And together the three women formed a triangle as highly charged as its counterpart off the coast of Bermuda.

*Not to mention as dangerous.* He'd known this unhappy day would come. He just hadn't reckoned on split knuckles and spilt blood.

"Mum, stop?" Maura repeated, incredulous. She gave Henry a hurt look. "Your poor old mum's just defending herself, love. Look at my face! Your precious Kate attacked me. Broke my nose. All because—"

"Kate," Tony thundered.

The parlor's acoustics weren't as impressive as the kitchen's, but the result was similar. Maura halted in mid-rant, mouth hanging open.

Color flooded into Kate's face. Her left hand curled around her right, concealing the freshly-applied plaster.

Only Louise seemed glad to see him. Drink halfway to her lips, she paused, staring at Tony with undisguised fascination. "Look at you! A peer of the realm." She sipped. "Thought you'd be taller."

"Kate." Tony adopted a determinedly civil tone. "Forgive me for intruding. I believe I caught you unawares. I see we have guests. Please introduce these ladies to me."

That dissolved Maura's paralysis. Perhaps because, according to tradition, social inferiors—"commoners"—were always introduced to lords and ladies, never the other way round, a convention she seemed to find offensive.

"Oi! If you haven't heard, Jane Austen's dead, *Lord* Hetheridge, and Charles Dickens ain't looking so hot himself," Maura said, slurring a bit. "Guy Fawkes is the horse I bet on. What's more, this is the twenty-first bleeding century, and I can introduce myself, thanks very much. I'm Maura Wakefield." Putting down the icepack and drink, she advanced with right hand out.

Henry was trembling all over. Stepping behind the boy, Tony ignored Maura's demand to shake, resting his hands on the boy's shoulders instead. Beneath the typical schoolboy layers—hooded jacket, cable knit sweater, button-down shirt—the tremors lessened. As Tony waited, he watched from the corner of his eye as Maura slowly withdrew her hand. Her mortification was of no concern to him. He wanted Henry to feel safe.

"Perhaps you should go downstairs?" he asked the boy. "Wait for dinner with Harvey? It's sure to arrive soon."

"I can't. They're arguing over me." Henry pushed his glasses up the bridge of his nose. "If I can't go to Robbie's, I'm staying here."

"Of course. In which case—" Tony looked from adult to adult "—we'll strive to keep matters civil. Perhaps even cordial. Now, Ms. Wakefield—Maura, isn't it? Forgive any rudeness a moment ago. I was simply concerned about your son. As are you, of course." Smiling, he crossed the room, took her hand in both of his, and shook it warmly.

Apparently that was the very last thing she'd expected. In surprise, she looked vulnerable, and when vulnerable, her chin trembled just the way Kate's did.

"I'm Anthony Hetheridge," he continued. "My friends call me Tony. I hope you'll do the same. It occurs to me I really ought to beg your forgiveness for eloping with your sister. It was terribly selfish of me. I do hope you'll let me make it up to you."

Maura looked starstruck. She didn't seem to want to let his

hands go. Gently freeing himself, Tony threw in a bow from the waist, the sort of thing considered overdone anywhere outside Buckingham Palace. Maura managed a tremulous smile; Kate emitted some other sort of noise. He didn't dare look in her direction.

"Marvelous," Louise cooed. Belting back the last of her Dalwhinnie, she sprang up, seemingly cured of the various afflictions—backache, knee pain, flat feet—that had prevented her from seeking gainful (legal) employment her entire life. "Kate! Introduce me. Never mind all that about Guy Fawkes and anarchy in the UK. I want it done proper."

"Tony." Kate sounded like a person under extreme duress. "This is my mum, Louise Wakefield. Mum, this is my husband, Tony."

"Title," Louise said out the side of her mouth.

"Lord Hetheridge. Baron Wellegrave."

Thus cued, Tony gave the old woman a longer, deeper bow, imagining Queen Elizabeth II in a conservative suit instead of Louise in her FUBU tracksuit and trainers.

"*Enchanté.*" Louise dropped a passable curtsey.

"Mum," Kate and Maura groaned.

"Bloody hell, I'm only human. First time I ever met a person of quality."

"I'm a baroness, if you didn't notice," Kate ground out.

"Nobody likes a braggart, Katie." Plopping back on the settee, Louise splashed more scotch into her glass. "Now that we're all acquainted, Tony, love, let me clue you in. Our Maura's been through the wringer—all the way through, mind you. No thanks to your lot at the Met, always hounding her for this and that, but no hard feelings, either. Them doctors gave her a boatload of diagnoses, too, because that's what doctors do, diagnose. So Maura went to hospital instead of prison. But she done her time and now she's out, so—"

"Out, as in a halfway house," Kate cut across her mother. "Pending conditions."

"—and it's high time poor little Henry was back in her life," Louise finished serenely. "High time he was in my life, too. I need my grandson. I have a right to him." She took a sip. "You've done right by him, Katie, but being rich isn't the same as being God. You can't bully poor Maura just because you bully everyone else. You can't expect her to slink off, tail between her legs, when her only child's happiness is at stake." She lifted her glass at Tony. "Good stuff, this! Smooth as a baby's bum."

"Bully poor Maura? What are you on about?" Kate cried. "Bullies get things. I've never had a thing from either of you, not once in the whole of my life. Practically raised myself, didn't I? Found work and paid the bills when you scarpered. Nicked food when I had to. Chatted up the landlord to keep a roof over our heads. And as for you...." Kate swung toward Maura with such fury, Tony feared he might have to physically restrain her. "*You* flushed your life down the karzi, not me. All I did was keep Henry from going into care. I've seen the system from both sides, and it's rotten. I wanted him to have stability! A good, safe home with his own blood. And *this* is the thanks I get?"

"I don't—I wish you wouldn't—" Henry faltered, beginning to tremble again.

"Look what you've done!" Maura accused Kate. "Look at my poor boy's face. Is this your game? Tell him how terrible I am? Poison him against me?"

"Of course. That's our Katie, always keeping score," Louise said. "Probably expects me to apologize for all those Christmas mornings when she didn't find her heart's desire under the tree. You held me to impossible standards, Katie. Judged me night and day. It's etched in my memory, carved in my bones. So when it comes to young Henry, I know—"

"You don't know!" Henry exploded. "This is stupid. You're all so—so—stupid!"

Before Tony could concur, albeit in slightly more diplomatic language, Kate said in a voice of dead calm, "Mum. I don't expect you to apologize because I never got what I wanted under the Christmas tree. We never *had* a Christmas tree. And if your memory's so sharp, answer me this: when is Ritchie's birthday?"

Louise blinked. "What?"

"Ritchie. My brother. Your son." Kate folded her arms across her chest. "He's in his room, playing with his Legos, thank God. Do you know he's an artist? He does things with Legos that are good enough for galleries, Mum. One of his pieces will be shown at a Legoland fair next month, which you'd know, if you ever bothered to call. You've been in this house for two hours and you haven't even asked about him. When is Ritchie's birthday, Mum?"

"This isn't about Ritchie, it's about Henry," Maura sniffed. Wiping her eyes, she tried to get down on one knee in front of her son. Perhaps because of the fraught atmosphere, perhaps because of the whiskey, she failed in that attempt, overbalancing and falling on the carpet.

Henry backed away, tears spilling down his cheeks. As Tony helped her up, she whined, "Henry! Baby! You still love me, don't you? You understand I had to go in hospital, I had to get well...."

"Tell me what day Ritchie was born," Kate continued, still locked on Louise. "Amaze us. Never mind the year, the day and month is good enough."

"Katie." Louise rose with all the dignity available to an inebriated senior citizen in designer trackies. "Never mind that art nonsense, Ritchie's a lost cause. Not because of me, because of you. You stole him from me. Bribed him and lied to him and made him forget me. But you won't do that with Henry, because you're giving Maura custody."

"I don't want—" Henry tried to interject.

"I don't take orders from you," Kate shouted at Louise.

"Henry's my son," Maura put in.

"I'm right here!" Henry cried. "Doesn't anyone care what *I* want?" Whirling, he tried to dart out of the parlor, but Tony blocked his escape.

"You have to stand your ground," he whispered in the boy's ear. "Run now, and you'll never stop."

Forcibly turning Henry to face Kate, Maura, and Louise, Tony said, "Well, ladies? It's a fair question. Do any of you care what he wants?"

Kate made a shocked sound. "How can you ask me that?"

"I would die for Henry!" Maura surged forth as if to embrace the boy.

"No!" Throwing himself against Tony, Henry sobbed noisily into his coat. Unsure how to respond, either to the gale of emotion or the death grip around his middle—it was his first time being seized by a weeping child—he decided to just carry on.

"I await your answer," he told Louise. "Do you care what he wants?"

"Kiddies don't know what they want. Or need. That's why God made adults, innit?"

"Terribly sorry, milord," Harvey announced jubilantly from the door. His uniform had been replaced, his comb-over back where it belonged. "Scotland Yard is on the line. They've rung your mobile several times, sir. Must be a satellite issue."

Tony, infamous among his younger colleagues for switching off his mobile when it suited him, nodded as if carrier failure was obviously at fault. "Who called?"

"Dispatch, milord. There's been a homicide. SCO19 has been summoned. The scene may still be hot." Harvey kept his face blank, as if he took no pleasure in casual use of Met lingo, but satisfaction radiated off him in waves. Tony knew how much his manservant enjoyed coming to the rescue.

"What's a hot scene?" Henry asked.

"One where the bloke what did it might still be loitering

about," Louise said wisely. "Bloody hell, Katie, don't you let the little bugger watch *Crimewatch*?"

"What's the address?" Tony asked Harvey.

His manservant indulged in an infinitesimal pause for effect. "Twenty-four Euston Place, milord."

Kate caught her breath. "But that's...."

"In this very neighborhood," Tony agreed. "Just down the street. Therefore, though it pains me to do so" —he smiled—"I fear I must ask our guests to leave."

"Right. We'll bugger off. But we're taking Henry with us," Maura announced. "You can't just leave him in this drafty old house while you and Kate go gallivanting."

"Madam, I shall be with him." Harvey said haughtily.

"Oh, sure, a butler. Might as well put Ritchie in charge."

"Ritchie can look after me. He looks after me just fine," Henry said, defending his chief nemesis with a fervor usually reserved for Jedi knights. "He's older than Kate."

"He's been daft every day of his life and you know it," Maura snapped. "And a butler isn't your blood. I'm your mum, and I'm taking you home."

"Maura, I swear to God—" Kate balled up her fist, crinkling the plaster across her knuckles.

"Kate, please." Hetheridge didn't meet his wife's eyes. He didn't need to; the force of her glare could have been felt from orbit. Turning to Maura and Louise, he said, "I understand your position perfectly, ladies. But a certain expression applies. I've had it said to me countless times, yet never had occasion to use it myself." Resting both hands on Henry's shoulders, he said, "Not without a warrant."

# CHAPTER 2

Detective Sergeant Kate Wakefield Hetheridge still found it difficult to omit the "Wakefield" and supply the "Hetheridge," even in the privacy of her own thoughts. Several times since returning to Scotland Yard as a married woman, she'd introduced herself to new colleagues as DS Wakefield, resulting in cleared throats and curious glances. Everyone at the Yard, including file clerks, secretaries, and janitors, seemed aware she'd been featured (briefly and coolly) in newspaper society columns. Many could quote entire paragraphs of the tabloid coverage, which had been colorful and expansive. "Beggar Bride and Geriatric Beau Baffle West End," published in a scandal rag called *Bright Star*, was now required reading for the Metropolitan Police Service, judging by how often Kate heard about it. Only in the fame and title-obsessed world of *Bright Star* could a career detective, who'd paid her own way since her teens, be called a "beggar," and a fit, handsome sixty-year-old be called "geriatric."

*He'd deny the "handsome" part*, Kate thought. That triggered an automatic flood of fondness, which she mentally squashed, incinerated, and cursed out of existence. She was furious with him, and he deserved it. So what if she accidentally introduced herself as DS Wakefield at the crime scene? Maybe she'd do it on purpose while he was in earshot.

"Kate," Tony called from the other side of the bathroom door. "They've cleared out. Walked them halfway to Green Park Tube station myself. Shall we…?"

She said nothing, perversely hoping he'd blunder again. Since their marriage, he'd occasionally muddled personas, adopting what she thought of as "Guv mode" at home, or "Tony mode" on the job. Just now, a command—"Shall we get on?"—had nearly issued from CS Hetheridge's lips. But then it fragmented into the gentler "Shall we…?" as he no doubt remembered they were still at home, and on the husband front, he was still in trouble.

Kate leaned over the basin, scowling at her reflection. Her cut lip was obvious. There was no concealing it with makeup, so she settled for extra mascara and a liberal application of powder. As for her shoulder-length blonde hair, it was hopeless. Gathering it into a ponytail, she twisted the mass into a bun. If this murder case turned into an all-nighter, the clips would eventually work free, probably at the worst possible moment. She didn't care. At least she had on one of her nicest suits, dark and sober and scarcely bloodstained. Maura and Louise had descended on Wellegrave House just as Kate arrived home, and what with all the shouting, she'd never had time to change out of her professional attire. This tailored suit from Harrods was still a prized possession, something she'd purchased soon after joining Hetheridge's team, in hopes a more conservative appearance would help her up the ladder.

*Before I leapfrogged everyone by marrying the boss….*

She knew better, of course. But *Bright Star* believed it. Her archenemy at Scotland Yard, DCI Vic Jackson, believed it. Maura, who considered herself eternally victimized and Kate a scheming pseudo-saint, believed it. No doubt Louise, the absentee mum who refused to stay absent, believed it, too.

*I expect that of them,* Kate reminded herself. *They always assume the worst. It's Tony who should know better. Who should never ask me if I care what Henry wants, especially in front of them.*

"Kate?" He rapped on the door.

She sighed. She hadn't shot the bolt, yet he still didn't enter, not without an invitation. Perhaps the people who'd reared him, all those terribly impressive sorts who stared down from portraits on the landings, would have considered that impolite, even between man and wife? In her old flat, she'd had to lock the door to keep Ritchie and Henry from bursting in, often to referee an argument while she tried to use the loo.

"Here I am, guv." She emerged from the bathroom. "All present and accounted for, sir."

Tony was prepared for the walk to 24 Euston Place, his over-coat buttoned and scarf wound around his throat. He'd also obtained Kate's newest coat, a Christmas present from him to her, which he passed over now. Full-length and cut from brilliant red wool, wearing the coat usually made her feel extravagant, glamorous. Now, as she slipped into it, she felt ridiculous, an utter fraud.

"Mum and Maura took the Tube?"

"Yes."

"I wonder you didn't put them in a black cab. Guv."

"As a matter of fact, I offered that very thing. Sergeant." His eyes twinkled. "They declined."

"I'm surprised you took no for an answer, given how madly you campaigned to get on their good side."

"My dear DS Hetheridge. If you believe Sir Duncan Godington is the only man of your acquaintance who uses charm as a weapon, you haven't been paying attention." Taking her hand, Tony examined the plaster on her injured knuckles. "Does it hurt?"

"Not as much as Maura's nose."

"No doubt."

She pulled her hand away. Black suede gloves were in her coat pockets. As she fished them out, she told herself to drop it. But even as she resolved to focus on the upcoming investigation, Kate heard herself say, "How could you ask that?"

"What? If it hurt?"

"You know what. If I cared what Henry wants."

"I only meant to redirect the discussion toward what matters most. Things seemed to be going off a cliff."

"It always does with them." Kate worked her aching hand into a glove, hoping it would prevent swelling as the night wore on. "Do you think I *don't* care what Henry wants?"

"Of course not."

"Because the worst thing about being trapped by those two wasn't getting decked. It was feeling like my husband, the person who's meant to trust me, has lumped me in with them. Like even you see me as one of them, a Wakefield to the bone."

He sighed. "That wasn't my intention. As far as how I see you —let me point out, it's not me who keeps forgetting you're called DS Hetheridge now."

Kate couldn't answer that. Instead, she pulled on the other glove, buttoned up her coat, turned up her collar and checked herself in the mirror once more. And she was fine, absolutely fine, until Tony put his arms around her. Then a hot tear slid down her cheek, burning a trail in that freshly-applied powder.

"I meant what I said about the warrant," he told her. "I'll have a word with my solicitor tomorrow. Henry wants to stay with us, he's accustomed to us, and surely the courts will see it our way."

"A judge will grant Maura access the moment she applies," Kate said bitterly. "At the very least, she'll be in this house night and day, bringing all her chaos with her. Telling Social Services a butler and someone like Ritchie can't handle child care. That you and I work round the clock, while she can devote herself twenty-four/seven."

"If I could solve this for you tonight—now—I would," Tony said.

"I know," Kate sniffed.

"There is something else, though, that we *can* solve...."

"I know, guv. Murder in Mayfair. Is it difficult, sliding from chief superintendent to husband and back again?"

"You have no idea," he said, and she couldn't tell if he was joking or not.

The night proved bracing enough to clear Kate's mind. Euston Place was, as always, quiet. The street was scrupulously clean, all wheelie-bins tucked away, trees and shrubberies manicured. Terraced houses, many erected in the mid-1800s according to their lintel stones, were mostly pale with an occasional splash of new paint; under the glare of so many security lights, those bits of green, blue, and red stood out like rouge on a corpse. Among the eaves of the detached houses, CCTV cameras stood sentry, revealing an upper crust obsession with robbery Kate found amusing. Criminals who frequented Euston Place weren't of the purse-snatching or house-breaking variety. They were international robber barons, purveyors of televised filth, and politicians, to name only a few.

"Who lives at number twenty-four?" Kate asked Tony.

"I'm ashamed to say I don't know. When I was a boy, my father knew all his neighbors. Hated most of them, but that's another story. These days, they keep their eyes on the street as I pass and I return the favor."

"At my old building, I was on nodding acquaintance with everyone. Mind you, we weren't all mates. One slag banged her doors at all hours. And this tosser played gangster rap every—oh. Look, guv!" The honorific slipped out automatically as they turned the corner. "Blue lights."

Twenty-four Euston Place was an aggressively modern, blindingly white three-story house. Fully detached and made of poured concrete, it stood alone in a treeless gravel courtyard. Such isolation put forth the unmistakable impression that no naturally-occurring thing on earth cared to rub elbows with the house, and the feeling was mutual, thank you very much. Everything about it was asymmetrical. Oddly spaced windows, unbalanced roof, and no columns or pediment, just a vast porch burdened with what appeared to be a heap of red wheels and gyros.

"Crikey. What's that meant to be?" Kate asked.

"Art, I fear," Tony said. "I suppose a shrub in a planter was all too obvious."

Like most residences, number twenty-four stood awash in halogen security lights, giving it a sort of radioactive glow. It wasn't just violently modern, but futuristic: a life support cube from some bleak tomorrow, teleported smack into the heart of Mayfair.

Affixed to number twenty-four, Kate saw a large nameplate, white with red letters, that read EAST ASIA HOUSE. It was decorated with the block-cut silhouette of an elephant, also in red.

"Good God," Tony murmured, startled. "That red heap *is* meant to be art. And I am acquainted with who lives here, slightly. Granville Hardwick. Only I've never heard his home called Twenty-Four Euston Place."

"What's it usually called?"

"The White Elephant. The neighbors were so upset when he built it, a protest group was actually formed. The REB: the Society to Reverse Euston Brutality. 'White Elephant' is the nicest thing they call this house. As for Hardwick, they say he's obsessed with self-promotion. Provocative, vainglorious."

"Whew. Around here, getting a reputation like that must take some work," Kate teased. But gently; after all, it was now her neighborhood, too. "Whatever happened inside, things seem under control." She indicated three panda cars, a yellow plastic barrier, half a dozen uniformed officers, an ambulance, and a forensics van. It was all very much business as usual, including a few gawkers who'd edged as close to the perimeter as possible: a bald man with a dog and a grandmotherly sort with two small girls. The dog's tail wagged; the small girls fidgeted. "Can't be a hot scene."

"Is that so? Check the rooftop to your left."

It took a moment for Kate's eyes to adjust from the garish white house to comparative blackness. When the roof finally swam into focus, she saw a man in a bulky Kevlar vest positioned against a chimney, rifle at ready.

"Oh."

"And behind us," Tony continued. "Atop the trattoria on Westbury."

Turning her head as unobtrusively as possible, Kate picked out two more armed SO19 officers, so well-positioned as to be almost invisible. If a suspect tried to flee East Asia House, he or she would pass directly through the officers' sights. "How did you notice them?"

"How could I not? I owe police snipers my life." He referred to that event, long before Kate came to Scotland Yard, which had sealed his reputation as ice cold under pressure. "Therefore, I tend to look for them when approaching a scene. Let's clear those civilians before we pass the barriers. Sharpshooters or no, unneeded distractions are dangerous."

Warrant card in hand, he approached the elderly woman with the girls. Withdrawing her own credentials, Kate approached the bald man with the Alsatian on a lead. Its gray muzzle lifted, tail thumping its master's leg in friendly anticipation. The man, however, narrowed his eyes. Then he pointedly turned his back on her, staring at East Asia House as if it were the most interesting thing in the world.

"Excuse me, sir. I'm DS Kate Wa—Hetheridge. Scotland Yard." Though the bald man's face remained averted, she held up the warrant card anyway. "I must ask you to go. Let the police conduct their business."

The man said nothing. The Alsatian tugged at its lead, giving Kate a happy bark as its tail wagged even harder.

"Sir. Did you hear? I'm DS Hetheridge of Scotland Yard," Kate repeated firmly. "I'm ordering you to clear off. Now."

"Hetheridge, eh?" The man gave Kate a sidelong glance. Perhaps sixty years old, he had a doughy face, trimmed mustache, and beady black eyes. "Very well. This is a public street, DS Hetheridge, and I am a British citizen. I've lived here forty years, never mind the accent," he said, imitating an Indian cadence thicker than his natural one, "so I know my rights. I pay your salary, and I'm telling you to leave me in peace."

This sort of response wasn't uncommon. According to recent UK opinion polls, the police ranked low in public esteem, just beneath sales clerks and traffic wardens.

"Sir, this is for your own safety, as well as the sake of an ongoing criminal investigation." Kate kept the warrant card up. "If you disobey my direct order, you leave me no choice but to ask a constable to remove you."

"Madam," the man replied, as certain sale clerks might address a troublesome customer. "I have four barristers and thirteen solicitors in my family. I've done nothing wrong, and I—"

"Sergeant!" Tony called. He'd already warned the grandmotherly sort off. She was walking away with small girls in tow, grumbling aloud all the while. "Must I send for a PC?"

"Should he?" Kate prompted the bald man. The dog let out another friendly bark, prompting a stern command from its master in Hindi.

"My, my. The noble Lord Hetheridge himself," the man said viciously. "Always where he shouldn't be, taking what doesn't belong to him."

"What are you on about?"

"He has a great deal to answer for," said the man, pulling his knitted scarf over his mouth and nose. "And he'll get what he deserves, in good time. Come, Mani."

Mani the Alsatian whined but obeyed her master. Watching them go, Kate committed the image of man and dog to memory. As she rejoined her husband, she asked, "Who was that?"

Tony gave him a cursory glance. "No idea whatsoever."

"Well, he knows you. And doesn't seem to like you very much."

"Is that so?" He shrugged. "Try not to take it personally. I don't. Every time I send a murderer to prison, I alienate a fresh handful of people." He led Kate toward a semi-circle of plastic barriers strung together with blue and white police tape. "These days, the only enemies that concern me are the ones inside Scotland Yard."

"What's that supposed to mean?"

"Never mind. Good evening, Constable Kincaid," he said, greeting the young man behind the barrier. Kate was once again impressed with his powers of recollection, which extended even to uniformed officers he saw two or three times a year. "Put us in the picture, will you?"

"Of course, Lord Hetheridge." Kincaid's tone and face were professional, but his unironic use of *Lord* marked him as an admirer. At the Yard, Hetheridge's inherited title was never invoked, except as a form of reverse snobbery. "The victim is the homeowner, Granville Hardwick. Unclear if the motive is theft, revenge, or a spur of the moment fight. Our efforts to secure the scene were, er, not entirely flawless. We, er, worked hard to follow procedure. I had men everywhere, neighbors kept stopping and hailing us. One tried to peek in a window, and we had to caution her. It wasn't intentional, sir, but—"

"Just say it," Tony cut across him, not unkindly.

"Half the team checked the house's basement and ground

21

floor. The other half searched upstairs. There was, er, a small wardrobe in a bedroom. And because the square footage is so large and all the lights were out, I—that is to say, *my team* and I —we, er—"

"Passed over a suspect?"

Kincaid winced. "Yes, Lord Hetheridge. I'm sorry, sir. She emerged from the wardrobe just as the techs began dusting for prints. Said the passage to Narnia failed."

"Beg pardon?"

"The, er, wardrobe, sir. It didn't take her to Narnia."

"I see. May I presume she's now in custody?"

"Yes, sir, but she's been no help. No ID on her person. Answers questions with complete rubbish. We're still working on her name."

"What about the forensic team? Still at it, I suppose?" As always, Tony sounded slightly put off by being permitted into the crime scene only after it was processed. In his youth, senior detectives had enjoyed full access, which sometimes allowed them to solve cases more quickly. Other times, they smeared irreplaceable evidence with fingers and ground subtle traces beneath heels, leading to a mistrial or acquittal in Crown Court. Nowadays, in what Kate considered a perfectly rational change of policy, the Forensic Medical Examiner went in first, assisted by a squad of CSIs. They took samples, dusted for prints, photographed key details, and digitally filmed the scene in three hundred and sixty degree slices, assembling a flawless 3-D image for future study. To Kate, it was the best possible use of technology. To Tony, it was another attempt to replace human ingenuity with a web of interlocking policies. Old-fashioned copper that he was, he valued a seasoned detective's instincts above even advanced scientific analysis.

"Tony! We're ready for you." From East Asia House's doorway, a tall man in blue overalls, gloves, and booties beckoned. It was FME Peter Garrett, his plastic-fronted hood under his arm, revealing that trademark deaths-head grin. "Go round to the forensics van and get your protective gear. You and your bride need to do this one by the book."

The van had both back doors propped open. Inside, on a folding chair, sat a tech wearing a dirty yellow vest with highly reflective patches, a copy of the *Evening Standard* in his lap.

"That's it, step right up ladies and gents, step right up," he called to Kate and Tony. "I'll take your coats, I'll take your scarves, I'll take your purse, too, blondie, and promise not to paw through it too much."

Tony gave the man a sharp look. Kate didn't like the idea of handing over her bag to anyone she didn't know; most of these techs were contract workers, not Met employees, and once in a blue moon, valuables went missing. She glanced at her husband in mute appeal.

"There's nothing for it. Peter always enforces the letter of the law when there's significant blood spatter."

"Oh, there's more than blood in there, guv. Brains, too," the tech continued in his boisterous Cockney manner. "Right slaughter in that house. Someone must've hated the poor bugger."

Tony, in the process of stepping into an overlarge, overlong pair of filmy blue overalls, gave the tech a longer, more pointed stare.

The tech laughed, showing a mouthful of crooked teeth. "No offense, guv'ner, no offense! You two are old school, eh? Hearts breaking for the dearly departed?"

"Something like that," Kate said, reluctantly handing over her purse. "So if you were allowed inside with the crew, how'd you land back out here, minding the little blue booties? Too much carnage for your delicate tum?"

"Nah, love. These are austerity measures. Used to be, we had a newbie to mind the van while us old pros worked. Now the Met's frozen our wages. Claim they're too skint to hire new blood. So a twenty-year man like myself draws van duty, babysitting the evidence baggies. But mustn't grumble," he said, passing a plastic-fronted hood to Hetheridge. "While I mind the van, I can read my paper. Have a fag. Get a nice view of how the other half lives."

"Speaking of that. I don't suppose you had a look at that bloke hanging about? Bald man with an Alsatian?" Kate asked as she put her hood on.

"I did. Didn't want to leave, that one," the tech agreed, handed Kate her own overlong, overlarge blue coveralls.

"Notice him doing summat strange? Snapping pics or recording video with his mobile, maybe?" she asked, stepping into them.

"And here I thought Scotland Yard was all loafers, and me and my mates were the genuine heroes." Another flash of those crooked teeth. "He was coming up the street when our van arrived. Playing it cool, just walkies with the mutt, right? But he didn't move on when the pandas rolled up. Loitered about, watching the house, long after that big blighter did its business. In my book, that makes him a conspirator. Probably a lookout. So how's about it, blondie? Do I make the grade?"

"Not quite. The correct way to address my colleague is Detective Sergeant, for a start," Tony said, zipping Kate's overalls up the front. "But did you say your van arrived before the first police cars?"

"Too right, guv. We're the psychic murder squad. Gonna have our own program on Sky TV." The tech sounded stroppy now; Tony's reproof must have struck home. "Naw. We were all dispatched at the same time. Our van just beat the pandas. The bloke what found Mr. Hardwick called it in as murder. From what I can gather, the unies didn't believe him and arrested him on the spot. Your prime suspect, signed, sealed, and delivered? I call that easy work, milord."

"My name," Tony said pleasantly, reaching past the tech to obtain Kate's booties, "is Chief Superintendent Anthony Hetheridge. I'd ask yours, so I could mention it to your superior officer," he said slowly, maintaining eye contact for what felt like a very long time, "but I fear I'll simply forget it. Just as I'll forget you, the moment I walk away. Carry on babysitting the evidence bags. The work suits you—so long as they're empty."

Tony turned away. Kate spared the tech a pitying glance, mouthing the word "Whoops."

"For the love of—" He shook his head, horrified. "Why didn't you give me a wink? That was *Lord Hetheridge!*"

"Was it?" Kate grinned. "Oooh, he's dead sexy. Must dash!"

Falling into stride with Tony, she said, "Not sure if I buy Mr. Working Class Hero's lookout angle. But don't forget, the man with the Alsatian mentioned you. If that's a coincidence, it's a big one."

"We'll look into it. Though it beggars belief, doesn't it? A scenario in which one conspirator circles the crime scene, in full view of witnesses, while the other sticks by the victim till he's arrested?"

"Fair point. Now tell me, do you plan on getting angry every time some tosser calls me blondie?"

Tony looked surprised. "I wasn't angry. Only pulling rank. I don't believe you've ever seen me angry."

"Maybe not. I'm usually angry enough for both of us. But I've seen you displeased. I've watched that look come over your face."

"Which look?"

"You know. The one that says the peasants plowed the wrong field, or the scullions made off with the silver. That's it," she cried, delighted. "No wonder that poor tech almost soiled himself. I'm all a-shiver!"

"Tony?" Peter Garrett called from the doorway of East Asia House. "Are you two coming inside or embarking on a second honeymoon?"

"Coming," they replied in unison.

The concrete steps were stamped with more block images of elephants. On the porch, a huge GH, painted in gold, made Kate wince. She didn't belong to the cult of Mayfair, wherein the phrase "grade II listed home" represented the highest possible good, and the term "Georgian-inspired" meant the homeowner was at least, well, *trying*. Still, Kate appreciated the neighborhood's relentless symmetry, its understated grace: pediments, black-lacquered iron fences, steps inlaid with black and white tile. But this? Elephant silhouettes, an incomprehensible art installation, a gigantic gilt monogram? Kate found it all a bit repellent. So members of the Reverse Euston Brutality group must have been positively suicidal.

*Or homicidal. Confessed killer on the premises or no, we'll need to interview the entire group. Maybe Paul can handle that. He's a genius at knocking on posh doors and getting under the residents' skin.*

Tony seemed to read her thoughts. "I require a bit more assistance," he told Garrett. "Would you be so good as to have someone call the Yard? I'd like Dispatch to round up my other detective, DS Bhar."

The forensic medical examiner's face split into a familiar toothsome grin. "No need, old chap. He's inside already."

Kate blinked at Garrett. "What? The first responders called DS Bhar before they called us?"

Garrett kept his smile in place, but it began to look pained. "They did. A, er, *witness* wanted him." His emphasis on the word "witness" transformed it into something closer to *suspect*. "She's an older woman. Quite loud, quite insistent. Wouldn't take no for an answer, actually. I believe she's called Sherry … Sharon…."

"Mrs. Sharada Bhar?" Tony sounded neutral. But judging by the look in his pale blue eyes, one could be forgiven for concluding scullions had made off with the silver, the china, and perhaps even the Bentley.

"That's it, Sharada Bhar." Garrett's smile flagged. "She insisted DS Bhar be present. It seems the man they arrested for killing Mr. Hardwick is her, well, boyfriend, as it were."

## CHAPTER 3

E ast Asia House's interior was as idiosyncratic as its
future-shock exterior. In the foyer, a neon sign covered
an entire wall, spelling out WELCOME three times in
block letters. However, the first few letters of each word had
been deactivated, leaving this, over a meter tall and glowing like a
red hot poker, to confront visitors:

ME

ME

ME

*Ego, much?*

Kate used her smartphone to take a picture. The rules on
crime scene photography via mobile devices were still a bit
woolly. Taking snaps was one thing; transmitting those images in
any fashion, even to one's private cloud storage or personal hard
drive, was quite another. Attempting to enter them into evidence
after personal storage? Also potentially disastrous. Yet despite the
dedication of the Met's crime scene techs, Kate liked taking

photos for her own personal reference. It gave her an illusion of control in a system almost too vast to imagine.

"Have you met Mrs. Bhar's boyfriend?" she whispered to Tony as they followed Garrett.

"No, but I've listened to Paul grumble about him. A genuine American cowboy, to hear him tell it, called Wainwright."

"That's right. Buck Wainwright," Kate said. "Not to justify murder, but that welcome sign would put anyone off. How do you suppose an American rancher knew a London art dealer?"

The tunnel-like foyer bent twice, taking Kate, Tony, and Garrett around funhouse-style corners before depositing them into what seemed like a waiting room. There was bland furniture, an oval table, and a muted flat screen TV showing a montage of paintings and sculptures.

*It's an infomercial,* Kate realized. *Hardwick plays an infomercial about himself in his own house?*

The video seemed intended to educate guests about Hardwick's triumphs, judging by the number of times his company, Hardwick Happenings LLC, cropped up in the captions. And for every picture of modern or post-modern art—gold lamé-wrapped trees, giant anvils suspended above teacups, David Beckham rendered in Weetabix—there were several "action" shots of Hardwick himself: breaking ground before a new gallery, being interviewed on a TV chat show, sipping sake in a trendy Japanese restaurant. To Kate, he looked a bit like Andrew Lloyd Webber, with red cheeks, thin lips, and limp hair, yet lively eyes and a boyish smile. That face would have been at home in any issue of *Punch* from 1841 to 1900. Still, Hardwick's suits were youthful, his female companions were beautiful, and his forelock was frequently dyed some Day-Glo color like lime green, orange, or hot pink. Was that hair a signal to creative types? A sort of Open Sesame for the art world?

Kate snapped two more pictures, more from habit than interest. This room was pristine. No blood, no body, no signs of a struggle.

"Where's the body?" she asked Garrett.

"This way."

If the waiting room was bland, the room to follow was even blander: raw stuccoed walls and a concrete floor. Kate took it to be "industrial-chic," that soulless intersection between a debtor's prison and a South American sweatshop. Denied windows and relentlessly gray, the space offered no television, sound system, bookcase, or sofa.

"What is this?" she asked her husband.

"A gallery."

She looked again. If this was Hardwick's personal gallery, then what it held must be art. Kate saw bits of wadded toilet tissue arranged on a silver platter. An unframed canvas stapled with church jumble adverts. Brown and gold turkey feathers glued into the shape of a sombrero. And in the center, occupying pride of place, a naked female mannequin arranged in a handstand, bolted to her pedestal. Up her legs someone had spray-painted,

PLASTIC

THE OTHER WHITE MEAT

Kate thought, *I don't know much about art, but I know what I like. This looks like nothing but a lot of wank. Probably means it's priceless.*

Still, at the far end, the gallery contained one gripping, emotionally affecting piece. It was Granville Hardwick, face down in his own blood.

In death, he was smaller than in his infomercial. Dressed in khaki chinos, a blue pinstriped shirt with white cuffs and collar, and a lime green vest, he'd slipped out of one shoe as he fell, revealing a lime green sock. His hands had been pre-bagged by Garrett and the forensic techs; any DNA evidence under his nails, or defensive wounds on his fingers, was so valuable it had to be protected right away. Through the clear plastic, Kate noted no wedding band, just a gaudy pinky ring. Given his position, it was impossible to make out Hardwick's features. But despite all the blood in his hair, she noted a flash of lime green.

"Blood's congealing. Ambient temp feels like 15 or 16C," Kate said. "Did Hardwick die this afternoon?"

"Almost certainly," Garrett said. "But don't quote me in advance of the official report." Nodding at the ominous wall splatter, he asked, "What do you make of that bloodstain pattern?"

"Killed by a single, massive blow to the head."

"And there's the murder weapon." Tony indicated the hefty marble statuette which lay beside Hardwick, painted with gore.

"The bloke minding the van said Buck Wainwright's been taken into custody," Kate told Garrett. "The alarm was on standby and there's no sign of forced entry. Looks like Hardwick opened the door to Buck, and Buck killed him. What else did you want us to see?"

"Ah, but that would be telling. No doubt you've attended at least one of my lectures. Now's your opportunity to put that knowledge into action." For one who could pass as Death's body double, Peter Garrett's voice was surprisingly hearty. And his toothsome grin looked sincere—alarming, but sincere. "However, before you begin… Lady Hetheridge, forgive me for veering from the strictly professional, but it's a pleasure to make your acquaintance at last." Garrett's bony hand fastened onto hers with unexpected strength. Even through blue nitrile gloves, the touch was icy. "I do hope you enjoyed your honeymoon. How does the life of a baroness suit you?"

"V-very well," Kate stammered. Why did she always respond like an idiot? Best to get back to the job.

She moved closer to Hardwick's corpse. The smell of violent death—copper, urine, and feces—was overpowering, but she didn't flinch. At a crime scene, uniformed PCs always watched from the periphery, and heaven knew coppers liked a juicy bit of gossip. Bad enough how the rank and file derided Scotland Yard's "Toff Squad." Showing even momentary weakness would be grist for the mill, and Kate couldn't allow that.

She went back to the blood spatter. Four huge spots marred the wall, soaked into its rough, porous surface. Each spot was a dark round center surrounded by a halo of smaller points. Together, the four spots looked like a cluster of dandelions gone to seed; a bouquet, rendered in blood.

Something caught her eye on the opposite wall. Multiple craters, each over an inch deep. It took Kate a moment to realize those craters were roughly the size of a man's fist. Someone had battered the walls. But when? During the rage that had preceded the murder, or the despair that followed?

"Did you have a look at our suspect's hands?" she asked Garrett.

"I have. They'll soon be black and blue. Well done, DS Hetheridge. The first crew overlooked those marks entirely. Until I pointed them out, they assumed it was all part of the décor." Garrett gave a disapproving sniff. "But there's one more thing."

From his position beside the corpse, Tony pointed at a pool of mostly congealed blood. Two long smears emanated from it, dried and irregular. "Can these be drag marks, Peter? I think perhaps they are. Unless someone stepped in the blood. Slipped in it?"

"My theory is someone did indeed track through it," Garrett said. "I think those are shoe prints he or she took the time to rub out. I asked a technician to examine the pattern. Perhaps the shoe size can be extrapolated, if the thinnest swipes are cataloged and eliminated. If that size matches your prime suspect, I doubt Johnnie Cochran could get him off. If it doesn't, the defense will run riot."

"I agree," Tony said. "Kate, are you ready for him to turn the body?"

She nodded.

"Ah, but let's have a closer look at this first," Garrett said, lifting the murder weapon. A statuette of veined white marble affixed to a thick base, the item was half a meter tall. Kate guessed it weighed nine or ten kilograms, judging by how Garrett used both hands. As he brought it up for their inspection, an arm dropped off. Which still left plenty of limbs; as far as Kate could see, the figure possessed three additional arms, two legs, and four hooves, all in a tangle. Alone on the floor, the broken arm looked rather forlorn, clutching its miniature club daubed in red.

"Have a good look, please, before I bag it," Garrett warned.

Rising, Tony turned to Kate. "Will you take us through it?"

"Sure, guv. Our killer is right-handed. He killed Hardwick with a single blow to the back of the skull. The parietal bone, I think. Since Hardwick was about five foot seven, the angle suggests his killer was the same height or taller, and probably held the statue by the base, judging by that negative space." She indicated a clean area on the bloody statuette. "Not sure if that's a two-handed grip, which means the killer could be female, or a one-handed grip, which suggests a male."

"Anything else?"

"That PC out front said he wasn't sure if the motive was theft or revenge. The body shows no signs of overkill. Maybe it wasn't personal?"

But even as she said it, Kate's eye was drawn back to the battered wall. *Something* personal had transpired in this room.

"Prints have already been lifted," Garrett assured them as he gently bagged the statuette. "Two partials made in blood. And the techs may recover more latent prints in the usual ways—Super Glue, ninhydrin, laser luminescence. To say nothing of touch DNA."

Tony made a disbelieving sound. Kate felt much the same. Notorious for false positives, touch DNA mostly belonged to the world of defense barristers, often to conjure up reasonable doubt. By locating eight or ten skin cells, usually left by a CSI or copper in the line of duty, touch DNA could get an entire crime scene ruled contaminated—and therefore inadmissible—torpedoing an otherwise solid case. When it came to Scotland Yard in general, or prosecutors in particular, touch DNA was rarely a friend.

"Go on, have your laugh," Garrett said serenely. "I'll order the tests all the same." Now that the statuette was properly sealed in its clear evidence bag, he placed it on its base, allowing Kate to view it properly.

"Yet another piece of art I can't comprehend. What's that even meant to be?"

She expected shrugs or sarcasm. Instead, Garrett and Tony said at once, "Giambologna." Then, nearly in unison: *"Hercules Beating the Centaur Nessus."* They looked as pleased as if they'd simultaneously buzzed in the winning answer.

Kate must have looked nonplussed. Garrett said, "It's quite all right, DS Hetheridge. Back when Tony and I were at school, and Stonehenge was merely a gleam in some prehistoric Celt's eye, art was considered essential. And the ability to discuss it, the mark of a gentleman."

"Hang on. Are you telling me this poor bugger was done in by a famous work of art?"

"Not at all," Tony told her. "He's telling you Mr. Hardwick was killed by a rather tasteless reproduction of a famous work of art. An item that hardly fits the room, wouldn't you say? This space is devoted to post-modern art, probably all originals. Whereas this type of item is… well…."

"Vulgar?" Kate asked sweetly. "The sort of thing someone who doesn't belong in this neighborhood might pick? Ordered from a home shopping channel in the middle of the night?"

Tony, clearly sensing the danger, said nothing. Garrett, however, looked pleased all over again.

"Yes, precisely. This must have come from QVC or somewhere equally ghastly. Why would Hardwick possess such a thing? Whatever you think of all this" —he gestured around the gallery— "it's nothing if not consistent."

"Perhaps it was a gift?" Tony suggested. "Something the killer brought into the house?"

"Good thought," Garrett said. "Which brings us back to the question of overkill and personal malice." Gently, he rolled Hardwick over, out of the congealing blood. "It's true, the man was killed with a single blow. But look what that blow did."

Kate saw that Hardwick's skull was ruptured. As Garrett moved him, a trickle of cerebrospinal fluid leaked out, carrying bits of grey matter. But even in death, Hardwick's face retained a genial, boyish cast, the corners of his mouth tilted up in a smile. His eyelids were shut, which looked peaceful, but something round and pinkish-white stood out on his cheek. For a split second, it didn't register. Then Kate realized a slender cord extended from beneath his eyelid to the blob on his cheek. Her stomach dropped. Hardwick's eye was knocked out on its stalk.

*Don't think of it as knocked out. Think of it as dislocated. Displaced,* she coached herself, shifting her gaze to Hardwick's jaunty bowtie as she waited for the nausea to pass.

"Chief Superintendent Hetheridge! What a relief." Surging into the crime scene, Sharada Bhar, mother of DS Deepal "Paul" Bhar, made for Tony, which amounted to throwing herself at Hardwick's corpse. "Someone senior is needed. These people have made a terrible mistake."

With a growl of frustration, a uniformed PC shot after her. The man surely meant to preserve the peace, to say nothing of the evidence, but when he caught her by the shoulders, Sharada shrieked. Her cry, high-pitched as a little girl's, was probably heard in Wembley. And *that* summoned her son, already hard on the PC's heels. Darting in, Paul laid hands on the constable, spun him around, and bellowed, "Don't you touch my mum!"

*"Stop."*

Everyone froze. Even Kate, well-accustomed to her husband's commanding nature, stood rooted to the spot. For his part, Paul literally ceased in mid-grapple, still hanging on to the constable's shoulders.

The constable, equally shocked, made no attempt to free himself. Like Paul, he seemed afraid to breathe. Sharada, essentially untouched, nonetheless managed to look wounded to the core. She was dressed in her usual manner: long skirt, bright sweater, gold rings on every finger. Behind her overlarge spectacles, her equally overlarge eyes looked as hurt and pleading as a greeting card puppy's. Paul had warned Kate about that. He claimed his mother's seeming helplessness was an evolutionary adaptation, like the sweet whiff of a carnivorous plant.

As for Paul, he still wore his office attire—charcoal Prada suit, Gucci shoes, pink Ferragamo tie, and enough Acqui di Parma to announce his coming around corners. He cut a dashing figure these days, or would have, except for his tendency to put his foot in it, time and time again. Still, Kate ached for him. His comically arrested look of horror made it clear. He'd leapt to his mum's defense so instinctively, he'd never guessed his chief was on the premises, much less bearing witness.

"DS Bhar." Tony didn't sound cold. He sounded positively frigid. "Release that officer."

"Yes. Yes, of course. Sorry, mate," Paul babbled. He took his hands off the poor PC. Then, ludicrously, began patting the officer's shoulders, possibly in an attempt to restore the man's personal space. "No offense meant. I only wanted to—"

"Now get out," Tony said, cutting across him.

"Guv." Paul stopped patting the hapless PC. He looked as stricken as his mother. "I'm completely out of bounds, I know. But this is madness. They've arrested Buck. He discovered the body, stumbled upon it. Then Buck rang Mum and Mum rang me, and before we knew it—"

"Detective Sergeant Bhar. Forgive me for being unclear." Hetheridge stepped as close as the corpse between them permitted. "Speak not another word. Touch not another object. Get out *now*. And present yourself in front of my desk at oh-eight-hundred hours tomorrow."

Paul's mouth worked. Kate knew it went against his deepest nature to keep silent, even when ordered to do so. She faced a similar problem; it took an act of will for her not to leap to his defense. And not because he was right. Protocol was clear; having learned his mum and her boyfriend were at a murder scene, he should have done anything, absolutely anything, but show up at said murder scene. Much less insert himself into the investigation, manhandling a PC in the process. Such conduct was indefensible. But every instinct cried out for Kate to defend him anyway, simply because he was a mate. Loyalty was encoded in her DNA, just as verbal recklessness was encoded in his.

Paul kept silent. Kate kept silent. So far, so good. In his case, self-preservation must have finally kicked in. As for her, she had little choice—Tony was not only her guv, he was her husband. That didn't make the moment any better, or Paul's expression any easier to bear.

"Lord Hetheridge, I beg you!" Sharada would have clambered right over Hardwick's corpse if Bhar hadn't stopped her. The collision between mother and son made her look at the body—really look at it, taking in what that tabletop reproduction of *Hercules Beating the Centaur Nessus* had done.

"No." Sharada went rigid, hand to her throat. "My Buck couldn't have done this. No, no, no—"

"Sharada." Tony's use of her given name sliced through her incipient hysteria. Going to her side, he placed an arm around the trembling woman's shoulders, turning her away from the dead man. "Would you accompany me into the next room? I'd like to interview you personally. Let's get to the bottom of this, shall we?"

"Y-yes," she quavered, clinging to him. "Buck wouldn't—he couldn't.... That man's eye. His eye!"

"We'll make sense of this together, I promise," Tony said. Without looking at Kate, he ordered, "DS Hetheridge, go to the suspect. Interview him here, now, and if circumstances warrant, arrange his processing."

"Yes, guv." Kate gave Paul a sympathetic glance. *Steady on*, she mouthed, but he was already slinking away.

# CHAPTER 4

At the back of Hardwick's gallery was a door. Blindly steering Sharada through it, Tony was relieved when they entered a proper living room complete with typical amenities, including a comfortable place to sit down. After placing a constable on the door to guarantee no more disturbances, Tony escorted Sharada to the sofa. It was hideous: Barcelona-style with purple upholstery and vinyl throw pillows. The walls were worse, covered with pop art paintings of four-color blondes and advertising logos. Still, there were tissues, utterly normal tissues, and that was a start. Sharada, glassy-eyed and shaking all over, didn't seem to notice anything else.

"Here we are," he said, placing the box before her. She might go through them all before the pre-interview was done. Some men quailed at a woman's tears, but he'd learned to endure them, even analyze them, as heartlessly as an entomologist examined bugs under glass. He was utterly immune—so long as they weren't Kate's.

"I regret I can't offer you a cup of tea, Mrs. Bhar, but with any luck, this will soon be over. Now." He seated himself in the opposite chair. "Begin at the beginning. Leave nothing out."

"Buck didn't hurt that man." Sharada announced. Decades of living in London, not to mention penning several romances, had given her full command of the Queen's English, but her accent was thicker than usual. "He's not a killer. I saw his hands, but he works with them, he's very physical, he gets into squabbles and rows like any man. Those bruises don't prove—"

"Mrs. Bhar. Sharada," Tony interrupted, again capturing her attention through use of her given name. "Would you like to help Mr. Wainwright?"

"Of course!"

"Then answer my questions as completely as you can. First. Did you know Granville Hardwick?"

"No."

"Why did you come to his house tonight?"

"Buck called me."

"When?"

"Oh." Blinking, she pushed up her sleeves, checking two bare wrists. Then she looked around the room, craning her neck to peer at the ceiling. "I didn't wear a watch. I can't find a clock. I'd answer your question, Lord Hetheridge, but I seem to have misplaced my purse."

"Call me Tony. And forgive me," he said gently, not wishing to worsen her incipient hysteria. "But your bag is on your shoulder."

"What?" Removing it with some consternation, Sharada opened the oversized tote and delved within. Each item she discovered was placed on the coffee table. A wallet stuffed with Boots receipts and five pence coins. A beaded change purse, also overstuffed. An ereader. A compact. A lipstick. Keys. More keys. A tin of mints that called itself "thermonuclear-strength." Another handful of loose coins. Just as Tony feared he must pose the original question a second time, she came up with the last item in her bag, a smartphone.

"*There* you are. Phone!" she barked at the device, so loud he flinched. "Show me my call log."

The phone, apparently knowing what was good for it, obeyed. Sharada passed it over so he could see the screen.

"It says seven o'clock. That's when Buck rang me—seven-oh-two, to be precise. From his mobile."

"What did he say?"

"He didn't make much sense. He sounded dr—" She stopped. "Confused. That's it, confused. He said something bad had happened, and he needed me here at once. Gave me the address. When I asked him what was wrong, we were cut off."

"He disconnected?"

"No. Buck would never do that. He's never rude to me, never abrupt. It's only he gets a bit muddled sometimes. Probably hit the wrong button. And I am telling you," she continued, taking on the lecturing tone her son liked to imitate, "Buck wouldn't hurt a fly. Not even a wicked, despicable little fly everyone hated. Those officers were very wrong to—"

"Wicked?" Tony interrupted again. "Despicable? Are you referring to Mr. Hardwick?"

"Yes, of course."

"I thought you said you didn't know him." He handed the phone back to her.

"I hadn't been introduced to him," Sharada said, getting flustered all over again. "But I knew of him. Half of London knew of him."

"Have you visited this house before?"

"No. And I wasn't about to take the Tube at that time of day. Our station is mental, completely mental, from four to seven. Grown men fling themselves into the cars in front of little old ladies while hooligans push, shove, and trample anyone who hesitates. I took a taxi, after I checked GPS to estimate the distance. See? Open GPS!" she commanded the phone with such violence, an onlooker might have suspected Tourette's.

"Recent trips? Yes. There it is." She thrust the phone back at Tony. "I've never been in this house before. Neither has Buck, not more than once or twice. Wait," she corrected herself with an air of palpable desperation. "I mean, I've never been here and neither has Buck. Yes. That's my final answer."

"There's no need to invoke quiz show phrases," Tony said, struggling to keep his temper. "I assure you, I'm not here to trick you. I simply require the truth." He didn't care to be reminded of DS Bhar's latest blunder; better to compartmentalize that until it could be dealt with properly. But although Sharada didn't particularly resemble her son, and certainly didn't sound like him— Bhar had mastered "received pronunciation" to a *T*—all this rambling and backpedaling inevitably called her son to mind.

"I'm interested in why you called Mr. Hardwick despicable," Hetheridge continued. "That indicates strong disapproval, does it not?"

"Phone!" Fortunately, Sharada's device was protected by one of those shatterproof cases, or else her grip might have cracked the glass. "Okay, Google. Search for—"

"Sharada, please. Let's put technology aside and just talk." Carefully prying the device out of her hands, he placed it on the coffee table beside the rest of her handbag detritus. "I vow not to interrupt again, if you vow to tell me precisely what you discovered after alighting from your taxi."

Sharada stared at him. She looked trapped, or on the verge of another breakdown. Then, dabbing her eyes with a tissue, she gave a loud sniff and began—not where he'd asked, but at the beginning.

"I met Buck in a pub, which I cannot tell Deepal because he would not approve. I only wanted some dinner. But the dining room upstairs was packed, and it was Friday night, so the front was overrun with men. A huge knot of men, from the taps to the glass doors and spilling out into the street, all of them hoisting pints, arguing, wagering, roaring. I detest the way they roar in pubs. Englishmen!" She shook her head disapprovingly, then seemed to recall to whom she spoke. "No offense."

"None taken."

"It was as bad as the Tube. But I was famished, so I fought my way inside, in search of a barstool. I wouldn't have found one, except Buck stood up. One gentleman in the entire place, and him an American, if you can believe that. And do you know he insisted on ordering for me? A plate of roast beef, boiled potatoes, and ginger ale with two maraschino cherries. I'll never forget it. He's a Texan, you know. Calls me 'little lady.'" A note of pride crept into her voice. "Mind you, Buck is six foot five in his cowboy boots, so perhaps to him, I *am* little. That, or his eyesight is wanting. To myself in the mirror, I look as big and lumpy as two dogs under a blanket." She indicated her bosom and matronly curves, which included a bonus curve smack in the middle.

"He asked me what I did," Sharada continued. "He was very interested when I told him about my latest book, *A Dashing Deadly Spy*. Have you finished it yet?"

Hetheridge blinked. What promises had DS Bhar made in his name? "Er… I have so little time…."

"Oh! I sent a copy to your office. Your assistant must have mislaid it. I'll pack another with Deepal's lunch. But as I was saying. Buck told me his life would make a good story. Usually when people say that, I tell them I'm full up on good stories, thank you very much, and sort them quick. But Buck's life *was* interesting. Sagebrush and cattle. Steel guitars and cowboy lullabies. I won't say he charmed the pants off me, because Deepal wouldn't approve of that, either. Besides, I'm a lady. I never wear pants. But Buck and I have been together ever since."

"I see. And how long is that?"

She did some quick arithmetic on her fingers. "It doesn't seem possible. But only eight."

"Months?"

"Weeks. Which might not seem like a long time, Lord Hetheridge. *Tony*," Sharada said, clearly delighting in the use of his Christian name. "But at our age, we cut through the nonsense, don't we? Focus on what matters. True soul mates recognize one another almost instantly, and love creates unbreakable bonds, wouldn't you agree?"

He realized she meant his swift courtship of Kate, and their equally swift marriage. What precisely had Bhar shared? Tony cleared his throat. "You and Mr. Wainwright are engaged, then?"

"Engaged?" Sharada refilled her purse by sweeping everything on the coffee table back into its depths. "Of course not. I'm still married to Haresh, even though he's been living with that slut for fifteen years. And Buck's divorce from What's-Her-Face isn't settled. Another detail Deepal would find distressing, so I haven't told him. He's such a delicate boy. The way you reprimanded him was a bit harsh, don't you think? Even if he was technically in the wrong, I *do* hope—"

"I promised not to interrupt, but only if you told me what you witnessed when you entered this house," Tony reminded her.

Another stricken look. "I want to help you, Tony. I truly do," she said. "But I can't help remembering what Deepal always says. The thickies talk and talk. Even when they're not guilty, they talk themselves into a corner. The clever ones lawyer up."

"But we're only chatting," Tony lied. He had to; his first duty was to the murdered man in the gallery, not Sharada Bhar. "If you're unfamiliar with the house, how did you enter?"

"Buck let me in. He was all alone—well, we thought he was alone. I suppose that nutter was up in the wardrobe. The woman the constables are detaining in the kitchen. But poor Buck! When he opened the door, he looked dreadful. I know he felt terrible Mr. Art Man was dead, despite the affair with What's-Her-Face."

"I'm sorry. The affair with who?"

"What's-Her-Face. Mrs. Wainwright. Buck's wife." Sharada scowled.

"So that's what made Hardwick despicable in your view? His association with Buck's wife?"

"Soon to be *ex*-wife," she corrected. "And no, of course not, good riddance to her. It's the money Mr. Hardwick was so awful about. Unbearable, really."

At last, Tony scented the meat of the interview, as a shark scented blood in the water. Conversationally, he said, "I suppose if Buck and his wife were still married, any money she spent could be considered Buck's, too. Did she buy art, by any chance?"

"Tons! Ordered it through Mr. Hardwick's gallery and expected Buck to foot the bill," Sharada said. "When he refused, that's when the harassment started. Emails, phone calls, ambushes in pubs. Just last week, Buck and I were having a nightcap, and Mr. Hardwick turned up on pretext of having a drink—in Buck's hotel, if you can believe it. Money, money, money, I'm sick to death of it. If I'd had enough in the bank, I'd have settled the account myself, just to make that grinning, green-haired monkey disappear forever." Sharada looked slightly taken aback by her own outburst. "Er... nothing but good of the dead, naturally."

"Naturally. I must say, if I were Buck, I might have found Hardwick's appearance at my hotel a touch over the top," Hetheridge said.

"He did. He'd had a few, you know. Told Hardwick not to cross him again or there'd be blood."

"You heard Buck say that?"

"Exactly that. 'If you ask me for money one more time, make no mistake, there will be blood,'" she recounted, attempting an American accent. Only after she repeated the threat did she seem to realize what, precisely, she'd disclosed.

"Of course," she quavered, trying to backpedal, "someone who doesn't know Buck might jump to conclusions, but it was just male posturing. Chest thumping. I'll bet Mr. Art Man made enemies everywhere he went. There are probably a hundred men in London who've threatened to kill him this week."

"Quite possibly. But only one was found at the scene of Mr.

Hardwick's murder, and only one has been taken into custody."
Tony gave her a moment to absorb that, again reining in his
private sympathy. Eight weeks didn't seem like a very long time
for a romance, particularly between mature adults. But as she'd
pointed out earlier, he'd personally experienced the heady
madness of attraction, fascination, and love—not in eight weeks,
but eight days.

"So. You received a call," Tony said, taking up the thread
again. "Hired a taxi to Mayfair. Was let into East Asia House
sometime after seven pm by Buck Wainwright. The alarm wasn't
ringing, there was no sign of a struggle, and Buck seemed alone,
in a state of distress. Did he show you the body? Tell you what
happened?"

Fresh tears glistened in Sharada's eyes. Like many before her,
she'd been tripped up by habit—the habit of telling the absolute
truth. And if she'd related even half of this to the uniformed PCs,
it was no wonder Buck was in custody.

"I'm sorry. I can't tell you, Tony." Mopping her wet cheeks
with another tissue, she gave a defiant sniff. "I'm not a thickie.
This is where I lawyer up."

Soon after her declaration, Sharada Bhar was permitted to
depart, provided she present herself at New Scotland Yard the
next afternoon, solicitor at hand, for a taped interview. Yet
despite this impasse, Sharada remained stubbornly convinced she
had a right to remain near Buck Wainwright, even if she wasn't
permitted to see or speak to him. Compelling her to exit the
crime scene proved nearly as difficult as ejecting DS Bhar. In the
end, the only way Tony could avoid threatening her with arrest
was by reminding Sharada her son was surely home by now,
awaiting her safe arrival.

"You're right." She dug in her handbag, coming up with that phone again. "Missed call log! Nothing? Messages? Still nothing." She frowned at the screen. "Deepal hasn't called. Hasn't texted. And Tony, you were so stern with him. He idolizes you. I hope he hasn't done something drastic."

As far as Tony was concerned, a truly drastic action from Paul would be to experience contrition, or renounce his reckless ways, or simply arrive at work on time for a change. "I'm sure he's fine," he told Sharada, by which he meant safe in a pub, drowning his sorrows in a pint. "The sooner you're home, the sooner you can reassure yourself."

"I suppose. But will you check your mobile to see if he's called?" She gave him a wide-eyed, pleading look.

Reluctantly, Tony withdrew his phone and turned it on. Immediately he was confronted with three missed calls, all in the last hour. None were from Bhar. All came from his immediate boss, Assistant Commander Michael Deaver, who'd even taken the extraordinary measure of sending a text. Deaver was resoundingly, unshakably negative. Some men saw the glass half empty, but Deaver saw it half full—of hemlock. Yet even by his standards, the text message was bleak.

**It's done. Sorry.**

Tony stared at the words. He stared at them for so long, his mobile's power-saving scheme kicked in, darkening the screen. He was still staring at the black rectangle when Sharada asked, "What's wrong? Is it Deepal?"

"What? No." He forced a smile. "Go home to him, please. We'll continue our discussion tomorrow. Now I really must carry on. Excuse me."

He wandered back through the house, half-aware of what he was doing, taking in details with a dispassionate eye. In East Asia House's gallery, the scene had been properly sorted. Granville Hardwick's corpse was gone. FME Peter Garrett had departed. Even the CSIs had packed it in, leaving behind only key areas marked with yellow crime tape.

Tony's usual habit, when an unwelcome turn of events disordered his thoughts, was to painstakingly reorder them, sorting valid concerns from rubbish ones until he felt balanced again. Yet Deaver's text had done more than disorder his thoughts; it had swept them away altogether. What remained was an ominous swirl of emotions, circular as a whirlpool and leading down, down, to some place inside himself he'd never been and didn't want to discover.

*Kate.* The thought came to him like a life preserver. Almost an hour ago, he'd ordered her to interview Buck Wainwright. If Buck had proven obstructive, she might still be in East Asia House. He could ask a PC to help locate her. If Buck had been cooperative, she might be escorting him to the Yard. He could ring her mobile and—

Wait. Was he actually proposing to interrupt a crucial interview? To ring Kate in the midst of what might be a taped murder confession? All so he could moan and whinge? Bleat about his *feelings*, for heaven's sake?

*Bugger that. Those Wakefields put her back to the wall. Even after I cleared them off, she didn't ease up, not till we reached the crime scene. Work is her salvation. I can't poison that for her. I won't.*

"Chief?"

Turning, Tony found himself confronted by PC Kincaid and another young constable, this one pale and stout as a blond fireplug. "Yes?"

"DS Hetheridge accompanied the suspect to New Scotland Yard," Kincaid said. "But she asked us to keep the other witness in the kitchen till you could speak with her."

"Other witness?" Still struggling inside, Tony spoke without thinking, and immediately regretted it. PC Kincaid looked taken aback, as though he'd witnessed an embarrassing mental lapse.

*The old lion opens his mouth to roar, revealing toothless gums.* That black inner whirlpool threatened again, ready to swallow him whole, even as the shorter, stouter PC piped up.

"He means Mrs. Tumnus. The lady in the wardrobe looking for Narnia."

"I see. Thank you. And you are...?"

The blond fireplug tried to exchange glances with PC Kincaid, who chose that moment to examine the floor. He cleared his throat. "Sorry, sir. PC Fannon, sir."

"Very good. Tell me, Constable Fannon, what is the definition of a vulnerable witness?"

"Er. Yes, sir. Definition of a vulnerable witness, sir," Fannon stalled. "Er... below the age of eighteen. Or physically disabled. Or mentally impaired. Sir."

"Correct. And what constitutes mental impairment?"

Fannon again looked around for assistance, but Kincaid remained in a fugue state while the other uniformed officers drifted away. "Er... low IQ? Learning disability?"

"PC Fannon, I'm disappointed. You don't sound terribly familiar with the Ministry of Justice's Vulnerable and Intimidated Witness Guide. It specifically includes persons who suffer or appear to suffer from psychiatric disorders. Now what did you tell me? That this potentially frightened, traumatized witness is married to—whom? Mr. Tumnus?"

Fannon coughed into his fist. "Sorry, sir. Took us awhile to find her ID, but her right name is Miss Georgette Sevrin, sir."

"I see. Then who is Mr. Tumnus?"

"He's... er... you know...." Fannon grew increasingly desperate as Tony waited. "Well, he's a *faun*, innit? But sir, I'm not just taking the mickey. That woman isn't off her trolley. She's putting it on, I swear she is."

It was time to show mercy. "Perhaps you're right. Let's find out, shall we? Constable Kincaid, see that we're not disturbed. Constable Fannon, take me to her."

~

PC Fannon led Tony into the room he called Granville Hardwick's kitchen. Evidence did suggest it was, indeed, a kitchen: the presence of a stainless steel refrigerator, for one thing, and a matching cooker, for another. Beyond that, Tony—who had the distinction, for good or for ill, of never having decorated a room in his life—believed he was looking at another in-home gallery, one even more provocative than the one in which Hardwick died.

It was monochrome for a start, the walls and ceiling painted burnt orange, the floors and backsplashes covered in matching orange tile. In place of normal overhead lighting, two enormous lamps blazed overhead like twin suns. Affixed to adjustable arms, they had clearly been designed for operating theaters. And the art? Black-and-white framed photographs, not so much pornographic as gynecologic, hung above food prep and dining surfaces. The pictures were so large, magnifying that most female of regions to such a degree, the effect ceased to be human.

*Is that the point?*

Not for the first time, Tony wondered about the victim's tastes, including his seemingly limitless desire to incite. Constructing a house guaranteed to alienate his neighbors, confronting his girlfriend's husband in a hotel pub, even decorating his kitchen in a manner that might put guests off their food—perhaps there was some truth to Sharada Bhar's assertion that Hardwick had plenty of enemies besides Buck?

"Sick, aren't they?" The voice was high, querulous. "Granville loved women. When he didn't hate them, I mean."

The kitchen table looked like a repurposed surgical instrument table, the steel type on four wheels. Metal stools, the kind that swiveled, were arranged around it. On one such stool sat Georgette Sevrin, turning this way and that like a six-year-old, though she must have been fifty. Her floral poplin housedress was zipped up to her chin. Her carpet slippers were stained, her wild brown hair uncombed. As she turned, enormous specs with magnifying lenses transformed her eyes into ping pong balls— very round, very white, and bouncing in all directions.

"Good evening, Miss Sevrin. I'm Chief Superintendent Anthony Hetheridge."

"How do you know my language?"

Beside him, PC Fannon made the tiniest of sounds, a sort of incipient cough.

"Just lucky, I suppose," Tony said. "May I join you?"

"Please yourself." She swiveled a half turn, jerking back as he approached. "Not there! It's occupied."

It was—by a toddler-sized baby doll he'd been on the verge of sweeping aside. As dolls went, it spoke less of idyllic childhoods and more of direct-to-TV horror movies: naked, glassy eyes, yellow hair standing straight up. A crack ran along its forehead.

"That's Ramona." Still riding the stool, Georgette lifted her legs like a little girl, the bottoms of her carpet slippers flashing by. "Question her first. She saw everything."

"Yes, well, thank you very much. Perhaps I'll get to her in a moment." Taking a different seat, Tony glanced at PC Fannon to see if the man had caught what just happened.

*If he did, he has a remarkable poker face.*

"Forgive the necessity of questioning you during this very distressing time. But as I'm sure you're well aware, Granville Hardwick is dead. Did you see what happened?"

"Told you. Ask Ramona." Seizing the doll, she plopped it onto the stainless steel tabletop. "Talk to her, don't be shy."

Another incipient cough from Fannon.

"Constable, I trust you're taking notes? I intend to revisit that Ministry of Justice guide with you when we've finished."

"Yes, sir." Frantic throat clearing and the tap of stylus on smartphone. "Getting it all down, sir."

Georgette began cooing at the doll, murmuring reassurances, stroking her stiff blonde hair. Every few moments she glanced wildly around the kitchen, eyes ping-ponging in every corner, the Coke-bottle lenses so distorting, it was impossible to gauge her sincerity.

"Do you live here, Miss Sevrin?"

She nodded.

"For how long?"

"Since the accident."

"And when was that?"

Two long, slow blinks behind those lenses. "Don't really *do* time, actually."

"A week? A month?"

"A year," she said uncertainly. "What's that, Ramona? Oh. Ramona says two years. She wasn't in the car crash. She remembers things better."

"And why do you reside here? What was your relationship to Mr. Hardwick?"

"Brother-in-law. Ex brother-in-law. On account of the divorce from my sister. Also on account of him being dead."

"It's a bit unusual, living with a former in-law, is it not?"

Those distorted eyes did their unsettling dance again. Then Georgette covered Ramona's ears and whispered, "I'm Granville's ace in the hole. His get-out-of-jail-free card with the troublesome ladies."

"What does that mean?"

"Gran had loads of women," Georgette said. "Sometimes they got clingy, wanted to sleep over, wanted to move in. That's when he brought me down for tea. An hour with me and they wanted to go home again, sharpish."

"Considering his former association with your sister, did you approve of all these women?" Tony asked. "Or of being used to chase his inconvenient dates away?"

"Oh, well, it's to be expected, I suppose. Triumph of the underdog and all that. In school, no bird looked twice at Gran. Couldn't buy a date in an all girls' school with One Direction tickets stapled to his bum. Then he grew up, discovered the art racket. Made a name for himself, made money. That brought the gold diggers out, my sister chief among them. In those days I was the third wheel."

"Younger sister?" Tony guessed.

She nodded. "When it fell apart, Gran tested his wings. Set out to discover just how far a homely little man with a lot of dosh could take it. Started dating Harrods lingerie clerks, the ones who model. Then young actresses, pretty faces with walk-on parts. Then married women, proving his worth, showing how he could even steal other men's wives if he wanted. I should have taken a page from my sister's book, washed my hands of him, but...." She looked around the kitchen again, big white eyes bouncing into every nook and cranny. "The crash. He was driving. I was the passenger. The lawyers haven't settled yet. Ramona handles counsel for me, but I can't go back to work." She laughed as if "work" was the funniest thing in the world. "I can't look after myself. I need someone to take me to the shrink on Tuesdays. I need my meals brought up. I need chocolate Hobnobs at four o'clock and a hot bath at half-eight...."

"Splendid, Miss Sevrin. It appears that with regard to certain daily rituals, you do, as it were, *do* time. Who brings those meals up to you?"

"Molly, the housekeeper. She left early because Gran was in a state. A bit shouty."

"I see. And who was he shouting at?"

"People on his mobile. His solicitor. His estate agent. Someone called Buck. And then…." Another wild look around the room. "The killer. I don't care for shouting, so I left Ramona on guard downstairs and went into my wardrobe. That's why she seen whodunit and I didn't." Georgette pushed the doll toward Tony. "Ask her."

He studied Ramona's fright-wig hair and cracked plastic skull. He wasn't overly concerned with his dignity; in pursuit of justice, he'd done stranger, not to mention less fruitful, things than interrogate a piece of plastic. And so he addressed the doll. "Who killed Granville Hardwick?"

Georgette answered for Ramona in a treacly voice meant to sound like a little girl's. "You did, guv'nor. Saw you do it."

"Indeed." Rising, Tony signaled for PC Fannon to do the same. "Thank you for your time, Miss Sevrin. Some constables will remain with you until a social worker arrives to arrange care." He jerked his head to Fannon, who followed him back into the gallery. It was out of Georgette's earshot, provided they spoke quietly.

"Chief." PC Kincaid looked eager. "What's the word?"

Tony turned to Fannon. "Proceed."

The constable consulted his notes. "Well, sir, as regards the application of the em-oh-jay's guidelines: Miss Sevrin qualifies as a vulnerable witness. Subject disclosed a history of mental illness after a car crash. Her doll Ramona may represent a fractured ego. She could have multiple personality disorder, in which case indiscriminate treatment from the police might cause further harm."

"Is that what you think?"

"It is, sir."

"Well, I think you were right the first time. She's putting it on." The constables goggled at him.

"Because—because she said you were the murderer, sir?"

"Because of red spots along the hem of her housedress and blood on the soles of her carpet slippers. Granville Hardwick's blood, unless I'm very much mistaken. Call back the CSIs, process her flawlessly, and remember this well, gentlemen," he said, looking each man in the eye. "Never give a suspect a miss simply because they behave like a nutter. She's been living here since a car accident for which Mr. Hardwick was likely responsible. Perhaps he sought to appease her by voluntarily taking on some of her care. Or it may be that someone else caused the crash, and they were suing that individual jointly, in which case her pretense of mental distress served Hardwick, too. I expect you to find out, Constable Fannon. I want to know everything about Georgette Sevrin: her former profession, any previous lawsuits, and all details about the accident."

"Yes, sir."

"Your instincts are good. But in future, open your eyes." Tony turned to Kincaid. "See that she's kept here under observation until we have the green light to formally interrogate her. Just because I'm convinced she's not a vulnerable witness doesn't mean it's wise to proceed without formal input from Social Services. It's no good grilling Miss Sevrin under the lights, so to speak, if her statements are ruled inadmissible because we failed to dot an i or cross a t."

"I'll put it in your hand by tomorrow afternoon at the latest, sir," Fannon vowed.

Tony started to agree, but then he remembered. Those emotions he'd temporarily stuffed down threatened to emerge. And if the whirlpool opened, it led nowhere but down.

"Giving it to the team is good enough," he said, grateful he could always sound calm and professional, no matter what sort of fiasco raged inside his head. "DS Hetheridge, DS Bhar, etc."

"Of course, sir."

On the way out of East Asia House, he checked his mobile. Nothing new, just Deaver's text.

**It's done. Sorry.**

Tony hit delete. He still had a few hours. It was time to get back to the Yard.

# CHAPTER 5

**B** har *gets sent home. Tony interviews Mrs. Bhar. And I get first crack at the prime suspect,* Kate thought, unable to contain a surge of jubilation. There was nothing like a murder confession to chase away a bad mood.

The PCs led her to the back parlor, where Buck Wainwright sat under uniformed guard. All four officers had chosen to remain standing, two facing Buck and two on the door. The most stone-faced among them had her baton out, ready against her palm. That one would make SO19 one day, Kate thought, or Counter Terrorism. And her aura of grim preparation didn't seem over the top.

At around fifty, Buck Wainwright wasn't a young man. Nor was he an ostentatiously fit one, in the manner of sports drink adverts. Yet he was tall, hard, and lean, with broad shoulders and an air of authentic danger. Men like Buck became strong through hard work, not workouts; they gained endurance in the world, not inside a gym. Even on the seat his guards had provided—a pouf fit for a child, forcing him to sit awkwardly, his knees almost to his chin—Buck looked like he could unfold those long limbs at any moment and come up swinging.

"Hello, Mr. Wainwright. I'm DS Kate Wa—*Hetheridge* of Scotland Yard. I work with Paul Bhar."

"Ma'am." His gray hair was shaggy, his mustache squared off in the style called a horseshoe. He wore old school jeans, copper riveted rather than designer, and battered cowboy boots inlaid with red roses. His shirt was white and open-throated, revealing a puff of chest hair the color of steel wool.

*If he bludgeoned Hardwick, he changed clothes afterward. That white shirt is pristine.*

"I've seen the body," Kate said and paused deliberately. When hoping to elicit a confession, she did her best to exude a sort of weary knowingness, as if all had been revealed, and she only needed to mop up. Leaving long, ominous pauses between each sentence often encouraged the suspect to fill in the blanks with their own guilt and paranoia. "I discussed the forensic evidence with the FME. Saw the blood spatter." Another lengthy pause. "Is there anything you'd like to tell me?"

Buck stared at her. His eyebrows, thick and steel gray, were so heavy they nearly obscured the small brown eyes underneath. "Aren't you supposed to say you're here to help me?"

Kate turned to the officers on the door. "Find us two proper chairs, will you? Ta." Taking a step closer to Buck, she said, "I am, ultimately. You called 999. Here we are. So why don't you tell me what happened?"

Buck sighed. When the officer dropped the chair in front of him with a disapproving *thwonk*, he gritted his teeth as he shifted off the pouf, unable to conceal his hands in the process. They looked like half-inflated balloons. In some places, the skin was badly abraded, a net of hardening scabs; in others, white scar tissue shone through, tough as dragon hide. These were new injuries, then, over a map of old ones.

Kate held up her own scabbed knuckles. "Look at that. We're practically twins."

The twin steel caterpillars lifted, small brown eyes boring into Kate. "Who'd you deck?"

"My sister."

"Because she hit you first?"

"Because she said the wrong thing." Kate took a seat opposite him. "I've always had a bit of a temper."

"No alcohol involved?"

"Not on my side."

"Oh. Well. I should tell you, ma'am, I'm a drinking man. Sometimes I drink too much."

Kate nodded. Seeing he expected a follow-up question, she said nothing. The silence stretched out uncomfortably for almost a minute. Then, as she'd known he would, Buck spoke of his own volition, saying far more to fill the hateful quiet than he would have in response to a question.

"I'm not happy Hardwick's dead. Not sad about it, either. He knew how to push my buttons. Strutting little bantam rooster thought the sun came up to hear him crow. When Sunny and I separated—Sunny is my wife, you understand, soon to be my ex-wife—she flew to London to visit her sister, Maisie. Maisie's an artist. Not a real one like Thomas Kinkaid. One of those phony baloney finger-paint types. Anyway, Maisie introduced Hardwick to Sunny, and don't you know, it was like red meat to a coyote. The fox chewed his way into the henhouse. Get what I mean?"

Kate nodded again. Already roosters, coyotes, foxes, and hens had figured in Buck's narrative. Did all Americans require a barnyard to tell a story? Or just Texans?

"So—Sunny wanted to split up? Fine. I was always a faithful old dog, sleeping under the porch, but she'd stopped throwing me bones. And she wanted to replace me with *him*, a little weasel with bad teeth and soft hands? Fine. But here's the kicker. She had this notion I owed her, ma'am, and owed her big. She thought until the divorce was final, she could live high on the hog in London and let old Buck foot the bill. Can you believe that?"

Again, Kate nodded rather than interrupt the flow of verbiage. A weasel, hog, and quite likely a hound dog had joined the mix.

"Sunny even used our joint credit card accounts to buy art through Hardwick," Buck continued. His tone remained calm, but his injured hands started to shake. "Ten thousand pounds' worth of junk you couldn't give away at a garage sale. Do you know how much that is in US dollars? Sunny doesn't work. She's never worked, not even in the home. We had a maid, a cook, and no kids. What did she have to worry about but keeping up with her TV shows, while I took care of the ranch and the hired help? Not to mention US Fish and Wildlife. Like the world really needs to protect the endangered Gonzales springsnail. Ma'am, you ever seen a Gonzales springsnail?"

"No."

"I have. Googled it. Worthless creature. Ever see one on my land I'll stomp it, or give it both barrels."

"So you owed Mr. Hardwick about twenty thousand dollars?" Kate watched a flush creep up Buck's neck. Murder suspects often worked to project tranquility. Usually they insisted all was sweetness and light, even with an estranged spouse or hated creditor lying dead in the next room. Buck seemed incapable of this; frustration came off him in waves. As did the stink of alcohol.

*Even if he showered and changed before ringing 999, he reeks like a drunk tank. Must've been a massive binge.*

"*He* claimed I owed him twenty thousand," Buck continued. "More, with late fees. I earned it, she spent it, and my lawyer?" He gave an incredulous laugh. "Called it an 'expensive lesson.' Says I should have closed our joint accounts the day she flew to London. Should've taken steps. Steps! Isn't that what the law and lawyers are for?"

"So you were stuck."

"That's what he said. Now where I'm from, ma'am, this sort of dispute doesn't have to clog up the legal system. Doesn't even have to end in violence. Where I'm from, when there's a misunderstanding, even over money, men can talk it over. Come to Jesus. That's what I had in mind when I decided to see Hardwick one last time. Discuss it, man to man."

"Today?"

Buck nodded.

"What time?"

"I'm not sure. I'd had a few," he muttered, gaze dropping.

"How many?"

Buck cleared his throat. "A few," he repeated, still not making eye contact.

"And how did the meeting go? The, er, 'come to Jesus?'"

"No messianic figures turned up," Buck said morosely. "Hardwick told me to pay him directly, or pay through the courts, plus legal fees. Called me a berk and a pillock. Maybe he didn't realize I've been over here long enough to know what that means. That's when I hit the wall. At least, I think I hit it. Who else could have left those marks?"

"You're not sure?"

"No, ma'am. I got what they call a blackout temper," Buck said softly. "Something flips the switch inside my head and I... I...."

He was trembling from head to toe, overcome with shame. Recognizing her moment, Kate did what she'd been trained to do: go for the throat.

"Hardwick was sleeping with your wife. Emptying your bank account. Laughing in your face." She leapt to her feet. "You reek like a distillery and look like you went ten rounds with a brick wall. But scaring Hardwick wasn't enough, was it? You finished it, didn't you? Dashed his brains out!"

"Yes," Buck whispered. "I must have."

"Right. Now we're getting to the truth. Good." Kate interjected an artificial note of compassion into her voice. Hurling that accusation at Buck, she hadn't felt angry. And now that he'd accepted responsibility, she felt no true softening. Altogether, Kate felt nothing for Buck, not even contempt. Emotions might come later, when the job was done and she had the luxury of sentiment. Now, the only feelings she cared about were his—his fear, his self-pity, and his desperation for absolution. She had to stoke those passions, keep them in play, until she placed him in front of a camera and drew out his full confession, word by golden word.

"Buck Wainwright, I'm charging you with the murder of Granville Hardwick," she said, reciting the standard right-to-silence caution. "You do not have to say anything, but it may harm your defense if you do not mention when questioned something which you later rely on in court." At this point, Kate usually took her prisoner by the arm, as being taken into literal custody often had profound psychological effect. But Buck topped her by close to a foot and outweighed her by five stone. So Kate stepped back, letting the stone-faced PC with the truncheon do the honors.

"On your feet, sunshine," Stone Face barked, sounding more like Peckham's Most Wanted than a uniformed officer of the law.

"Anything you do say may be given into evidence," Kate finished as Buck stood. He looked miserable, desperate, ready to die. But still better than Granville Hardwick, zipped into his plastic body bag. "All right, Mr. Wainwright. Let's go to the Yard, get a medic to see to your hands, and get this sorted."

Kate's impatience to interrogate Buck notwithstanding, his arrest had set a painstaking process in motion, no part of which could be expedited or omitted without jeopardizing the Crown's case.

By her estimate, it would be another hour or two before she'd have the opportunity to take him through his story again, point by point. That meant there was time for a detour. So when she left East Asia House, she walked back to Tony's place—*their* place —to look in on the boys.

To her great relief, Henry was asleep. She wasn't ready to talk to him yet. But in the morning, she owed him an explanation, perhaps even an apology. *She* knew she cared about what he wanted, that she would do anything for him, even act against her own wishes if they violated his best interests. But perhaps at not quite nine, he didn't know that or felt shaken by what he'd witnessed. Tomorrow, she'd make it right.

Ritchie, who kept highly individual hours, was still up, watching his favorite Blu-ray, *The Lego Movie*. Since receiving it as a Christmas gift, Ritchie had given the film an unswerving devotion that put Henry's *Star Wars* obsession to shame. In the morning, Ritchie watched it while eating breakfast. In the evening, he watched it again with the commentary on. Any attempt to interrupt this pattern resulted in a meltdown. Fortunately, Wellegrave House was large enough to accommodate Ritchie's viewing patterns. Back in the old flat, commandeering their lone telly for a single program, day in and day out, would have tested Kate's patience and pushed Henry to the brink.

"Did you get something to eat?" Kate asked, leaning over the sofa to hug Ritchie from behind. He accepted the embrace with his eyes still locked on the screen.

"Yes."

"What did you have?"

"Takeaway."

That was better than a Cornetto and Coke, a duo he would eat at least as often as he watched *The Lego Movie*, except Harvey wouldn't allow it.

"Sorry family dinner was scuppered," she said, mussing

Ritchie's curly brown hair until he swatted her hand away. "You know the drill. Work calls, and I have to answer. Catch the bad guys and put 'em away. I'm leaving again in a few and might not be back till after midnight."

"Okay. Where's Tony?"

Kate bit back a smile. There it was again—her brother's growing fascination with the new man in his life. Henry had fallen for Tony almost as quickly as she had. Ritchie was thornier. He didn't relate to others in the traditional sense, didn't hold what might be called normal conversations, took little interest in most people he met. But after all his tantrums and breakdowns about leaving their South London flat, he'd settled into Wellegrave House. And though he'd done so with utter indifference toward its history, antiques, and comparative splendor, he'd latched on to one feature—Tony.

"Also working. Remember, he's the chief."

"Beefeater?" After his visit to the Tower of London, Ritchie conflated all police officers, and indeed all of Scotland Yard, with the venerable yeoman warders. She suspected that in his mind, Tony spend a portion of each night guarding the White Tower and performing ceremonies to do with Queen Elizabeth's keys.

"Something like that."

"Who was shouting before?"

"Shouting?" she stalled. "I didn't hear any shouting."

"Sounded like Maura. I hate her. Manky minger."

Kate swallowed a laugh. Ritchie's animosity didn't surprise her. He'd spent most of his childhood terrified of Maura, especially when she turned up loaded or high.

"Richard Wakefield, that was a very rude thing to say about your own sister. Who taught you that?"

"Henry. I wasn't supposed to tell you. Snitches end up in ditches." Breaking contact with his beloved red and yellow bricks, he turned to her and added, "I don't want Henry to go."

Kate caught her breath. "Oh, Ritchie, baby. Henry isn't going anywhere."

"But he cried." Ritchie's breath quickened. "Cried and said he had to go. That Maura will turn up and take him away, and no one can stop her."

"I beg your pardon." To assure his full attention, Kate not only plopped down on the sofa beside him, but dared to pause the movie. "I'm not just your mouthy little sis. I'm Detective Sergeant Kate Wakefield. No one is taking anyone out of this house without my permission. And if they try, I'll force them through Traitor's Gate and lock them up in a dungeon."

Ritchie considered that. He said nothing, but his breathing slowed, and finally he touched the remote, restarting the movie. Meltdown averted.

"All right, love." She kissed his cheek, laughing as he tried to shrug away. "I'm off to right wrongs and keep the city safe." But as she turned to go, Ritchie said, "Hetheridge."

"I told you, Rich. Tony's not here. Knowing him, he'll nap behind his desk and work straight through tomorrow."

"Not Tony. You. You aren't Kate Wakefield now. You're Kate Hetheridge, aren't you?"

"Oh. So I am. Thanks for that, stinker."

"Things have to change."

It was her own phrase, words she'd repeated to him time and again, ever since she'd accepted Tony's proposal. And it had been one thing to expect Ritchie to live by those words, knowing she was in full control of said changes and would always do her best by him. But suppose Maura was actually permitted to regain parental responsibility for Henry? Suppose some ivory tower magistrate, nurturing fantasies of absolute social equality and foolish enough to believe Maura's tales of rehabilitation, ruled that Henry belonged with his so-called mum?

*I've held the family together despite all the disappearances*, Kate told herself. *I'll keep it together through reappearances, too.*

"You're right. Things do have to change. And that's for the best," she said, hoping at least one of them believed it.

~

"Wonders never cease. The cavalry's arrived," DCI Vic Jackson said in tones of mock astonishment as Kate stepped off the lift. "Who knew the poshies worked after six o'clock?"

As he frequently seemed to live at Scotland Yard, she wasn't surprised to find him casting gloom over the detectives' bullpen, his not-inconsiderable hindquarters parked on some poor bugger's desk. Never the radiantly healthy sort, Jackson, who was known for surviving on fags, office coffee, and powdered doughnuts, looked significantly worse than usual.

"Crikey, you dead or summat?" Hardened as Kate was to the man's unshaven jowls, foul breath, and dandruff-bedecked shoulders, she couldn't help but goggle. "Zombie apocalypse kick off and claim you first?"

Usually such abuse seemed to energize him. Tonight, he looked startled. "No need to get personal," he said, gaze flicking to the linoleum floor.

*If I didn't know better, I'd think I hurt his feelings.*

But the moment that came to Kate, she instantly rejected it. To have hurt feelings, one must first possess feelings, and DCI Jackson did not. He harbored no sentiment, no hopes, no dreams, no inner life whatsoever. Within his overtaxed veins, shriveled by nicotine and clogged with dietary fats, coursed no mortal blood, only sexist jokes and racist remarks.

"Why're you loitering about?" she asked. "Busted down to DI again? I hear there's an opening for a copper in Snowdonia National Park. Deep in the heart of Penrhyndeudraeth," she said, rolling those Welsh *r*'s with relish. "Mountain air! Feral goats! Perfect for a man of your talents."

"You'll see your precious Bhar there first," Jackson said, eyes flashing. "Word's already spreading about his latest cock-up. But never mind that. Your little insinuations and slights don't even register. I'm bulletproof, ain't I? Every last one of you tossers wakes up wanting to be me and cries yourself to sleep at night having failed again."

*Wow. He even* sounds *hurt,* Kate thought, mystified. At the far side of the otherwise deserted bullpen, two constables she recognized as part of Buck's escort appeared. They craned their necks in her direction, too polite to interrupt senior officers. Ordinarily she never missed a chance to escape Jackson's presence, but now her sleuth's curiosity was piqued.

"Vic." Kate moved closer. "Seriously, you sound funny. Even smell funny."

"Shove off!"

"I mean it." She forced herself to take another sniff. "You reek of... soap? And—mouthwash? Definitely mouthwash, loads of mint there, maybe a twinge of vomit." A new suspicion dawned. "Flu! Vic, if you have flu, you have to go home. And believe you me, if I catch it from you and spread it around home and end up surrounded by whinging half-dead males, so help me I'll—"

"I don't have flu. I'm fine, fit for duty, and thrilled to be here!" Jackson cried, voice breaking on the last word. "Now shove off. And mind you address me as 'sir' from here on. Respect my rank, DS Hetheridge."

Kate blinked. He almost never addressed her by name, either the old or the new. Since his last brush with dismissal, for calling a rookie detective constable "Wonder Wazzock," he'd abandoned such epithets as "Carpet Muncher Kate," sticking to safer labels like "you," "her," or "it." Even more astonishing: he was trembling all over. His eyes shone, not with fever, but....

*Tears. Good grief. Those are actual human tears.*

She froze. Talk about long day's journey into night. Tony had witnessed the Wakefields at their worst. Maura had threatened a custody battle, Bhar had disgraced himself again, and his mum's handsome Texan? Confessed murderer. All that Kate could accept. But DCI Jackson weeping?

"Oh, look! Those PCs need me," Kate babbled. "Must dash. I, er, have a confession to hear and reports to write. Scads of reports. An insane number of reports. Feel better soon," she cried over her shoulder, fleeing headlong out of the bullpen and into the stone-faced constable from Peckham.

"Sorry! What's the story?" Kate gave the PC an apologetic smile that was, unsurprisingly, not returned. "Did Wainwright request counsel while I was *en route?*"

"He did not. Spoke not a word, ma'am," the constable replied. "And now we're all shipshape and Bristol fashion. CSIs took away his clothes and shoes, swabbed his skin, did a buccal, inked ten, and wrapped him in white. I added a four-piece suit and popped him in Two."

Kate nodded. Translated from the copperish, it meant Buck's personal items had been seized and catalogued. His hands and face had been rechecked for trace evidence, and DNA had been obtained by cheek swab. Fingerprints had been taken, though "inked" was a misnomer. In Greater London, actual ink had been replaced with a digital scanner. As for "wrapped in white," that referred to the tracksuit assigned to detainees whose apparel had been soiled or seized. Once placed in remand to await trial, Buck would be permitted to dress in his own clothes. His "four-piece suit" (hand-cuffs, waist chain, leg irons, and keyhole guards) would also go away, unless he demonstrated further propensity toward violence.

"Wainwright's in Interrogation Room Two," Kate repeated. "Anything else?"

Stone Face swapped a look with the male PC.

"What?"

The male PC said, "Well, *she* turned up, but we sent her packing."

"Who's she?"

"The prisoner's girlfriend. DS Bhar's mum, ma'am." Stone Face remained stone-faced, but her eyes sparkled. "Brought two of her sisters for backup. Big ladies, both sixty if they were a day, jabbering in Hindi and English at the same time. PC Loomis here almost took a fingernail to the eye. Long, pink, and crusted with glitter."

He nodded. "Dead scary when I had to tell them to leave. Mrs. Bhar warned me there were four barristers and thirteen solicitors in her family. Said one would turn up any minute to take over the prisoner's defense."

"I explained Mr. Wainwright had waived his rights and only he could reinstate them. Members of the public couldn't assign him counsel against his will," Stone Face continued. "That's when the aunties started shouting, 'Deepal! Deepal!' Like he was a hotel clerk who could get them an upgrade."

Kate winced. Though she'd never met Bhar's aunts, Gopi and Dhanvi, she'd heard all about them. Sharada's squat, vertically-challenged sisters favored hot pink caftans, designer handbags, and towering hairstyles they considered "elongating." According to Bhar, his mum's sisters were like Sharada on steroids: pushy, prone to hyperbole, and infamous for butting in where they didn't belong.

"They cleared out, didn't they?" Kate asked.

"Only after I threatened to arrest the lot."

"I see. Well. I know I can rely on you both to keep this quiet," Kate said, trying to imitate Tony's way of tucking a threat inside an expression of confidence, "You've been the model of discretion and professionalism. Let's keep it zipped. We don't want some spendy solicitor digging up rumors and innuendo about police connections to the suspect, do we? Getting our man sprung on a technicality?"

"No, ma'am." Loomis's expression had gone from polite to faintly overawed.

"No, ma'am. You can count on us, ma'am." Stone Face practically snapped out a salute.

For a heartbeat, Kate was overjoyed. It was all about clear communication. Respect. A firm but fair hand! Then suspicion pricked her.

Turning, she found Tony standing behind her. It seemed that just before her impromptu speech, he'd exited the lift and crossed the bullpen, arriving in time to lend gravitas to her use of his management technique.

"CS Hetheridge."

"DS Hetheridge." He smiled. "May I sit in on your interrogation?"

"Of course." She waited till the constables were gone, then took him by the lapels of his bespoke Italian suit, fingers sliding beneath heavy wool. It felt good. "So tell me. How do you do it?"

"Do what?"

"Carry on like God's in his heaven and all is right with the world, despite what's happened?"

She expected him to laugh. Instead, he stiffened. "What do you mean?"

"I mean you. You're perfect." Kate was reasonably certain she'd married a human being. Yet here at the Yard, he was dauntless, unflappable, and forever in the right place at the right time. Not only indefatigable, he managed to look distinguished and charming, while her hair slipped out of its untidy bun and her stomach growled and grumbled.

"Sounds like you're hungry. We can stop by the canteen first," he said. "Pick through whatever remains."

"No thanks. The canteen's cold lasagna is fatal. A Coke and some crisps will be good enough. Sir," she added, tacking on the honorific as another uniformed officer passed through the bullpen. "Can I get you something?"

"I'm fine."

"Of course you are. Like I said—perfect, at least in your

natural habitat. You are the Yard, and the Yard is you." Kate expected the analogy to please him but instead, he seemed to go cold.

*What is it with everyone tonight?*

"Forget it. Just give me two shakes." And Kate, nearly as baffled by her husband as she was by Jackson, hurried off to find a vending machine.

# CHAPTER 6

Before Tony entered Interrogation Room Two, he stepped into the observation anteroom for a look at Buck Wainwright. It was always good to take a glance ahead of time, to judge the suspect's demeanor from afar.

In days of yore, only two-way glass had separated the detainee from note-taking detectives. That had led to a certain amount of theatrics from those awaiting interrogation: tears, impassioned oratories, even an unnerving, unblinking gaze directed toward the glass. And the sort of suspects who exhibited this latter behavior tended to share key traits. They were male, unusually tall, physically strong, with a history of violence and a concurrent history of substance abuse. As new breakthroughs in genetics arrived, the conclusion was XYY syndrome, a genetic abnormality that resulted in reckless, easily angered, mentally subnormal "supermales."

But since the nineteenth century, all who attempted to identify wrongdoers by type instead of actions had failed. Cesare Lombroso, the man who in 1911 had posited that all criminals shared a weak chin, low slanting forehead, and abnormal body hair, was soon discredited. The XYY fable had been similarly binned, which was lucky for Buck, who some criminologists would have loved to shoehorn into their "supermale" theory. He certainly looked the type, sitting upright at the table and gazing straight at the primary camera. Hardly seeming to breathe, he sat utterly still, like a man dead, a corpse unaware the end had come.

"Good evening, sir," PC Gulls chirruped from her seat by the monitors.

"Good evening, Constable." During his team's last high-profile case, PC Gulls had volunteered to cull five minutes' crucial footage from hundreds of hours of CCTV film. She'd done the job quickly, accurately, and without complaint, despite its daunting nature. Tony thought highly of her, but around the Yard, the sentiment was far from universal. Short and slight, with elfin dimples and a mop of curly brown hair, Gulls's upbeat demeanor had engendered considerable ire. Grimmer, wearier colleagues took to calling her names: PC Gullible, the Hobbitess, Bilbo Slaggins.

That last was, in Tony's view, an inexcusably lazy attempt at humor. Gulls was the furthest thing from a slag; any country that prided itself on sophisticated wit ought to do better. So he'd quietly leaned on the worst offenders, suggesting they devise a nickname capable of making *him* laugh or else desist. No one, it seemed, possessed such faith in their comedy stylings. Now PC Gulls was known only as PC Gulls.

"Anything to report?" he asked.

"No, Chief. They sat him down about a half-hour ago. He's been waiting like that ever since. Someone said he killed an art dealer. It wasn't Granville Hardwick, was it?" Gulls asked.

"It was. You've heard of him?"

"After last week, I reckon anyone who reads the *Daily Mail* has. Then again, I might be their last reader. They don't call it *Daily Fail* for nothing." She tittered. "Our killer must have stood at the head of a very long queue. You want to see?"

Tony nodded.

Turning to an auxiliary monitor, Gulls opened a search engine, typed "Granville Hardwick," and hit enter. Tony was astonished by the results. For a man who'd never impressed him one way or another, his erstwhile neighbor certainly garnered a lot of hits.

"Constable. Would you be so good as to let me drive?"

"Sure, Chief." Gulls scooted her wheeled chair aside, and Tony seated himself. After a few clicks, he was soon looking at a photo taken just three days before, at a gallery fête. It was captioned, *Granville Hardwick drums up interest in the* Tribal Rhythms *installation by shaking his maracas with Sunny Wainwright.*

To Tony, Hardwick looked like most of the male guests, except for his lime green forelock: middle-aged, middle height, expanding middle beneath a red silk cummerbund. His date, Sunny Wainwright, was an altogether different matter. She had long, straight, spun gold hair; a glowing tan that seemed to scream good health, never mind the dermatologists; full breasts, narrow waist, and legs that went all the way up. He'd seen her many times before, albeit with a different name and face, turning up repeatedly in his line of work.

*The sort of woman men kill for.*

Yet even as he felt an odd stab of pity for Sharada Bhar, he pushed the idea aside. Men killed for all sorts of reasons. Often they named a woman as the cause: an ex-lover, mother, sister, or boss. The media, and in particular novelists, loved it when the woman was sophisticated, sexy, worldly. Somehow her desirability made the story sizzle, as if the man who'd committed murder couldn't be held guilty in the face of such carnal appeal.

The other society snaps were more of the same. Mayfair's wayward art dealer clearly preferred a certain type: tall, female, and called "Mrs.," yet not Mrs. Hardwick. In photo after photo, Hardwick courted the spotlight beside the not-quite-exes of professional athletes, C-list celebrities, and entrepreneurs. There he was, attending an unveiling beside curvaceous Mrs. Barney

Leeds, whose husband was a footballer best known for punching out his coach; clinking champagne flutes with Mrs. Declan East, wife of a noted playwright and opinion columnist; posing on the red carpet next to Mrs. Jimmy Quarrels, married to a TV chef better known for tantrums than soufflés.

*If not for Buck Wainwright's arrest at the scene, the spouses of Hardwick's other lady friends would have formed quite an identity parade*, Tony thought. The man's dating proclivities made him a crime of passion waiting to happen.

"Chief, I hope you don't mind my asking, but—any chance I could sit in on the interrogation?" Gulls sounded eager. "I always get shut out of interviews unless the witness is a crying child. In that case, they come to me straight away, but only till the kiddo's sorted with a mug of hot chocolate. Then the real questions start, and I'm out on my ear."

That didn't surprise him. Gone were the interrogation rooms of his youth, where tobacco smoke hung ominously overhead, suspects were routinely threatened or cursed, and certain laws were suspended altogether. But even in an era when interviews were digitally recorded and cigarettes were *verboten*, the interrogation room remained a fraught place. Allow a sweet, smiling, optimistic officer into the mix? To many, it must have felt like madness.

"I'm open to the idea. Provided we set some ground rules first," Tony began. But as Gulls nodded eagerly, someone said from the doorway,

"Am I too late, then?"

"Almost, DS Hetheridge," he said lightly, choosing to ignore the note of annoyance in his wife's voice. She was exhausted and on edge. He'd permit her another hour's work, then pull rank and send her home. What unforgiveable selfishness had tempted him to unburden himself to her? Thank goodness his better nature had prevailed. To PC Gulls he said, "I believe two officers at the table is sufficient. But next time. That's a promise."

"No worries, sir. It's only natural you'd prefer her," Gulls said in her usual cheery tone. "Oh!" Her eyes widened. "I don't mean because you're married, sir. Ma'am. I just mean, well, because you've worked together for so long. Well, not *so* long, a few months. But you worked together the entire time you dated, and now that you're married, I should never expect to take priority over...." Mercifully, she stopped.

"I don't think we've been properly introduced," Kate said brightly. "You're Gulls, right? The one who analyzed all those hours of Hotel Nonpareil footage? I'm Wakefield, at least in my own mind, but everyone else calls me Hetheridge. Ever so pleased to shake your hand." Crossing the room, she performed the action with gusto. "Well done, that. Maybe next time we'll catch Sir Dunc in the act."

"Oh, if he puts a toe over the line, I'm your man. I mean, woman." Gulls was practically quaking with relief. "We're sure to have another crack at it. Killers like Duncan Godington don't stay quiet for long. Not that I'm *hoping* for another murder...."

"We quite understand your sentiment. Now if you don't mind, DS Hetheridge and I will begin the interrogation of Mr. Wainwright," Tony said. "Observe carefully, PC Gulls. A quiz may follow."

"Yes, sir!" Gulls burbled happily. Kate didn't roll her eyes—she'd come a long way in professional deportment since exiting Vic Jackson's team—but Tony could practically feel the energy his wife expended not to scowl, sigh, or otherwise express disdain for the junior officer's enthusiasm.

"I know you have a thing for hard luck cases," Kate began the moment they were out of earshot.

"Yes, indeed."

"I mean, Paul can be a nightmare...."

"Ah, the near-incalculable sins of Paul Bhar," he agreed archly.

"And probably some people thought I was hopeless...."

Tony managed not to smile.

" … but *she* ought to be a primary school teacher! She should be reading nursery rhymes on the CBeebies bedtime show. She's not cut out for police work," Kate finished, one hand on the door of Interrogation Room Two. "What will she do in an interview, offer the suspect tea and ask about the time his mummy made him cry?"

"Perhaps."

"But that's just—" Kate stiffened, releasing the doorknob as the light dawned. This time, Tony did not conceal his amusement.

"Certain things, like black ties and firm handshakes, never go out of style. Good cop-bad cop is as classic as they come. But I'm too, let us say, *seasoned* to make a believable good cop. The moment I'm introduced as Chief Superintendent, no suspect worth his salt will believe I'm in his corner. As for Paul, he performs better now—a sense of humor helps—but you, my love, couldn't play the good cop if your life depended on it. In most interrogations, I fear you might surge over the table and try to beat the truth out of our man."

"I would never," Kate muttered. "Too many cameras."

"Indeed. But PC Gulls, despite her yearning for truth and justice, is polite and kindly right down to the marrow. Would she ask some hardened, uncooperative detainee to unburden himself about his mum?" Tony chuckled. "Perhaps. And who knows what such an individual might reveal to an officer who seems so harmless?"

Kate studied him. Tony thought she'd argue the point, or perhaps shrug it off. Instead she looked right, looked left, seized him by his Windsor-knotted tie, and kissed him, long and hard. When she let go, he pulled her back into his arms, not caring who passed through the corridor and witnessed their embrace.

"What was that for?"

"Because you're you, and I love you. Besides, I needed a kiss, after all the hell I've been through."

"When did you start thinking of investigations as hell?"

"Not the murder. My family. Now." She jerked a thumb at the door behind her. "Would you rather go in cold or hear what he told me?"

Despite three wall-mounted video cameras, all of New Scotland Yard's interrogation rooms included a tabletop audio recorder to commit the interview to posterity. Tony had no idea if such duplication were deliberate, as in a failsafe, or accidental, as in typical bureaucratic waste. In some branches of UK government, the right hand didn't know what the left was doing; in the Met, as far as Hetheridge was concerned, the right had no notion the left existed, much less how it entertained itself in the dead of night. But he hadn't survived, even thrived, in such a complex environment by tilting at windmills. Therefore, despite multiple audio/video feeds, he switched on the tabletop recorder, reciting his name, Kate's name, the date, and all other salient details. And as was his habit, he did so as slowly as possible, drawing out the process for one reason: to test Buck Wainwright for guilt or innocence.

It was a ludicrous yardstick, one he'd never disclosed to anyone, not even Kate, lest she conclude he was losing his wits. But perhaps two-thirds of the time (according to his unscientific estimate) the test yielded fruit. An innocent detainee was impatient. Eager to make eye contact, eager for reassurance. Innocent detainees often started babbling before the first question, or gasped aloud when the charge was read. The very words "charged with murder" produced a visceral reaction in people who'd never knowingly broken the law, who prided themselves on a blameless life. To be consigned to a featureless, forbidding room and be forced to listen as Hetheridge oh-so-slowly recited the identifying data in an equally forbidding tone? It made them desperate to speak, to argue, to leap out of that institution-style plastic chair and make someone, anyone, listen.

Then there was the guilty. Killers tended toward manipulation. Some tried to seize control with a calculated facade. They smiled happily ("Observe how innocent I am.") or they smiled sadly ("I shall forgive your allegations.") or they assumed Zen-like calm, believing that to appear untroubled was the key. Still others adopted stony silence. Legs locked together and arms wrapped tight across their chests, they scowled at the floor as he made them wait, wait, wait. Perhaps they imagined an innocent man would be too furious to speak. Anger was, after all, their go-to emotion, how they responded to virtually every situation.

Last came the habitual criminals, those who committed their crimes as a way of life, either to make a profit or fulfill some deep, dark need. Many remained blank as Tony went through his routine. Sociopaths did whatever they wanted, examining their fingernails or picking at scabs. Psychopaths, prone to thinking themselves dead clever, liked to gloat. Such flashes of sly contempt had often convinced Tony of their guilt long before questioning commenced.

But Buck Wainwright was difficult to categorize; he displayed bits of all these behaviors. Sometimes he stared straight ahead. Other times he focused on Tony, gaze intense. Was it calculating? He thought so, until he uttered the word "murder" and saw a flash of shock in Buck's eyes.

"Mr. Wainwright, as you just heard, I'm Chief Superintendent Hetheridge. My intent is to help you get this sorted as soon as possible. For that to transpire, I require your complete honesty. Can you give me that?"

There it was again in Buck's eyes: shock, humiliation, misery. He looked like a cornered animal, and Tony had barely begun.

"Tell me about how you met Mr. Hardwick. Describe your relationship with him."

"Through my sister-in-law, Maisie. She lives in Shoreditch.

Specializes in stuff that makes a velvet Elvis look classy. Dumpster-dives, drags in a kajillion things Goodwill would veto, and hot-glues it together while burning a doob."

Tony pondered this as he occasionally pondered conversation in Mandarin, of which he had only stock phrases. When Oscar Wilde described England and the United States as two countries separated by a common language, he'd had no idea what was to come.

"So your sister-in-law sifts through rubbish, fetches it home, and assembles it into 'found art.'" Sensing Kate about to interject, he concluded triumphantly, "Whilst smoking marijuana."

"You got it." Buck smiled weakly. "In fact, you sound just like her. Maisie was born in San Antonio. Nowadays her fake English accent puts Madonna's to shame. Anyway, my wife and I— Sunny's her name—were having problems. We married too young, I reckon. Couldn't have kids, got frustrated trying to adopt. She had all these hobbies: salsa dancing, yoga, meatless cooking. Meatless! Can you believe that?" He shook his head. "Me, I worked. Threw myself into my daddy's ranch. Before he passed, I'd taken it from a broken down piece of desert to what it is now: one hundred thousand acres of prime real estate, with the finest herd of Black Angus cattle in the Southwest, if I do say so myself."

"Happy marriage?" Tony asked.

Buck passed a hand over his face. "Whaddya think? I already told Miss Kate here"—he nodded politely in her direction—"I'm a drinking man. Always have been. But a working man, too, and one never interfered with the other. I'm up with the sun, I honor my commitments, I pay my bills." He spoke with the bone-deep assurance of one who'd justified his behavior with those three statements for many, many years.

"I did say *complete* honesty, Mr. Wainwright."

"So I drank. It never interfered with work till Sunny left. Then things got out of hand." His gaze swept over the table as if noticing it for the first time. "No ashtray. I suppose smoking's off-limits?"

"I'm afraid so." Tony regretted those modern health and safety regulations. Nothing loosened up a nervous interrogee like sweet, soothing carcinogens.

"Figures. One day the federal government will tell me I can't smoke outdoors on my own land. What I wouldn't give to see the Marlboro man kick some politically correct butt."

"Didn't he die of cancer?" Kate asked. It was the first time she'd spoken, and already she sounded like the stereotypical bad cop going for broke. Tony expected Buck to bristle, but he didn't.

"Probably. You remind me of Sharada, Miss Kate. She found my cigarettes in a trouser pocket and dumped them in her cat box. Dared me to pick 'em out of the litter." Buck chuckled. "Maybe that's why losing Sunny hit me so hard. I'm nothing without a woman to pull me up by the short ones."

Tony held back a smile. He would have commiserated, if not for his wife's presence. Another disadvantage to spouses working together.

"Anyway. With my wife gone and the place empty," Buck continued, "I bought more land, acquired more vacation property. Shifted funds around, selling this and developing that. Rode into the mountains, cleared brush, spent my evenings at a joint called the Hitching Post. Drank more tequila than I ever have in my life. Anything to keep from hearing myself think. I was almost at peace, telling myself Sunny was off playing hooky with Maisie and sure to come home any day. Then a friend—son of a friend—had to up and tell me about Twitter." He shook his head bleakly. "You know what Twitter is, Mr. Hetheridge?"

"Sadly, yes."

"You got that right. Amazing what people do these days to entertain themselves. Phones! I don't even like to talk on a phone, and this boy spends every waking minute staring at one," Buck said. "Anyway, turns out Sunny was on Twitter. Tweeting, that's what they call it. Sharada lit into me when I called it posting. Sunny had been tweeting night and day about her 'return to romance.'" Buck's mouth tightened; his eyes went cold. "And not just lovey-dovey stuff. Not just pictures of her and Hardwick at parties, hugging and kissing. No, sir, Sunny went all the way, putting it out there for the whole world to see. She tweeted, 'I can't wait to divorce my husband's sorry ass and marry Granville, the man of my dreams.'"

*There it is,* Tony thought. *The smoking gun, as it were, in the form of a seventeen-word tweet.*

# CHAPTER 7

B ut even as that passed through his mind, he recalled Buck's look of shock at the word "murder." And although the motive fit, experience suggested the circumstances didn't. Yes, rejection, contempt, and humiliation formed a familiar unholy trinity, but it was a rare man who did in his romantic rival instead of his wife. Even someone like Buck, tall and strong, was statistically most likely to vent his rage on the hundred and ten pound woman he knew, not an unknown man who might fight back. Moreover, a successful rancher like Buck, used to delegating unpleasant tasks, was far from alone in the world. Why would he fly to London and personally beat Hardwick to death? Whether for business or pleasure, rich men who murdered their competitors almost always outsourced the kill.

*He did mention tequila. When sufficient alcohol is involved, all other factors go out the window.*

"So you were angry enough to kill someone." Kate still sounded resolutely bad-cop, despite—or perhaps because of—Wainwright's obvious warmth toward her. "Is that what brought you to London? Sunny's tweet?"

Buck looked embarrassed. "Do you remember when I said I

have a blackout temper? Well, truth is, I'm a blackout drinker, too. Not all the time. Not every day, or even every week. Up with the sun, commitments honored, bills paid, I swear to God.

"Anyway. I was doing shots at the Hitching Post when that boy took it upon himself to show me Sunny's tweet. I stormed out, went to the store, and bought myself a dad-burned smartphone after swearing I never would. Last thing I remember is going through her public account, looking at every picture, reading every word. A few hours later, I woke up on an airplane. Forty thousand feet above the Atlantic."

"You flew from the United States to England during a blackout?" Kate gaped at him.

"It's not the strangest thing tequila's ever made me do. I guess it might sound far-fetched if you don't know any drinkers, Miss Kate, but—"

"I know drinkers," she cut across him. "Go on."

Buck's gaze lingered on her hand. It had puffed a bit, the plaster across her knuckles stained with blood. "So. Even drunk, I managed to book first class. The people are snobs but the seats recline all the way back, and when your legs are as long as mine, that's worth a pretty penny. Took another four hours to touch down in Heathrow, and by then I was sober. Sober in jolly old England without a friend in the country, unless you count Sunny. Which I don't."

Kate looked sidelong at Tony. It was just a quick flick of the eyes, but enough to reveal she was verging on another outburst, or what some interrogators called "forceful redirection." He shook his head fractionally. Perhaps Buck was deliberately stalling. Or perhaps this slow, detailed buildup to the simple question "How did you meet Mr. Hardwick?" contained nuggets of information that would mean everything, later.

"Since I'd come such a long way, I decided to confront Sunny. Ask her why she never told me she'd met someone else, much less wanted a divorce," Buck continued. "I knew she was staying with Maisie, so I took a cab to Shoreditch. Spent awhile pacing in front of her building. During the flight, I thought about telling her where to go, getting up in her face, you know? But standing there in my right mind, hungover in a strange city, all I wanted to do was…." He trailed off, looking ashamed.

"Find a pub?" Tony suggested gently.

"Yeah." Buck brightened. "Makes sense, doesn't it? I was staring down the barrel of another twelve-hour flight. Best to calm my nerves. Put myself in a good mood first."

"Wait." Kate put a wealth of skepticism into that one word. "Are you telling us you saw a tweet mentioning divorce, flew into a rage, traveled all the way to England, then decided to go home without even talking to Sunny?"

"Yeah. That's what I'm saying. Sure I was furious over that tweet, but as I stood outside Maisie's building, I realized Sunny probably never guessed I'd see it. She knows how much old Buck hates phones and technology." He shrugged. "I reckon she was just happy. Happy to be moving on. So yeah, I hailed a cab and told the driver to pick a bar, nothing snooty, no rap music or kids with blue hair. He dropped me off at a corner joint called Lucky's, and it was the luckiest day of my life."

"Mrs. Bhar said she met you in a pub," Tony said.

"Yup. I gave her my seat. Bought her a ginger ale with two maraschino cherries, and she loved it. Sharada doesn't care for liquor or beer. Not even a glass of white wine. She's a real lady."

"I cannot pretend to know Mrs. Bhar well. But regarding her ladylike qualities, I'm inclined to agree," Tony said. "So be assured I mean no disrespect when I call her an unlikely choice for your, er, rebound romance. My staff did a cursory check on you, Mr. Wainwright. You and Sunny share a fortune of over twelve million dollars. It's not uncommon for a man of your means to divorce and start anew. But for you to do so with a woman like Mrs. Bhar…."

Buck's eyes narrowed. "What do you mean?"

"What do you think? She's older than my iPhone and weighs more than a postage stamp," Kate snapped. "Men in need of an ego boost don't fall for women like Sharada Bhar."

Planting his shoe firmly atop his wife's foot, Tony applied pressure until she squirmed. Buck, for his part, absorbed the statement in silence. Tony expected an angry outburst, but he smiled.

"Miss Kate, when you own some land and a few head of cattle, pretty women make themselves available. Young. Giggly. Looking to go clubbing and drink mojitos and spend money. My money." He sighed. "I tried that route, and they seemed to have fun, but I didn't. Reckon I still carried a torch for Sunny. Then that tweet laid waste to everything, burned the crops and salted the earth. So yeah, you're right, I went into Lucky's hoping for an ego boost. I gave Sharada my stool, fell under her spell, and found exactly what I was looking for." As he spoke of Sharada, Buck sat taller, sounded happier, and seemed unashamed at last.

"She listened to my story, the whole sorry mess. How Sunny and I met, built a life together, drifted apart. I showed her the tweet." He laughed. "Boy, did I get a lecture about 'unfollow' and 'block.' Then she told me about her husband, Haresh, and all the sh—stuff he pulled. Put Sunny's behavior in perspective, that's for sure. We talked and talked, and I didn't even drink that much. Saw her to her door, then hailed another cab to the nearest Holiday Inn. I was in London, so I figured, why not stay awhile? Besides, I wanted to see Sharada again. And every time we got together, whether we had dinner, went dancing, or stopped off for a couple of ginger ales, I forgot about everything but her."

"How long have you been in London, Mr. Wainwright?" Tony asked.

"I don't know. Eight or nine weeks. I manage the ranch by phone. My overseer's a good man, and my admin assistant's a genius. All I had to do was check in, tell them how my sabbatical was going. Hinted I might come back with a new bride."

Kate snorted—probably imagining Paul Bhar's reaction to his beloved mum disappearing overseas, deep in the heart of Texas—but even as Tony stepped on her foot again, Buck misunderstood that derisive noise and shifted to the matter at hand.

"All right. Fine. I didn't stay in London all this time just for Sharada. On day two, I called the credit card company to let them know I'd be running a tab overseas, and that's when I found out how much Sunny was spending. Not just on living expenses. Buying bullsh—sorry, bullcrap art through Hardwick with my money, which was the same as *giving* Hardwick my money."

"So after twenty, twenty-five years of marriage, you thought the money in your joint account belonged only to you?" Kate asked.

"I worked for it," Buck said stubbornly. "I sweated for it, I bled for it, I made it grow. All she ever did was blow it on her hobbies."

"To whom did you complain about this state of affairs?" Tony asked. "Sunny, or Mr. Hardwick?"

"Both of them. First Sunny, of course, but she wouldn't listen. Kept saying I was jealous, mean, a tightwad, you name it. So I tried to talk to Hardwick." Buck shook his head. "The first ten thousand pounds were gone. There was nothing I could do about it. I accepted that. But a week after I warned Sunny to stop, she did it again. Bought another ten thousand pounds worth of ready-made junk from that green-haired weasel. The credit card company denied my appeal. I told Hardwick I hadn't authorized it, but he didn't care. He as good as stole twenty thousand dollars from me and thought it was a big joke."

"When did you learn the credit card company denied your appeal?"

"Yesterday. No—day before. They called, I fussed and acted the fool, and then I... well...."

"Went to the pub?" Tony asked.

"Yeah. Drank a long time. Found myself on Hardwick's street,

Euston Place. Knocked on the door. He answered it himself. Big stupid grin on his face." Those steel caterpillar eyebrows converged, ominous. "I don't remember what all we said. I don't remember hitting the wall, but I saw the marks later. I've done stuff like that before."

"Then what happened?" Tony asked.

"I don't know. But I used to fantasize about hitting him. I wanted to beat his crooked teeth in. I wanted to knock him down and kick his sides and stomp on his face till there was nothing left. If Sunny picked that little weasel over me, I must be nothing, I must be the most worthless sumbitch to ever walk the face of the earth." This last was difficult to understand, as Buck's low baritone broke into harsh, panting sobs. Chains rattling, he held out his hands, redness transforming to black and blue, and cried, "Did I really kick and punch him to death over money? Money?"

Tony and Kate exchanged a look. The small hairs on the back of his neck had stood up, and she looked equally startled.

"Mr. Wainwright, this is very important," Tony said, sharply enough to cut through the man's sobs. "Do not speculate. What do you actually remember?"

"I—I remember him grinning at me. I told him it wasn't over. That I'd sue him for theft, extortion, undue influence. I told him he'd never so much as look at Sunny without remembering how I shook him down. Then I stormed out. To—to...." He broke into deeper, wrenching sobs, but Tony thought he said, "Find another bar."

There was nothing to do but let the man cry it out. *Should I fetch tissues?* Kate mouthed to Tony. He shook his head.

"Buck," he said when the weeping finally lessened. "This is very important. Before you went to confront Hardwick, which pub did you visit?"

"It was near Green Park. Yellow... something? Yellow Duke?"

"The Yellow Earl?"

"That's it."

"With whom did you speak, besides the barman?"

"I don't know. No one. Wait. There was a man out front. Had a German Shepherd." Buck wiped his eyes with his injured, cuffed hands, an operation that was painful to watch. "Woke up in my hotel room late in the afternoon. Maybe the evening—it was getting dark. There was blood on my hands. Blood on my shirt and jeans. I had the feeling I'd done something terrible, but I always feel like that after a blackout. Because I never really know till someone tells me."

"What then?" Tony asked.

"I got scared. Wondered if I took it too far with Hardwick. If I knocked his teeth out, maybe he'd sue me for assault, you know? Decided I'd best go back to his house and eat crow. Maybe even write off that twenty grand as the price of meeting Sharada."

"What about your bloodstained shirt? Your jeans?"

"I, er, didn't want any evidence, in case he did sue. Gave the maid fifty pounds and told her bleach out every drop, even if she ruined 'em in the process."

Tony sighed. "Mr. Wainwright. If those clothes had proven free of Mr. Hardwick's DNA, if the lab had determined the blood was yours and yours alone, it might have been sufficient to clear your name. You comprehend that, do you not?"

Buck closed his eyes. Fortunately, the storm of deep emotion had passed; what escaped him was only a groan.

"Keep going," Kate prompted. "You showered, put on clean clothes, arranged to have the blood evidence destroyed. What else? Place any calls, send any texts?"

"Never sent a text in my life. Never will, I guess, if I'm headed for prison. Most days, I keep the phone switched off so the durn thing won't beep or vibrate."

It was Kate's turn to groan. "Off as in, all apps shut down?"

"Off as in off, ma'am."

"Right. Lovely. So once we have Hardwick's official time of death, we can't use your mobile's GPS feature to place you, say, safely back at your hotel," she said. "Keep going. When did you arrive back at Hardwick's?"

"I'm not sure, Miss Kate. By then my head was pounding, and I was sick as a dog. I know it was full dark outside. I knocked, but no one answered. The lights were on. His car was parked out front. I tried the door. It was unlocked, so I went in and … and found him."

"What then?" Tony asked.

"Turned on my phone and called Sharada. She called Paul."

"Did you touch anything while you waited?"

"No. Well, except for Hardwick. Just his wrist, and then his throat, to see if he was really dead. Oh, and the statue-thingy lying beside him. It was bloody, so I put It down again, quick." As he spoke, he seemed to realize the full import of what he'd said. "Mr. Hetheridge, I have to ask—does your country have the death penalty?"

"We do not, Mr. Wainwright. For which you should be eternally grateful."

Buck was returned to his cell for the night. Next morning, he would appear before a magistrate, have the opportunity to retain legal counsel, and enter Her Majesty's Prison Service for remand. Given the evidence against him, not to mention his non-national status, he would be considered a flight risk, making bail unthinkable. The only real question was did the Met boast a facility safe enough to house an American millionaire without consigning him to week upon week of solitary confinement? If not—if, for example, the governors of HMP Wandsworth and HMP Pentonville declared their prisons unequal to such a task—a Category C training jail, such as HMP Brixton, might be a safer bet.

Wherever Buck found himself, he faced an uphill battle. Tony saw that clearly when he and Kate adjourned to the observation anteroom, only to be greeted by PC Gulls.

"Bloody hell, such a load of cobblers," she chirruped as they entered. "He's a gormless tosser and daft to boot! Talk about a job for Google translate. It's all horses for courses, I suppose, but I *parlez* more Farsi than whatever he was on about."

"CS Hetheridge thinks he's innocent," Kate said.

"What? I—" PC Gulls stopped and thought it over, then gave Kate a fresh smile. "Pull the other one."

"DS Hetheridge speaks the truth. Mr. Wainwright is guilty of many things, including abusing alcohol, trespassing, and interfering with a crime scene," Tony said. "I do not believe him guilty of murder."

"But he... but I...." PC Gulls glanced over the video monitors as if a surfeit of technology had cruelly misled her. "His story was vague. He had motive. He had opportunity. He even returned to the scene of the crime, and told us to expect his fingerprints on the murder weapon!"

"I never expected to hear myself say this, but I'm in your corner, Gulls. Hundred percent," Kate said.

"You heard the man. Since his arrest, he's believed he beat Hardwick to death with his bare hands," Tony said. "He didn't realize the statuette was the murder weapon."

"He was three sheets to the wind. Just because he forgot *how* he did it doesn't mean he didn't do it," Kate countered.

"He's made it to his fifth decade, or thereabouts, without a previous violent episode."

"So have you. But if *you* were hauled in spouting the same load of bollocks, I'd be forced to conclude there's a first time for everything."

Now she was just being difficult. Feeling warmth creep up his neck, Tony said, "I find it difficult to believe Sharada Bhar would consort with a man violent enough to kill. Particularly over a few thousand pounds."

"You heard him. He didn't inherit that dosh, he worked for it. Practically had every dollar named." Kate's color was rising; she looked like she had among the Wakefields, close to the breaking point. "And as far as Mrs. Bhar goes, please. If I had an espresso for every woman I've met who fell for a violent man, I'd never sleep again. Fact is, Sharada's as bad as her son, who happens to be a famous imbecile! You'll have to do better than that."

"I should *think*," Tony announced in thunderous tones, "I needn't explain myself at this point in my career. That someone would remember who I am and what I've accomplished time and again in public service."

"I just sat across a table from a man who sounded guilty as sin," Kate countered. "He admitted there will be fingerprints and touch DNA. He's cooked! So go on, guv, enlighten me. What on earth did I miss?"

"His innocence. I didn't hear it in his words. I saw it in his eyes."

"What?" Kate said.

"What?" PC Gulls said.

Kate went rigid. So did Tony. Slowly, painfully, he tore his eyes away from his wife. Yes; not only was the eager young constable still present, she'd been following their argument with rapt attention. More seasoned officers would have slipped out or feigned sudden, impenetrable deafness.

"PC Gulls. Still here, then? Right." He threw in a bit of throat clearing, which sounded desperate but allowed him to formulate his next words. "Because you were observing Mr. Wainwright via closed-circuit TV, it's quite likely the nuance I speak of may have escaped you. But early on, as I recited the formalities, he—"

"Sort of seized up when you said the word 'murder.' I did notice." PC Gulls's head bobbed. "Thought for a tick I'd cottoned on to something subtle. Then the whosits and whatsits piled up, and like DS Hetheridge said, his goose looked cooked."

"Subtle." Tony took up the adjective joyfully. "Yes. It was

subtle indeed, that sign from Mr. Wainwright. Miniscule yet compelling. Not one in a hundred young officers would have registered it. Well done. Now, if you don't mind, might Kate and I beg a moment to confer?"

"Of course." PC Gulls's eyes shone happily.

"Alone," Kate barked.

"Of course!" Beating a hasty retreat, Gulls closed the observation room door behind her.

Tony turned to Kate, regarding her coldly. She stared back, not giving an inch. This went on for what felt like a very long time. Then he started to crack, first smiling, then chuckling. Soon Kate dissolved into laughter. As she did, he pulled her close, and she didn't resist.

"Lord, I'm tired," she said. "That's the second time we've rowed tonight. Is it your new idea of fun, provoking me, or did Miss Bedtime Story really catch something I missed?"

"I think she did. But given the reception you had at home, plus a murder after hours, it's a wonder you're still on your feet, much less beavering away at the Yard. "

Kate waved a hand in dismissal. Seeing her bloodstained plaster, Tony caught that hand, bringing it to his lips. "Don't know why I said all that rot about my experience carrying the day."

"I've never heard you talk that way. You should do it more often. But I shouldn't have called Paul a famous imbecile," Kate said. "He's the best friend I've got. You won't really sack him, will you?" Before he could answer, she kissed him again, slowly, sweetly, just the way he liked it. His wife was tempestuous, there could be no doubt, but what followed the storms made each one a pleasure.

"Right. It's late. I move we go home and resume hostilities tomorrow. Do you concur, DS Hetheridge?"

"Completely, CS Hetheridge. Tomorrow it is."

# CHAPTER 8

fter his humiliating ejection from the crime scene, DS Deepal "Paul" Bhar stormed off to the Green Park Tube station, taking the usual line home but disembarking a stop early. When internal combustion reached dangerous levels, his best bet was a long, brisk, furious walk, letting his heels beat that impotent fury into the pavement.

"'Be at my office at oh-eight-hundred hours tomorrow morning,'" he muttered as he walked. It was bitterly cold. His breath plumed before him, but he was too angry to register anything but the wind. Each gust felt like a fresh slap in the face.

"C'mon, guv, sure you didn't want a bigger audience for that dress-down? Maybe engage *Bright Star* to run pictures on tomorrow's front page? And as for tomorrow, milord, where else would I be? I turn up at your office every morning at eight, right on time!"

*Unless you miss it by a quarter hour or more*, said a dissenting voice in Bhar's head. He ignored it.

"Should I have entered the crime scene without your permission? No. Fine. I accept that," he raged at a boxwood hedge. "I should be more like you, shouldn't I? Only someone with ice water in his veins and a sodden ash heap for a soul would hear of his mum *in the same room as a murder victim* and think, right-o, let's not be hasty! What's the proper procedure, old stick? Never mind if she's safe, never mind what happens to Buck. Is it done, old boy? Is it *done?*"

"Oi! Nutter!" a man shouted at Bhar from his front porch. "Keep raving, and somebody might call the cops."

"I am the cops!" Bhar bellowed, jerking his wallet from his coat and flashing his warrant card. "Careful I don't run you in."

"For what? Having a fag?" The man flicked ashes in Bhar's general direction. "Wanker!"

*Let it go. You're ranting at shrubbery. Probably his shrubbery, which appears reasonably innocent, as shrubbery goes*, that dissenting voice said.

Groaning, Bhar set his teeth, put his head down, and strode faster into the wind. Home was only three streets away. It was the house he'd shared with Sharada since early childhood, a piece of property his estranged father still owned, although Sharada paid for its upkeep. And theirs was a good neighborhood, safe enough, well-lit, dozens of CCTV cameras mounted on high. In dodgier surroundings, Bhar would have remained on alert, on guard against muggers, skinheads, or the proverbial man with a knife and nothing to lose. But so close to home, his focus swung inward, fury rising until he flung accusations at still another hedge.

"Does milord think I *enjoy* being an embarrassment? Does he imagine I pride myself on being the ginormous git who haunts Scotland Yard, destroying airtight cases with a single touch? Well, he can think what he wants, because I did what any son would do. And I will be there tomorrow at oh-eight-hundred, chin up, head high. Unwilling to grovel or beg or otherwise debase myself to atone for the allegedly unforgivable sin of—"

A harsh bark made him stop so abruptly, he stubbed his toe on the uneven sidewalk and went down. No sooner did he hit, hands and knees taking the brunt of the impact, then the dog was upon him, big and black and growling through bared teeth.

"The Grim!"

Since the previous autumn, he'd repeatedly seen a black dog he called, in a nod to one of his favorite book series, the Grim. A psychic had claimed it symbolized forthcoming change. But after Tony and Kate's marriage, after the revelation his mum was dating a mustachioed Texan, after being threatened by Sir Duncan and finding himself helpless to fight back, Bhar had expected the dark personification of his fears to vanish. What more could possibly befall him?

"Will I be sacked? Am I dying?" he babbled at the dog, still on his hands and knees.

*Get up. That brute wants to bite you, not psychoanalyze your dreams.*

His inner voice had a point. Scrambling up, Bhar tried to remember what to do when facing an aggressive dog. Should he run? No. Whatever this shaggy black beast was—part Newfoundland, part Chow, part hellhound—the race would be unwinnable. Should he try and stare it down? Wrong again. Bluffing a human was one thing. Trying to hoodwink a beast capable of smelling fear might be the last thing he ever did.

"Listen. I'm sure I look delicious. Odds are I probably am. But I've had a pitiless day and a positively catastrophic night." Using his softest, most soothing tone, Bhar focused on the dog's flattened ears. It was less terrifying than looking into those bright yellow eyes. "So if you'd consider not biting me, or tearing my throat out, or chasing me to perdition, I'd be ever so grateful."

The black dog's growl intensified. It poised to spring. Just as Bhar instinctively threw up his arm to defend his jugular, a man called,

*"Kaiser! Nein! Lass das sein!"*

The growling stopped. Rising out of its crouch, the dog whined, glancing in the male voice's direction. Then it refocused on Bhar, still hostile but less certain.

"Kaiser! *Hier! Hier!*"

With a second, more mournful whine, the dog turned and bounded away, dashing between parked cars and around a corner. As he ran, Bhar saw a flash of metal around the dog's shaggy neck, then heard the rattle of tags.

*Your omen of doom appears to be a wayward pet named Kaiser. Not quite worth worrying yourself sick over, eh?* the voice in head said unhelpfully.

Typical. His mum's boyfriend was probably a murderer. His guv was ready to show him the door. He hadn't heard from saucy blonde Emmeline or sensitive brunette Kyla in over a week; now even his own thoughts mocked him. There was nothing for it but to go home, brew a pot of tea, and wait for Sharada.

If the night Buck Wainwright was arrested was an unhappy one in the Bhar household, the next day proved grimmer still. Sharada, usually cheerful no matter what, arrived home in tears. She spent the night pacing, eating Haagen-Dazs ice cream by the pint, and researching various aspects of the criminal justice system. Naturally, she began her fact-finding mission by asking her son, who, personal failings aside, *did* enjoy the benefit of actually knowing what he was talking about. Alas, Bhar's truthful answers, however gently expressed, did not meet with Sharada's approval. Google, she decided, was a better resource than anything a mere Scotland Yard detective said. By 1:00 a.m., mother and son were no longer on speaking terms. Retreating to the relative sanctuary of his bedroom, Bhar set the alarm for six, hoping for an uninterrupted kip before facing his guv's displeasure in the morning. But soon after five, he was awakened by thudding, thumping, and an enormous crash.

"Mum!" he cried, halfway down the stairs. "What in bloody hell are you doing?"

"Don't be profane, Deepal." Attired in pinafore, kerchief, and yellow rubber gloves, she was taking a hammer to the living room wall. In the process of knocking a hole in the plaster, she'd unbalanced her curio cabinet, the source of the crash. It lay in the middle of room, glass doors shattered, its keepsake porcelain cups and saucers vomited onto the Turkish rug.

"Very well. Without profanity: what are you doing, Mum?"

"Buck needs an alibi. I'm providing one."

She looked so pathetic, held together by determination, adrenalin, and *Dulce de Leche*, all lingering resentment vanished.

"I see," he said more gently. "How exactly does demolishing our home establish his alibi?"

"It's clear to me what happened. That strange little man dealing his so-called art did something to provoke Buck. Buck punched the wall." Another blow landed with a *blam*. "So I'll say Buck came here, and I provoked him. He punched my wall." *Blam!* "Problem solved."

"Right. Mum, let's think about this." As he went to her, stopping her arm in mid-swing, the phone rang.

"Don't slow me down!" Sharada twisted out of his grip. "Answer that."

"It's probably one of our neighbors." Bhar caught hold of her again. "Seriously, Mum, let's assume you can stage this well enough to fool my guv. Remember my guv? The 'Lordly Detective' himself? In real life he's a lot harder edged than that randy bloke you wrote about. But fine, let's pretend he comes in, looks at all this, and agrees Buck injured his hands here instead of the crime scene. How will you explain your previous statement?"

"I'll recant. Say I'm a liar!"

"Yes. Well. Can't argue with that." As the phone mercifully stopped ringing, Bhar pried her fingers off the hammer. It was one of those tools that had been bizarrely reimagined for the ultra-feminine: smaller than average, with flowers printed on its pink vinyl grip. He held it behind his back.

"The guv's old-fashioned when it comes to self-confessed liars. He never believes anything they say. Same with most prosecutors, most magistrates, and the Crown Court in general."

Sharada's wide black eyes filled with tears. "Oh, Deepal. What am I going to do?"

He took a deep breath. Someone had to take control. And until a more qualified person showed up, that someone was apparently him.

"You're going to bed. No arguing! I'll clean up this mess and say sorry to our neighbors. Then I'll go to work, apologize to my guv, and find out what I can do for Buck."

*If you're still employed by the Metropolitan Police Service*, that voice inside his head added.

He stepped off the lift, expecting to smell breakfast. Despite his dread of facing Tony, breakfast was a constant in their work life, something he could look forward to when everything else went wrong. Even after the office snitches had complained in emails and special meetings, even after the guv had been forced to cover the cost out of his own pocket, breakfast remained a constant, elevating the worst morning. Thick toast, uncured bacon, eggs, baked beans, kippers in lemon butter, tomatoes, fried potatoes, black currant jam, good strong coffee and, if the previous night had been punishing, espresso. No matter how he felt after his morning commute, catching a scent of those dishes was enough to restore Bhar's default good humor.

Today he smelled nothing. Well—nothing edible. There was floor cleaner, a bit of burnt microwave popcorn, perhaps some lemon air freshener. That was all.

He checked his watch. Slightly after eight, which meant the food should have been waiting.

Entering the office, Bhar found the lights on and Mrs. Snell at her desk. She looked terrible. He'd known her to work through laryngitis, sinusitis, and the recent death of her mother, efficient and untouched no matter what the circumstances. This morning, her face was gray and her eyes were as puffy as Sharada's. She, too, looked like a woman who had wept all night.

"Good morning, Mrs. S! You seem a bit under the weather. *Downton* didn't kill off another Crawley, did it?"

"DS Bhar." Her tone dropped the office's ambient temperature by ten degrees.

"Mrs. Snell," he said more submissively, after a quick glance to make sure Kate wasn't around to overhear. "Sorry about that. It's only... where's breakfast? I know some of the yobbos complained, but I thought the guv pinned them to the mat."

"It's true, we were granted a reprieve. Yet that reprieve proved ephemeral, like much of this life." Mrs. Snell cleared her throat. "There will be no more meals served in this office. Health and Safety Regulation 208.1 B."

"I'm not familiar with that one," Bhar admitted.

"I imagine not. It was written yesterday and emailed as an addendum to the relevant manuals at oh-eight-hundred this morning." She tapped her wristwatch. "Which was six minutes ago, DS Bhar."

"Yes, well, traffic being bloody bollixed, I shouldn't think anyone would—" He stopped. "Oh. Right. I really am a disaster, aren't I, Mrs. S?"

She affected not to hear. "He awaits you even now, DS Bhar."

Bhar looked at Tony's closed office door. Taking a deep

breath, he squared his shoulders, announced himself with a single ceremonial knock, and entered.

The guv was swiveled toward the window and leaning back in his chair—far back in that way which impressed some and alarmed others. A few hoped that some halcyon day, he'd over-balance and fall on his brass.

Bhar took two steps toward the desk. Silence.

He took another step, well short of the guest chairs. It had been impressed upon him since boyhood not to take a seat before he was invited. Besides, this was England, and in England a man stood up for his dressing-down.

He cleared his throat. Still, Tony didn't turn.

There was nothing for it. "Good morning, sir," Bhar said. There was a bit of a quaver in the "good." Otherwise it sounded reasonably grownup.

The front legs of Tony's chair made contact with the floor. When he turned, he looked tired rather than angry. "Sorry I didn't hear you, Paul. Just enjoying the view. After all these years, I don't suppose the one on Victoria Embankment will be quite the same."

Bhar didn't know what to say. The move from the Broadway office, which had been New Scotland Yard since 1967, to the north bank of the Thames, wasn't on his radar. The slings and arrows of daily life kept him too busy to worry about new facili-ties, much less new views. "I'd best come straight out with it. I was dead wrong last night. I didn't think about anything except my mum and her welfare. Whatever reprimand you give me, I deserve."

Tony studied him. "Yes, well, I can't disagree. We've discussed this before. Every time you behave without thinking, you poten-tially damage the case, or even the Met. A letter has been entered into your file. And it goes without saying you're to have nothing to do with the Hardwick investigation."

Despite his willingness to accept any reprimand, news of yet another letter in his file cut deep. It took him so long to process the idea, Bhar nearly missed the implication in his guv's words.

"Investigation? I thought Buck confessed."

"He did. Yet the matter is far from settled. Beyond that, as you've proven yourself incapable of maintaining professional distance in this and other matters"—Hetheridge smiled strangely as he said those words—"I'm afraid I cannot discuss the particulars any further. Rest assured Kate and others to be determined will settle the matter, and Mrs. Bhar will be kept informed of Mr. Wainwright's ongoing status, as much as the letter of the law permits."

"You're saying it's not a wrap. He might be innocent. He might be innocent!" Bhar whooped. "Good grief, that's it, I'm saved. Just the *hope* of his innocence should be enough to keep my mum from going postal. No more rending of garments, no more gnashing of teeth. I might even eat a hot dinner tonight."

"Yeah, speaking of food," Kate said from the doorway. "Where's breakfast? And why does Mrs. Snell look like somebody died?"

"Take a seat, both of you," Tony said. That strange smile disappeared.

"I'm still knackered after last night, and I was really counting on coffee, or at least a cuppa, to bring me back from the dead," Kate said. "Give me two minutes, guv, just two minutes, I promise. Let me steal a mug of last night's brew, maybe a jam doughnut if Jackson didn't plow through them all, and—"

"Detective Sergeant Hetheridge. Be seated."

Dropping into the nearest chair, Bhar patted the one beside him. His pleading look to Kate went unnoticed—she was glaring at her husband, color already rising.

"He just took me off the Wainwright case," Bhar announced before she could say anything foolish. "Next step, the sack. You don't want to get it before I do, hey, Kate?"

That had the desired effect. Still looking mutinous, Kate sat down at last.

Tony didn't speak. The silence stretched out for ten seconds, twenty, thirty. Just as Bhar was seriously considering asking if they'd heard the limerick about the man from Capri, the guv said, "About the sack. I fear I've outdone you both. Assistant Commissioner asked for my resignation first thing this morning. I've given it to him, which was my only course beyond a protracted legal battle."

"What?" Bhar thought that stunned word came from his own lips, but after a moment's disbelief, he realized Kate had spoken. All he'd emitted was a faint wheeze.

"See for yourself." Hetheridge pushed a one-page letter across the table. Of ivory linen, it was folded once in the middle—hand-delivered, not posted.

**Dear Chief Superintendent Hetheridge,**

**After long reflection, I have no choice but to remove you from command, effective immediately. Given the many complaints received by fellow officers, public servants connected with the Metropolitan Police Service, and indeed various individual citizens over the years, your effectiveness is compromised beyond repair. Moreover, your personal relationships with certain other officers has given rise to frequent and persuasive charges of nepotism, particularly with regard to DS Deepal Bhar and DS Katherine Wakefield Hetheridge. As you've proven yourself incapable of maintaining professional distance in this and other matters, I request you resign your post and vacate your office by the end of the week.**

**Respectfully,**

**Michael Deaver**

**Assistant Commissioner, Metropolitan Police Service**

"The black dog," Bhar breathed.

"This is madness. Don't you dare resign. We can fight this!" Kate was on her feet.

"The black dog. The bloody black bollocking—"

"Shut it about the dog!" Kate screamed at him. "This isn't one of your harebrained psychodramas. This is real. It's serious." To Tony, she said, "They can't do this. You're a legend. You're the liaison to the rich and famous, and God knows those bleeding lunatics murder each other once a year. More than that, if Sir Duncan's in town."

"Ordinarily I would discourage such a show of emotion," Tony said. "But as I'm no longer your guv, I find I rather enjoy it. Warms the... what's the word? This region." He tapped the left side of his chest. "You know, where the knife goes in."

In spite of himself, Bhar laughed. Kate made a strangled, horrified sound and burst into tears.

Tony rose. "And that," he said, "concludes our last conference as a team. I've enjoyed working with you, Paul. Bite your tongue twice as much as you speak, and I feel certain you'll have a distinguished career."

He gestured for Bhar to stand up. Like a man trapped in a nightmare, Bhar obeyed. Then Tony took his hand, shaking it with warmth, good humor, and finality.

"This can't be happening," Bhar said.

"Why don't you go down to the canteen? Have a good hot breakfast," Tony said. "I believe the finer points are still being worked out, but the powers that be won't keep you at loose ends for long. Soon, someone will ring you with your next assignment."

"I just... it's only... I don't think I could eat."

"A cup of tea, then. Oh, and do stop on your way out and thank Mrs. Snell for everything she's done. She's just given the assistant commissioner her resignation, in solidarity with me, I fear. After so many years in the Met's service, she's taking the end rather badly."

Bhar tried to agree, but nothing came out. Kate was still weeping, hard and ugly. Putting his arms around her, Tony nodded toward the door.

"Go on, Paul. Give me a moment with my wife."

# CHAPTER 9

Crying made Kate feel guilty. And feeling guilty made her angry. So the more miserable and uncontrollable the tears, the more profound her guilt and anger. For years she'd combatted her emotions, always too close to the surface, by telling herself tears were for frightened children, or manipulative women, or broken men. Successful career detectives did not bawl uncontrollably at Scotland Yard. To do so reflected disastrously, not only on the woman in question, but on her superior officer. And that thought was too painful to be borne.

"You knew!" she accused Tony. "You knew all along this would happen if I married you!"

He said nothing, only held her.

"I didn't care about a piece of paper," she said through her tears. "We could just have been together, kept separate homes, different surnames. It would have been enough for me."

"But not for me. I wanted you as my wife more than I wanted this."

"This." Pulling out of his embrace, she wiped her eyes and

stared at him, astonished. "*This* is your career. This is your reason for living."

"No. I have a new reason for living now." His gaze was steady, honest, true. "I lost a job, Kate. A job I held for more years than I care to enumerate. And I had a good run. But times are changing, and you must admit, it's a touch ridiculous being married to a man who can pull rank on you at any moment.

"Still, if you're determined to view this as a Senecan tragedy, by all means, go to Mrs. Snell and attempt to cheer her up. I'm quite all right, Kate, I assure you. I happen to have many personal interests, most sadly neglected. I have Henry's fencing lessons. I promised to personally escort the boys to Legoland next month, to view Ritchie's work in the exhibition. I have my family estate in the country. Briarshaw ought to be managed properly, not left to rot. I have books to read, perhaps even a memoir to write…."

"That sounds bloody awful!" Kate cried. "Things need to stay as they were."

"But they couldn't," Tony said, cupping her face with both hands. "I suppose if the Met was famed for incorruptible leadership, if sexism and nepotism no longer existed…." He broke off, chuckling. "But alas, Scotland Yard is staffed by humans, run by humans, and judged from afar by still more humans. Nothing in that equation could permit us to continue working together in this fashion. By sacrificing me, a man who might reasonably be expected to retire in a few years, the top brass can assure Parliament and Downing Street that this institution moves with the times. Another privileged dinosaur sent packing."

Kate tried to absorb his words, his enviable calm, but once again her genetic predisposition for loyalty rebelled. Those same instincts that had urged her to defend Bhar, right or wrong, now cried out for her to burn down anything and anyone who harmed her husband.

"That letter," she sniffed, seizing the document and rereading it. "What a piece of work. Deaver's a right sod."

"He was my staunchest advocate. If it had been up to him," Tony said, "none of this would have happened. He fought them at every turn. He never thought he'd win outright, but given employment rights and protections, he thought he could hold them at bay for months, perhaps years."

"But *how* can this happen? How can they just send you packing, *boom*, without discipline first or a downgrade in rank? Vic Jackson's been busted down to DI a few times, but he always claws his way up again, no matter what he does."

"Vic's uncle is highly placed in the Ministry of Justice. He'll never be fired outright, not unless he commits murder. On camera. With something less than a sympathetic explanation when asked why."

Kate blinked at Tony. "You never told me that."

"As your commanding officer, it would have been highly inappropriate if I had. And truth be told, Vic takes no pleasure in the association. He's forever being given additional chances, when for years, I suspect all he wanted was to fail with finality. It's true, there are laws and procedures, and once a case is tried in the media, those procedures must be followed to the letter. But when the dispute is kept in-house, other remedies may apply."

She pondered that. An awful suspicion was dawning. One that probably would have come immediately to another detective, one without an emotional attachment.

"When you stopped Vic from sacking me. Made him look a fool. That's how you made an enemy of Vic's sodding uncle, isn't it?" she asked, referring to the day they'd met. "Then there's the time you took the Hotel Nonpareil case out Vic's grubby little paws. Another black mark. I'm right, aren't I?"

Tony was silent.

"Even so, you could have hired a solicitor. Fought it in court. Unless… unless they used me to make you go quietly. Held my career over your head to ensure you'd resign."

His only answer was a pained smile.

"Right. So. Everyone you've ever offended," Kate said, feeling as if she might scream. "Everyone you've tripped up or outperformed. They all considered your intention to marry a subordinate the perfect chance to force you out. And you decided to tell me now? After the axe fell? After it was too late to have my say?"

He still didn't answer.

"When did you know for sure?"

"Last night."

"Oh, my God! Why didn't you tell me?"

"To what purpose?" He spoke gently, but he was turning to stone, withdrawing behind those ice blue eyes. "Transforming an unhappy day into a deplorable one? Eliminating any hope you had for a good night's sleep?"

"Tony. Our whole relationship can't be nothing but you taking bullets for me. I'm your wife. You should have said something before we were married. At the very least, you should have told me the instant you knew." Her next words tumbled out angrily, helplessly. "Who *do* you confide in? Anyone? Anyone at all?"

He looked away.

Kate blinked back tears. *He's always kept his own counsel. I can't expect that to change overnight, just because we're married. I know he loves me. But he can't possibly trust me....*

She cut off that thought. She had to compose herself. Tony was mentally entrenched, that much was obvious. A typical Wakefield screaming match, complete with curses, ultimatums, and thrown objects, would get her nowhere.

*I have to wait for an unguarded moment. That's the only time I'll get an unguarded answer.*

Kate took a deep breath and managed a smile. "Okay. So what happens next? To the team? Me and Bhar?"

"Ah, well, a decision will made soon enough," Tony said, voice softening, visibly relieved. "An interim commander for a time, then a permanent assignment. I expect the Toff Squad, as it were, will ultimately be placed in the hands of someone younger and more in touch with the times."

"Hah! I'd like to see anyone else do what you've done. What a laugh it will be, watching the Powers That Be try and find someone younger and more politically correct who can do the job—who's proven at the job— *and* has a title."

Tony raised his eyebrows. "You think it will be difficult?"

"It's impossible. I wouldn't even know where to start."

"I would. I'm looking at her."

Kate went cold. "No. Oh, no. They couldn't... I'm not really a baroness...."

"I assure you, our marriage vows are binding."

"Those rich bloody bints won't accept a title by marriage."

He laughed. "They will in time. Never fear, I don't foresee you being promoted to chief superintendent tomorrow. But make no mistake—as the Hardwick case is unraveled, those at the top will be watching. Perform well, and new doors will open."

Finding that promise too difficult to absorb, Kate ignored it, sinking into the chair she'd leapt out of—when? The last half hour was a blur. That realization brought an unexpected rush of sympathy for Buck Wainwright, he of the blackout temper and inconvenient (or perhaps all too convenient) memory loss. Rage had gone off inside him like a hand grenade, obliterating all recollection. For Kate, the unjust demolition of Tony' career left her feeling the same: bomb-blasted, nothing but scorched earth.

"I know I have to focus on the Hardwick case, and I'm trying, believe me. Do you still think Buck's innocent?"

"Yes."

"Perfect. I have no idea where to go with that. Maybe Mrs. Snell had the right of it." Kate picked up the loathsome letter again, scanning the words for a third time just to torture herself. "I should turn in my resignation, too."

"Nonsense." Plucking the letter out of her hand, Tony tucked it into his breast pocket and sat in the chair beside her. "I mentioned yesterday that you've never seen me angry. Another word about resignation and you just might. As for the Hardwick case… I've always said when in doubt, establish a timeline."

"Yes. Well. Since Mr. I-Hate-Mobiles has done everything possible to make that difficult, I suppose it really is the place to start. That last pub Buck visited, the Yellow Earl, is probably his best chance of an alibi. Didn't he mention talking to a bloke with a dog? Wouldn't it be interesting if the man outside Hardwick's house was one and the same? But no—seems like Buck mentioned a different breed."

"He called it a German Shepherd. Which is American for Alsatian."

His memory never failed to amaze her. Just as Kate started to say so, she realized he was sitting next to her. "Why aren't you behind your desk?"

"I detest long goodbyes. There's probably some expectation I'll linger, take days to pack up, draw the whole thing out. Therefore, my vanity won't allow me to do less than depart as soon as possible. I've sat behind that desk for the last time."

"I'm sorry I fell apart." She lifted her chin and forced a smile. "Whatever you need from me, now's the time to say."

"Well, now that you mention it, I'd like you to find Paul. Sit down with him in the canteen. Have breakfast. Show the world you're completely unaffected. The longer you two exhibit signs of distress, the longer you'll be tested by those who scent blood in the water. For my part, I should be the one to escort Mrs. Snell out. Preferably to a destination with a quiet corner and a spot of tea."

"Masala Express should be open soon."

"I was thinking of the Albion Neo Bankside." He referred to a café by the Tate Modern with a gourmet menu and stunning views, including the Shard and St. Paul's Cathedral. "She appreciates an exceptional kedgeree, not to mention duck eggs on toast."

"Of course. You're the best boss ever."

"I was, wasn't I?" He smiled. "One last thing. Social Services is likely still grappling with a woman called Miss Georgette Sevrin. She resided with Hardwick and hid in the upstairs wardrobe. Remember that smeared track in Hardwick's blood? The one Peter Garrett called a footprint someone took the time to rub out? Last night, I noted blood on Miss Sevrin's carpet slippers. She'll need a careful assessment. A young officer called Fannon will deliver a dossier of her public activities to you sometime today."

"Fannon, eh? Another of your hard luck cases?"

"Possibly. Poor soul believed me when I pretended not to know who Mr. Tumnus was. Still, he saw right through Miss Sevrin's mental act, and she's a rather shrewd malingerer. She may also be a cold-blooded killer."

Despite her husband's dislike of lengthy goodbyes, Kate couldn't resist dragging it out as long as possible. But at last there came a moment when there was nothing to do but go, and as she did, that familiar sick throb at her temple became insurmountable. She needed coffee now. Not to mention privacy to digest all that had happened. She wanted nothing more than to find a Pret A Manger, plunk down the extortionate cost of a latte with three shots of espresso, and drink it in silence, preferably while staring at a wall.

But alas, she'd promised Tony she'd go to the canteen, put on a show, keep calm, carry on, etc. So off she went to find Paul.

He was already in the dining room, sitting alone like Billy No-Mates, parked at a table meant for four and disconsolately chewing a bit of toast. Ignoring the whispers, Kate braved the queue with head held high, getting coffee and a chocolate crois-sant. Her ongoing struggle to get back into the jeans size of her early twenties could wait; she was a career detective, not a model, and there was considerable comfort in gooey filling.

"Perkins smiled at me," Paul muttered when Kate sat down across from him.

"That bastard."

"Saunderson waved. I think he's trying to catch your eye."

"Of course he is," she said, tearing savagely into the croissant. "He worships Vic Jackson and would use me for target practice if there wasn't a law against it." She added cream to her coffee, then a reasonable amount of sugar, followed by an unreasonable amount. "Besides, he always hated the guv."

"He's not the guv anymore. And it's my fault. I made him look bad."

"Don't be daft. I'm the radioactive slag he married." The coffee was decent, for which Kate was grateful. As her headache started to recede, she forced herself to scan the dining room. Except for the two empty seats at their table, it was packed to the gills. Either all of Scotland Yard was off to an unconscionably late start, or work had been suspended in favor of watching the Toff Squad brought low: forced to eat an ordinary brekkie like ordinary people.

Derek Saunderson, a beefy, bucktoothed man who seemed to dislike women in general and Kate in particular, met her eyes. Holding her gaze, he gave her a slow, satisfied smile. Kate's first impulse was to get up, march over to his table, and knock those buck teeth down the back of his throat. What she actually did, in light of her promise, was visualize her husband's face—and smile back.

"It really is my fault," Paul was moaning. "I need medication. Therapy. Hypnotherapy, that's it, to keep me from saying what I think. Or doing what seems right. Those are the two habits that have ruined my life. I feel awful," he added so loudly, Kate gave him a sharp look.

"We're meant to be showing the world we're fine," she whispered, tearing off more croissant with her teeth.

"I'm not fine. I'm the opposite of fine. And what about him? The guv—I mean, the chief. I mean, Lord... er, he hates it when people at the Yard call him that...."

"Tony. Surely you've used his name before?"

"Once or twice. Felt unnatural." Paul shuddered. "In his office I was such a berk. News like that, and he practically consoled *me*."

"Yes, and then he consoled me, and now he's reassembling Mrs. Snell's soul from damp ashes." She reached for more croissant and found nothing but crumbs. This was probably how compulsive eating disorders started—shoveling down pastries as a balm against the rejoicing of one's enemies. Kate glanced in Saunderson's direction. No doubt about it: still rejoicing.

"But is he really okay?" Paul asked again. "Behind closed doors, you see the real him."

*Do I?* Kate washed down her doubts with more coffee. When this purgatorial breakfast was over, she intended to spend the rest of the day thinking about nothing but the case. Murder was easier than relationships; any detective would say the same.

"I should have offered to resign," Paul said.

"No. I tried. He came over all 'my lord' on me."

"How'd that make you feel?"

"Relieved. I've worked too hard for this. Giving up now is... well...."

"Unthinkable. I know. Uh-oh. Here comes Saunderson," Paul muttered, taking out his mobile and scrutinizing it with ersatz fascination. "Guess gloating from afar isn't enough."

Kate took another deep draught of coffee. If she was about to be arrested for visiting grievous bodily harm upon a fellow officer, she wanted to at least be properly caffeinated.

"Bhar. *Hetheridge*." Saunderson rolled the latter name off his tongue like a particularly scrumptious boiled sweet. "I heard the strangest rumor. Absolutely can't be right. I heard—"

"That old Derek's poncing around the canteen at this hour? When his report on the diamond district heist still hasn't hit my inbox?" DCI Jackson interrupted in his we're-all-mates tone, the one that always boded ill. "I heard that, too. Tell me it's bollocks."

Saunderson's chin, underdeveloped in the shadow of those big buck teeth, seemed to recede another centimeter. "Er, no, sir. That is, I'll have it to you by this afternoon. First thing tomorrow at the latest, sir."

"See that you do." Jackson watched Saunderson make his retreat, then turned to them. "Is this a bad time, DS Hetheridge? DS Bhar?"

There it was again. Her correct name, used without apparent malice. Kate was too confused by Jackson's rebuke of his crony to form a complete sentence. Bhar came to her rescue.

"No, sir. It's a good time." He picked up Kate's coffee, nodding for her to rise. When she did, he put the cup in her hand with an emphatic *go along with this* look.

"Of course, Chief." If that plonker could feign good manners, so could she. That was Bullying 101: the rules of the game were subject to change without notice. Kids who failed to perceive and adapt were doomed to a life of seized lunch money and purloined gym clothes. Kate had not forgotten; despite its sterling reputation the world over, there were times when life in Scotland Yard's canteen closely resembled the schoolyards of her youth.

They followed DCI Jackson out of the dining room. She expected him to revert to type the moment they were more or less alone, but no sneering abuse followed. So into the lift they went, the three of them plus a uniformed constable who offered cheerfully, "Lovely weather this morning, isn't it?"

No one answered. It was a long ride up.

The moment the metal doors parted, Jackson struck off toward his office, moving faster than Kate had ever witnessed.

He'd dropped a bit of weight, it seemed, or upped his caffeine, if such a thing were possible.

"Come through," Jackson said when they reached his office. Paul entered first. As the door opened, Jackson caught it... and held it for Kate.

*That's it. I'm having a psychotic break. Any minute they'll inject me with meds, and I'll see white coats looming all around....*

"Oh! Hello," said the matronly woman behind the reception desk. She had red plastic spectacles, three chins, and an infectious smile. "You're DS Hetheridge and DS Bhar, aren't you? Welcome! I've only just started working for DCI Jackson. Name's Joy."

"Hi, Joy," Paul said, admirably synthesizing warmth while Kate assessed Joy's workstation with a jaundiced eye. Judging by all the conspicuous happiness—yellow silk daisies, plush animals, and loads of cartoon smiley faces—the woman was a very new recruit indeed. Heaven knew what a few days' exposure to Jackson would do. Joy was overweight, black, and probably fifty, judging by the gray in her curls. She was the living embodiment of half his punchlines. Maybe someone at Scotland Yard hated Joy. Or maybe she'd been sent in wearing a wire, and not even Jackson's highly placed uncle would save him from what must surely follow.

"Two messages for you, sir," Joy told Jackson. "Transcripts sent to your email as requested."

"Thank you," Jackson said so politely, a new suspicion occurred to Kate. Was it *Joy* that had driven him to some kind of self-improvement scheme?

His office, it seemed, was not included in said scheme. It was even messier than the last time Kate had seen it. Unlike Tony, who preferred Spartan simplicity, Vic Jackson was a packrat at best, a hoarder at worst. Three large bookcases sagged, so over-burdened as to constitute a health and safety violation via threat of collapse. Kate spied thirty-year-old textbooks, tattered three-ring binders, legal pads, and loose conglomerations of paper.

Dozens of cardboard boxes were labeled ESSENTIAL DO NOT TOUCH in Jackson's messy, rather desperate hand. Isolated on one wall hung a twenty-year-old service award for Detective Constable Victor P. Jackson. Nothing else like it existed; it was a freak of nature, alone in the world.

Jackson went to his desk, or the collection of piles a concealed desk presumably supported. Rather than sitting down, he stood awkwardly beside his chair, as if debating whether or not to make a speech.

Kate exchanged looks with Paul. Once again, he seemed to be silently communicating something. Did he want her to follow his lead? Fine. When he sat, Kate sat, taking another slurp of coffee.

*Wish it were Irish.*

Tony kept a drinks trolley in his office, a cut crystal, single-malt scotch affair intended only for special occasions. Jackson had one, too, but less formal and subjected to hard use. Glancing about, Kate finally located it, pushed in a far corner. Gone was the middling vodka, the cheap whiskey, the wine sold by the jug. Now there was bottled water, fizzy pop, and those little prepackaged caffeine-and-vitamin shots.

"So. Right." Jackson looked briefly at Kate, then Paul, before aiming his gaze at his desk and keeping it there. "Let me begin by saying I've spoken to Tony. He's put me in the picture as far as the Hardwick case, no holds barred, everything he has. Which is, to be, er, *rigorously* honest, quite decent of him. Before I went down to the canteen in search of you lot, I had a look at Buck Wainwright's interview. At first glance, I thought the case was open and shut. But given Tony's years of experience, and his conviction Wainwright might be innocent, I agree we must explore all avenues before handing the matter to CPS." This came out stiffly, yet quickly, like an errant Victorian child stood up before the class and compelled to apologize. "Are there any questions?"

"What's happening?" Kate mouthed to Paul.

He gaped at her as if she were the crazy one.

"Was that a question, DS Hetheridge?"

"Sorry, er, Chief. It's been a wood chipper of a morning, and my coffee's gone cold. What *is* this?"

"All Tony's cases have been given to me for the interim," Jackson said. If he felt any triumph, it was well concealed. "You and DS Bhar are assigned to my command for the foreseeable future."

# CHAPTER 10

K ate found herself unable to form words to respond.
Which was fortunate, because all the words that came
to her were profane.

"Please excuse my colleague," Paul said with that same synthe-
sized warmth he'd applied to Joy at reception. "She worked quite
late last night and turned up early this morning, running on
fumes. We're both a bit off-balance, sir," he added, addressing
Jackson—Jackson!—with all the respect his rank deserved.

*This is real. This is happening. I'm back where I was when I met*
*Tony, only now there's no Lord Hetheridge to save me.*

"Don't apologize. The truth is...." Jackson paused. Perhaps
speaking the truth required muscles he'd permitted to atrophy.
"The truth is, I'd like to skip all this, whatever this is, and get
straight to the meat. Any takers?"

Paul nodded. Kate managed to nod, too.

"All right, Bhar, let's start with you. You bungled it with Hardwick, but Tony said you've been dealt with, so we'll say no more.
Clean slate. Do you have any open cases?"

"Two. Both sorted, minor details left."

"Perfect. New assignment. I'll email you the fine print,"

Jackson said. "Has to do with my favorite combination—cocaine and Albanians. The cartel is slippery, but one of the distributors put himself on my radar. Bloke by the name of Arjan Potka, goes by Arry. The case is built. There's an eyewitness willing to testify. She has the goods on Arry, lock, stock, and barrel. But then my lad in charge of the investigation pulled up lame, the witness got cold feet, and I've become too busy to massage her myself. I'd like you to take over. Charm the old girl, make her see sense. Convince her to go to court and put Arry the coke dealer behind bars forever." He frowned. "Which in today's Britain probably equals fifteen years or less, but I'll take what I can get."

"So there's no…." Paul took a deep breath. But lacking hypnotherapy or a brain surgeon's intervention, he still said what came to mind. "This isn't a murder case."

Jackson shook his head.

Paul opened his mouth again, and Jackson emitted one of his exaggerated sighs, the sort that typically preceded a torrent of abuse. Paul went rigid. So did Kate. So did Jackson, who seemed alarmed by his own response.

"Right. Er. Listen," he said after an uncomfortable silence. "There's two ways this can go. You can muff this, like you muffed Hardwick, not to mention Godington, and prove all the naysayers right. End up never working a murder case again, except in your dreams. Or you can take the assignment, no complaints, no skiving, get results, and prove everyone wrong. In which case, the next time your old pal Sir Duncan does it in the drawing room with a candlestick, you'll still be in the game."

Kate wanted to argue with Jackson. It was natural to argue with Jackson, to x-ray every sentence, to dispute every word. But what he was saying made sense, damn him.

"I won't muff this, Chief," Paul said, apparently having arrived at the same conclusion. "Which of your lads am I taking over for? I'd like a word, straightaway."

"Murdock. But now isn't a good time for a chat. He's at St. Thomas. Still in intensive care."

Paul took a moment to digest that. "Because of Arry?"

"Him, or the people Arry works for." Jackson shrugged. "I said it wasn't a murder case. I never said it was a feather bed."

"I'll handle it. I promise," Paul announced, synthesizing enthusiasm rather less convincingly. To Kate, he added, "See you around." Then he was gone, leaving her alone with Vic Jackson.

It was a situation she'd avoided ever since the previous summer, when he'd asked her to a pub, ostensibly to discuss a case. Thrilled to finally be treated like one of the lads, she'd met him in a back booth. There, he'd proceeded to open his mouth, unzip his trousers, and make a demand she'd never forget.

"So. DS Hetheridge."

"Chief." Did the memory of that night, and her near-sacking that followed, show on her face? Kate thought it must have, because he retreated to his broken-down office chair, which creaked in protest. Sitting half obscured by folders and files seemed to give him courage.

"I know I said let's skip the agony and get on with the misery, but the truth is, I need something from you."

*Of course you do.* Kate glared at him.

"I need you to listen to me."

She kept glaring, ready.

"That night. You know, in the pub. The things I said. What I did." Jackson cleared his throat. "It takes two to tango. There's two sides to every story, and nobody's ever blameless. Except that night. That night, it was down to me. You had no part. It was all my fault."

"If you're asking me to forgive—"

"I'm asking nothing," Jackson cut across her, sounding more like his old self. "Except for you to hear me say it. It was my fault. I was wrong."

"Yeah, too right you were. Back then, I was foolish enough to think if I played by the boys' code, they'd accept me," Kate spat at him. "I didn't turn you in to internal affairs because I thought it was the best way to protect myself. Now I've wised up. Say or do anything like that again, and I'll have you under investigation so fast, you'll be afraid to pull it out in the Men's, much less a pub."

"And so you should," Jackson muttered.

She waited. Her schoolyard training in Bullying 101 had prepared her for what should come next: a sob story about why it had actually been someone or something else's fault. Or perhaps a deeper look into her behavior, a recitation of her many attempts at revenge.

Jackson's chair creaked. He cleared his throat once, twice, a third time. Then:

"Since we're in agreement on the past, can we move forward to the Hardwick case?"

"Er. All right. Sir."

"Good. First order of business." He shifted a stack of desk-detritus, allowing them to see one another better. "Establishing a timeline for Buck Wainwright's movements on the day of the murder. I've already assigned constables to gather CCTV camera footage. If he's innocent, that might exonerate him. Especially if another person called on Hardwick around the time of death."

"What about the rest of the time-stamped data?"

"Such as?"

"Buck's hotel key card. His mini bar access. Credit card use at the hotel pub or that other spot he mentioned...."

"The Yellow Earl. I know the place. Know one of the barmen. I'll check it out," Jackson said.

"Then there's Euston Place. I understand there's a protest group solely devoted to East Asia House," Kate said. "I suppose I could go knocking on doors, see what people observed that day," she added, with no idea how helpful or unhelpful her new neighbors would be.

"Yes. Face to face with the bluebloods. That's the sort of task I'd have put to Bhar," Jackson said.

"But not me?"

"No. I suppose you're suited, being a resident and all, but not this time. Maybe I'll do it myself. Maybe I'll farm it out to someone special."

"PC Gulls?"

Jackson shrugged. "Now. About this Georgette Sevrin. I asked for a rush analysis on the blood on her clothes. Let me check the email...." More detritus was shifted, unearthing a mouse, then she heard some keyboard clicks. "Bingo. Initial check gives 95% probability the blood is Hardwick's. That's enough to clinch an interview. My court order for that has come through, too. But as far as a go-ahead from Social Services...." More clicks. "Nope, dead air. Looks like they ignored the emergency request Tony put through last night. Well, it's a new day. Let's light a fire under them, shall we?"

Joy was summoned to coordinate the conference call. All smiles and helpful remarks, she managed it easily once she excavated Jackson's phone. In less than five minutes, Kate and Jackson had Miss Sevrin's social worker on the line, a young man who sounded earnest, bright, and perhaps twenty-two. Kate tried to feel sympathy for him, but he was clearly operating under the assumption Miss Sevrin was an innocent bystander, menaced by jackbooted thugs. Therefore, he seemed determined to obstruct Scotland Yard as much as possible.

"I'm afraid Miss Sevrin responded poorly to her treatment by your agency," said the caseworker via speakerphone. "Strange surroundings, unfamiliar people, it was all too much. A night in lockup often sends vulnerable individuals into a dissociative state, which is what my client's experiencing."

"She wasn't in lockup," Jackson said. "She was in protective custody, which amounts to a private room with a comfy bed and a staff at her beck and call. Mind you, there's a great many states

I'd like to disassociate myself from, so if Miss Sevrin has the inside track, I'm all ears."

"By a dissociative state," said the social worker a touch sniffily, "I mean she has lost the ability to locate herself in space and time. She's adrift in a world of her own making."

"Like I said, precisely the state I've tried to achieve for eons. So I don't care if she's thinks she on the moon or inside Colin Firth's bedroom. She's a murder suspect, and we plan to interview her."

"That's not on the table. She needs medical reevaluation. An adjustment in pharmaceuticals perhaps, or—"

"Listen to me, you little—" Jackson interrupted, sounding precisely like the man Kate knew and loathed. Right at the moment, however, she rather enjoyed his reappearance and the shocked huffing sounds emanating from the speakerphone.

"A man is dead," she said, cutting across both of them, doing her best to sound as coolly authoritative as her husband. "We have a solemn responsibility to the victim, his family, and the public at large. In a murder case, deliberate attempts to impede the investigation will be met with the strongest possible scrutiny. So be advised, we are aware of the precise legal standard required to interview a suspect like Miss Sevrin. Our top consultant is double checking to ensure we've met it. You have twenty four hours to make her ready. That's all."

Silence. Then: "I understand. Can you interview her tomorrow at half-two?"

"I'll be there with bells on."

Jackson disconnected. "Well. That put him on the ropes." He sounded impressed. "Who's our top consultant?"

"Me. And Google. And a quick ring to Legal, if they can be arsed to put down the nine iron and pick up."

He nodded. "Step lightly, Wake—Hetheridge. I know we have more power on the front end than those heart-bleeders like to admit. But in the course of exercising those powers, if we say or do something a soft-headed jury might call coercive...."

"... whatever we collect will be ruled inadmissible, up to and including a murder confession," Kate agreed. "So Miss Sevrin's on my calendar for tomorrow. What about today?"

"I want you to look into Hardwick himself. Tony mentioned the man had an eye for the ladies. Three guesses where I'd start."

"His current girlfriend, Sunny Wainwright. I didn't get a look at the morning papers. Has his name been released?"

"No," Jackson said. "'Murder in Mayfair' was splashed all over, obviously, but without an address or details. The fact it was Hardwick should break by the afternoon edition, though."

*Meaning the time to interview Sunny Wainwright is now*, Kate thought. *When she has no idea her lover is dead—or will be forced to pretend as much.*

~

Upon arrival in the United Kingdom, Sunny had listed a flat in Shoreditch, leased to one L. M. Dase, as her residence for the duration. But L.M. Dase, presumably Buck's sister-in-law, Maisie, had either suspended her phone service or failed to pay the bill. Either way, Kate couldn't get through. She felt desperate to escape the Yard, so off to Shoreditch it was.

The Tube ride from St. James Park station on the District line, changing to the Central at Monument, then out at Bethnal Green, placed her within easy walking distance of L.M. Dase's address. And the Tube had been lightly-traveled and quiet, apart from a crocodile of French schoolchildren *en route* to Tower Hill. Kate felt a bit sorry for two American women, bewildered by the simultaneous rush to alight and board at one of Monument's busy platforms. Yes, in England, the queue was sacred. But boarding the Tube involved no queues, strictly speaking, and those who hesitated would be pushed past, left behind, or possibly flattened.

Shoreditch was part of Hackney in London's East End. In recent years it had become increasingly gentrified yet was still known for its street art (temporary) and its graffiti (permanent, at least until the Council took action.) Sometimes Shoreditch's street art was simple: chalk drawings on sidewalks or stickers all over a sign post. Other times, entire streets were transformed by spray paint; by giant sculptures erected on rooftops; even by fanciful decoupage, such as paper lilies blooming inside phone boxes. It was all left of center, unexpected, and mostly anonymous, although a genuine Banksy graced Rivington. Once upon a time in the Victorian era, rich young men in top hats and tails had gone slumming in Shoreditch, sampling its music halls and prostitutes, safely scandalized by how the other half lived. Now doubledecker buses packed with tourists trundled through, showing off a district that had become a sort of open-air gallery.

L. M. Dase's building, however, proved no tourist attraction. It was run down, the manager's office shut without explanation. A few neighbors opened their doors to Kate, frowning at her warrant card and claiming no knowledge of Maisie's whereabouts. Kate hadn't seen so many shifty looks and weak denials since Henry and/or Ritchie had caused the downstairs toilet to overflow. Either Maisie's neighbors were curiously wary of such inquiries, or she'd chosen a building where coppers weren't welcome.

*Wonderful. Sunny's an unemployed American on a tourist visa. It could take hours to track her down. I'm better off camping in this dank hall and waiting.*

Another option came to her. Pulling out her mobile, Kate opened Twitter and searched for @SunnyDase. The very first hit was the one she wanted. The profile picture showed a Mrs. America-style beauty, about forty, with cascading blonde hair and blindingly white teeth. A frequent Tweeter, Sunny's most recent submission to the digital void had been posted at half-two the night before. It read:

*I never felt more free. #nofear #noregrets*

That post was geotagged at someplace called Pure Silk, which turned out to be a City of Westminster dance club. Sunny's previous Tweet, time-stamped 12:03 the day Hardwick died, read:

*There will be consequences. #don'tbelievemejustwatch*

That one wasn't geotagged, but Sunny had attached a selfie. Her expression—scowling with lips pursed—was what Henry called "gangsta." He didn't do it very convincingly, and neither did Sunny.

*What do you know?* Kate thought, taking a screenshot for posterity in case Sunny later deleted it. *Buck's soon-to-be-ex just became a person of interest.*

Of course, as a human being with a stake in civilization, not to mention someone who hoped social media didn't obliterate every last vestige of common sense, Kate maintained healthy skepticism. It almost beggared belief that a murderer would Tweet her deadly intentions, then publicly rejoice when the deed was done. But experience had taught Kate there were all sorts of murderers. And some of them were, to employ a technical term, idiots.

Something else struck her. Glad she'd neglected to shut down her own little-used Twitter account, the suitably anonymous @katewake261, she used it to Tweet:

*@SunnyDase you're dead quiet. No pictures. OK?*

Now she just had to wait. Rather than head back to the Tube station, Kate lingered near Maisie's building, browsing through a street vendor's rack of pashmina shawls. Just as she located the very thing—snow white with a gold trim—her mobile pinged, indicating a response.

"Cheers," she told the vendor, handing over a tenner and tucking the folded shawl into her bag. Then she read Sunny's reply.

*Late start. Coffee and Red Bull first. My pretty face after.*

The Tweet was geotagged Xpression Xpress. To Kate, that sounded like a newsstand specializing in Cornettos and ciggies, but turned out to be a small private art gallery three streets over. Sunny, it seemed, was too sufficiently convinced of her own cyber celebrity to wonder why a stranger inquired after her. Not only had she answered, she'd specified her present location. Despite the popularity of cop dramas, detective novels, and true crime shows, some people saw no downside to putting their personal safety on the line.

*Behaving as if she's invincible might be a sign she was involved with Hardwick's murder,* Kate thought. Many killers enjoyed twenty-four to forty-eight hours' euphoria. During that "murder after-glow," as Bhar called it, the killer was most likely to boast to friends or issue dark hints. Or they might tuck away some grisly trophy, perhaps after suffering an overwhelming desire to return to the scene of the crime.

*Suppose Buck's story about being estranged from Sunny is just that, a story? Suppose they killed Hardwick together, for whatever reason, and his romance with Sharada is just a front?*

But it was too soon to breed theories. First Kate needed to meet Sunny, to get a feel for Mrs. America and her grot-art-creating sister.

Xpression Xpress was a dodgy rectangle squeezed between a launderette and a New Age shop. The gallery had no sign or lettered window to announce its presence, but nearby utility poles and one side of an abandoned café were covered in flyposts, all identical:

## NEW EXHIBIT!
## ART OR DEATH
## THE CHOICE IS YOURS

Judging by the altogether indifferent passersby, the public was opting for death. Then again, Shoreditch had art encoded in its very genes, which meant not only an innate seeking of truth and beauty, but a chromosomal state of rebellion. Common hucksterism wouldn't entice the locals; they'd walk a mile to avoid a hard sell.

Kate tried the door. As it swung inward, a bell tinkled and a variety of smells rolled forth: curry, incense, and marijuana.

Xpression Xpress's entryway was claustrophobic, three feet wide and twenty feet long, with a scuffed lino floor and dim lighting. Beyond that unpromising beginning, the gallery swelled into one vast, unpartitioned exhibition room with a ceiling so high, an upper floor must have been demolished to create it. The spotlights overhead were trained on various pieces of sculpture, some freestanding, some on pedestals. Sometimes Kate recognized the original materials: an aluminum bicycle repainted and twisted into a human female, or hundreds of broken crayons and dried up paint pots, rearranged to look like a flowerbed. She didn't understand more than half of it, at least at first glance, but she felt moved, uplifted, just by looking at those flowers or that sinuous steel woman.

*Buck, you may know Black Angus cattle, but you don't know bollocks when it comes to your sister-in-law's art.*

"Well, ain't you the early bird?" called one of two women picnicking in a corner as if it were the most ordinary thing in the world. On a calico quilt, they'd spread a late breakfast or early lunch: two Styrofoam takeaway containers of curry, plastic cups, and a bottle of red wine. The blonde, Sunny Wainwright, wore black jeans and an ivory sweater that fit her like a glove. The one who'd spoken, surely Maisie, had on a hoodie, yoga tights, and what appeared to be Army-Navy Surplus boots. Her brown hair was up in twin pigtails, half her face obscured by impenetrable black sunglasses.

"No, you can't use our bog," she continued, splashing more wine into a plastic cup. "No, we don't make change for the bleedin' launderette. And no, we bloody well ain't hiring."

"My goodness, Maisie, the poor lady has barely poked her head inside. It's bad manners to attack her." Sunny's twang matched Buck's or slightly exceeded it. "Maybe she's an art lover, you ever think 'bout that? You come on over, sweetie," she called to Kate. "We don't bite."

"Thank you." As she advanced, Kate pulled out her warrant card, holding it out for both to see. "My name is Detective Sergeant Kate Wa—Hetheridge. Are you Sunny Wainwright and L. M. Dase?" She used what seemed like the least objectionable pronunciation, *DAW-say*.

"Who called for police? No one called for police!" Maisie leapt to her feet. If she, like Sunny, hailed from the American South, she'd adopted the East End manner of speech quite well. "I know my rights. You have permission to touch nothing in this place, you hear me? Nothing. And no, I'm not L.M. *Daw-say!*"

"Maisie, calm down." Rising, Sunny stepped over the blanket, graceful in her red-soled Louboutins. "I am Sunny Wainwright, soon to be Sunny Dase." She pronounced it "daisy."

*Sunny Daisy?* Maisie *Daisy?* Kate thought. *No wonder those two left the States. Their parents are sadists.*

"And eventually, when the time is right, I'll be Mrs. Sunny Hardwick," Sunny added. But she sounded not the least bit convincing.

"Shut it," Maisie told her sister. "This cow isn't CID. She's one

of them, pretending to be filth, here for a shakedown. We're out!"
she told Kate. "Out, you hear me! Go bark up some other tree!"

"I assure you, I am CID, and this is official business. I'm investigating a murder. Granville Hardwick is dead." Kate kept her gaze locked on Sunny, the better to absorb every joule of her reaction. "My condolences. Now, I'm afraid I must ask. Where were you yesterday, Mrs. Wainwright?"

Eyes on Sunny, Kate never saw Maisie lunge. But the instant the artist slammed into her, Kate's self-defense skills took over. Pivoting with the impact, she brought her knee up, driving it into Maisie's chest hard enough to knock the wind out of her. As Maisie doubled over, Kate seized her by the hoodie, twisting the fabric tight around her throat. Dragging Maisie across the picnic blanket, sending takeaway and wine glasses flying, Kate thrust her against the nearest wall, yanking off those Yoko Ono shades and flinging them away. Sunny was shrieking, but Kate ignored that, roaring into Maisie's face,

"Right! You're under arrest!"

Maisie responded with only a choked noise. Relieved of those intimidating sunglasses, she was just a fiftyish woman with a pierced eyebrow and wide, terrified eyes. The tough gal defending her patch had been rendered helpless by two basic hand-to-hand moves Kate could have done in her sleep.

"Let her go! Please. She'll behave, I promise," Sunny cried.

Kate let go. On guard, she took a step back, still bristling with narrowly contained energy.

Maisie slid down to the wall. Clutching herself around the middle, she vomited red wine and curry all over her combat boots.

"You—you're really a cop?" she gasped at Kate.

"I'm a real cop. That's a real warrant card," she said, retrieving it from where it had fallen, "and you're really under arrest."

"Please, Detective, take a moment and reconsider." Sunny knelt at her sister's side, just shy of the vomit. "We're from Texas.

We know better than to attack the police. Maisie's just confused. People are turning up at her flat at all hours. We can't even sleep there now. Over the weekend, they started coming here, too, talking nonsense, making threats against Gran. You sounded like one of them. I even thought you said—said—"

"I did say it. Granville Hardwick died yesterday. He was murdered in his own home."

"Gran?" Sunny repeated blankly.

"Yes."

"Dead?"

"Yes."

"But—what about me?"

Kate didn't know what to say. Sunny stared at her, awaiting an answer. With her Botoxed forehead, collagen-plumped lips, and cascades of highlighted blonde hair, she looked like a flummoxed doll. Thrown For A Loop Barbie.

"Murdered." Maisie groaned and brought up a fresh torrent, retching miserably long after there was nothing more to come. "They killed him. We need protection. We need police protection, *now*, or we're next!"

"But Gran can't be dead," Sunny said, helping Maisie to her feet. "He promised me things. He was taking me to Paris. I can't be alone right now, I don't like being alone, it's not good for me. I need—"

"*Not everything is about you!*" Maisie screamed at her sister. "Gran put his foot in it, and now we're involved, whether we like or not. This is life or death, don't you get it?"

That got through. Releasing Maisie, Sunny tottered toward the sinuous bicycle woman, making it halfway there before she chundered all over her Louboutins.

"Listen," Kate told Maisie. "You're still under arrest, but whether or not I press charges remains to be seen. Tell me what's going on. Small words, short sentences. Don't leave anything out."

"Granville's not just an art broker," Maisie said. "He transports product out of London into Manchester, Leeds, Wolverhampton. Sometimes across the Channel. I didn't find out he was packing plastic baggies full of powder into my crates until one got diverted due a lorry crash and delivered back to me. I crowbarred the lid off, took out the pieces to see what I could salvage, and there it was—enough gear to keep a women's prison lit for a month."

"Heroin? Cocaine?"

"Either. Both. It's not like I can tell. I smoke a little weed, that's all. The hard stuff isn't for me." Maisie rubbed her sternum. "You hurt me."

"You attacked me. Suppose I had been one of these people you're so afraid of? You really think you could have taken me down?"

"I don't know. Used to be pretty good with my fists. Grow up with a name like mine, and you learn to fight early on," Maisie said miserably. "Guess the art world has turned me soft."

"So what did you do when you discovered the contraband?"

"Rang Gran. Gave the oily little weasel an earful."

"And he reacted how?"

"Like always," Maisie said. "Promises. Flattery. Then a list of things I needed to do so he could sleep easy. He was afraid the dealer would assume the crash was deliberate. That we'd diverted the box, listing it as destroyed in transit, so we could keep the gear and resell it ourselves. A little side-action for the middleman."

"I see," Kate said. "So did Hardwick come to collect the drugs?"

"Of course not. He told me to scamper down to bloody Brixton in the dead of night and return it to God knows who. I said no way, I don't want my throat cut in a back alley, thanks very much. I took it round back and flushed it down the toilet."

"I told her not to," Sunny offered. "I thought we should mail it back. With a note to say no hard feelings. And maybe cookies."

Ignoring that, Kate asked Maisie, "Did you flush all of it?"

"All of it. Burned the baggies in the grate. Told Gran he wasn't handling my art any longer, and we were finished. That should have been an end to it," Maisie said. "I reckon he told his connection he was innocent, and I was to blame for everything. That's when shady types started turning up. First they were friendly, just feeling me out, trying to get the gear back. Then they got serious. Said I had to reimburse them the street value in cash, or someone would die."

"Poor Gran," Sunny wailed, bursting into tears too loud and copious to be false. "Killed by drug dealers! Have you caught them? Please tell me you've caught them!"

"Actually, we've only arrested one man in connection with Hardwick's death," Kate said. "Your husband. Buck Wainwright."

Sunny stared at Kate. Then she closed her eyes and shook her head. "Oh, Buck. Buck. How could you do this to me?"

"We need protection," Maisie insisted. "I'll telling you, I'm next."

"All right. I'll arrange transport for the three of us to Scotland Yard," Kate said, pulling out her mobile. "We'll get this on record. I want names and addresses—every detail that connects Granville Hardwick to the drug trade."

# CHAPTER 11

"Right," said Mrs. Snell, a glint of steely resolve in her eyes. "This is a council of war, is it not?"

After kedgeree and three cups of tea, she no longer resembled the distraught woman Tony had led out of Scotland Yard via a concealed exit meant for officers undercover. He wasn't surprised how well she'd rallied. Mrs. Snell had that capacity to absorb and accept misfortune that he secretly considered almost wholly feminine. Women cried and raged as most men never dared. Then they dragged themselves up by their bootlaces and got on with it.

"As we lost the battle, I'd say, yes. War is the word."

"What about the legal strategy?"

"Dead. There isn't one I can live with." There was no need for further explication; Mrs. Snell understood. Even if the finest legal counsel promised to win him his job back, no force on earth could compel Tony to go along with what such a lawsuit would require: for him to take the witness stand and declare, as a matter of public record, how unfairly he'd been treated and what it had cost him to be forced out. He'd accept retirement first. He'd accept the firing squad first, if it came to it.

"Good. Personally, I find the notion of private investigation rather adventurous."

"As do I," Tony lied. He wasn't there yet and didn't know if he ever would be. But he'd raised the notion to Mrs. Snell some weeks before, during their last high-profile murder case, when Downing Street had exerted undue pressure, almost as if trying to intimidate him into failure. From that moment, they'd seen the writing on the wall, and Mrs. Snell had begun researching UK regulations for private investigators with gusto.

"What does your wife say?" she asked.

"We haven't spoken of it."

Mrs. Snell looked at her teacup.

"You disapprove?"

"I've been widowed for a very long time. What do I know of such things? Only...."Her gaze lifted. "As your administrative assistant, if you'd chosen to keep me out of the loop, I'd be gutted. I'd feel you didn't trust me."

Tony was startled. It was a day of firsts. His first day out of public service after more years than he cared to count. And the first time Mrs. Snell had issued a bare-faced rebuke.

"Forgive me if I seem to speak out of turn," she continued as if reading his mind. "But now that I'm no longer your subordinate, I suddenly have the need to express myself. Should the notion of a private investigation service pan out, and should you choose to engage my services under such auspices, no doubt I'll regain my former restraint."

"Perhaps restraint is overrated. And of course you must consider yourself on the payroll," Tony said. "Your first task? Begin the process for me to obtain that blasted license. I always used to say the government should make it a crime for unqualified PIs to harass private citizens and use investigation as an excuse for breach of privacy. I never guessed it would actually happen and put me in danger of arrest if I don't pass an online class. Or, heaven forbid, attend seminars."

"I think with your credentials, you'll be grandfathered out of any seminars," Mrs. Snell said. "If you'll forgive the terminology."

"It's appropriate. I'd surely be the oldest man there."

"I only fear the process won't be quick enough."

"Quick enough for what?"

She looked surprised. "Why, for you to clear up this matter of the dead art dealer, present the answers to the media, and humiliate Scotland Yard."

He laughed. "I can't fault you for dreaming big. But alas, Vic has charge of it now. If I managed such a thing, he'd be the one pilloried, not the people who forced me out. I couldn't do that to him."

Mrs. Snell's eyes narrowed behind her hugely magnifying lenses. "I'm not convinced this change in DCI Jackson will last. He's tried before."

"I haven't the foggiest what the future holds for Vic. But Kate's on his team, and she'll solve the Hardwick murder, I'm sure of it. Perhaps my license will come through in time for me to lend some sort of hand. But at the moment, I have no base of operations, unless you count Wellegrave House."

"Surely two of its rooms can be converted into temporary offices?"

"Let's go find out."

Rather than call Harvey, who certainly wasn't expecting to collect his employer in the Bentley at half-eleven, they took a black cab to Mayfair. The driver started grumbling as soon as he turned on Euston Place.

"I see your destination, but there's no getting close to it, sir," he told Tony. "Probably on account of the murder round these parts last night."

A *Best Buzz* news van, garishly decorated with its trademark, a cartoon bee with an overlarge stinger, blocked half the narrow street. Cameramen milled about. A striking brunette in a trench coat, either a celebrity reporter or someone determined to become one, paced the sidewalk with microphone in hand, rehearsing questions. From the cab Tony couldn't read her lips, but the questions were obviously of the "gotcha" variety, judging by how she paused to practice each one's corresponding reaction: astonishment, disbelief, or righteous indignation.

"Charming. The tabloid vultures descend to pick the art dealer's bones," Mrs. Snell sniffed.

"If only. That's not Hardwick's house they're camped outside," Tony said. "It's mine."

"Codswallop! How on earth did they find out? And why all this? The worst I expected was some sort of triumphant opinion piece in *The Independent.*"

Tony, who read *The Independent*, suspected its editors had larger concerns than yet another fossil purged from the Met. Perhaps *Bright Star* would run something, but only if every pop star, footballer, and royal in Britain spent the next two weeks leading blameless lives. His wedding to Kate had been covered because of its potential for disaster, but afterward, the tabloid's readership had returned to Justin Bieber, Joey Barton, and the Kardashians.

"I suspect this might be an altogether different matter," he told Mrs. Snell. "I'll see about it. Wait here."

She cleared her throat in a most unladylike fashion. "Hardly."

He looked at her, amazed.

"If I'm to be in your private employ, Lord Hetheridge, I think we shall have to negotiate new and different terms. I've had enough unquestioning obedience to last a lifetime. And if you intend to wade into that carnival of atrocious taste masquerading as news, you shan't do so alone."

It didn't take long for them to locate the eye of the scandal-rag hurricane: Louise and Maura Wakefield. The latter looked the worse for wear—uncombed hair, rumpled donkey jacket, cigarette in one hand and mobile in the other. She wore no makeup, but Louise had on enough for both of them. Foundation had rendered her face three shades darker than her neck. Once again she wore a FUBU tracksuit, this one sky blue, her hair tied up in a spangled kerchief. Her hand-lettered protest sign read:

**UNFAIR TO GRANDMOTHERS**

Another sign hung from the bars of his wrought iron fence. Less grammatically sound, it read:

**KIDS NEED MUM'S**
**NOT BUTLER'S**

"There he is!" Louise cried, catching sight of Tony. "That's the man who won't let me see my own grandson. Not without a warrant, he says! And me not knowing him from Adam. What's a geezer want with a little boy? Is he a paedo?"

The striking brunette whirled. Signaling her cameramen to follow, she glided between Louise and Tony, thrusting her microphone under his nose.

"Lord Hetheridge! Ann Spann, *Best Buzz* news. Congratulations on your marriage, sir. But some are asking—do you think it's quite fair, putting yourself between a mum and her son?"

"No comment."

"Documents obtained by *Best Buzz* indicate your wife, Kate, never adopted young Henry, and her sister Maura has applied for restoration of parental responsibility. In light of those facts," Anne Spann continued, checking the cameras to ensure she was optimally placed, "would you be adverse to allowing Henry's mum and gran to visit him now?"

"It's noon. He's at school."

"Shows what you know!" Louise crowed. "Little scrapper got sent home for fighting." Raising her sign, she tapped the word "unfair" with a sparkly fingernail. "Troubled, that one. We wanted to talk him off the ledge, but your almighty butler won't open the gates. My grandson is held hostage not a stone's throw away"—her voice quavered—"and there's nothing I can do about it."

"Sent home?" Tony repeated, wondering if school officials had called Kate. Would she turn up in the midst of this chaos, fly into a rage, and try to finish last night's fist fight? He cared little for the safety of Louise and Maura, but he had to prevent Kate from giving this gossip correspondent what she wanted: the sort of footage that made careers in the entertainment biz and ended them in the Met.

"Yes, my son was sent home, and no one could reach you or Kate, so the butler had to fetch him," Maura announced, crowding Louise to one side. "After you practically set the dogs on us last night, what could I do but try to see him at his school? He was having a break in the schoolyard when I got there. One of the posh boys called me a clot, and Henry slugged him. After the teacher broke up the fight, Henry said *my sister* taught him violence is the answer. Too right she did! Didn't she do this to me?" Maura demanded, pointing at her swollen nose.

Tony struggled to rein in his temper. Henry, though not yet nine, would never have said such a thing. Maura was trying to make the boy seem poorly-adjusted as a result of Kate's guardianship. And while Tony could forgive the cameras, the reporter, and the accusations in general, he could not forgive a misrepresentation of Henry's character.

"I'll thank you not to lie, Ms. Wakefield."

"You hear how he talks to me!" she screeched at Ann Spann.

"Thinks we ain't human," Louise agreed, grabbing the microphone to be certain she had everyone's attention. "I guess my grandson will be a poor little rich boy, alone in a big house. With nobody but a servant to pick up the pieces when he descends into violence."

Ann Spann nodded wisely. "A tragic picture," she said, wrestling her microphone away from Louise, only to thrust it back at Tony. "These ladies make a passionate case for continued involvement in young Henry's life. No doubt there are many advantages to living in *Mayfair*," she said, her added emphasis seeming to connote sleeping on stacks of cash, "but blood is thicker, eh? Some might call this proof of class warfare in modern Britain. So tell us, Lord Hetheridge, now that Mum and Gran have taken their case to the public, can you reassure us as to young Henry's future?"

"Indeed I can." Mrs. Snell stepped forward, and the Wakefields stepped back. Even Ann Spann visibly quailed at the sight of those blue-rinsed curls, the 1960s-era tweed suit, and that black leather pocketbook. Such unassailable correctness could be terrifying, even to those who ignored convention.

"And you are?" the reporter asked.

"I am Mrs. Snell. From this day forward, I shall be Master Henry's nanny, overseeing his needs when he is not at school."

"Oh, ain't that just like the rich. Hire another servant! Throw money at it!" Louise cried. "Listen, Ann. You need to pry into my Katie's life. Her job's dangerous. Got herself held at gunpoint awhile back. Always mixing it up with serial killers and the like. Never works less than sixty hours a week. And him!" She stabbed a finger at Tony. "Never less than eighty. Pull the records and see what kind of guardian he'd be. Don't be put off just because he has the high and mighty act down pat."

"Ms. Spann." Forcing himself to smile at the reporter, Tony held her gaze till she softened. "Might I make an announcement? Something I feel certain your viewers will find interesting?"

Without waiting for her to answer, he plucked the microphone from her hands as if it had belonged to him all along. Louise Wakefield was mistaken about a great many things, but in one respect, she'd pegged him right. He had the high and mighty act down pat.

"It's true, over the course of my career at Scotland Yard, I've worked eighty hours a week or more, serving the public. But this morning, I resigned my position to devote more time to my family. I have no objection to Henry's relatives visiting, if the courts choose to award access. I would never separate a child from his blood. But he's lived with my wife for several years, and stability is essential. This is about what's best for Henry, not the whims of adults. To that end...." He looked directly into the camera. "Kate and I will adopt him, and make him my heir."

After that declaration, it took some time for Tony and Mrs. Snell to safely retreat to the desirable side of Wellegrave House's nine foot gate. As they approached the house, Tony saw the curtains in an upstairs window ripple. Then they fell back into place as if a small boy, afraid of being seen, had left his vantage point.

*He's probably off to Google* Best Buzz *news,* Tony thought. *Heaven knows how quickly they'll have the footage up. An hour or two at the latest.*

His pulse still beat in his ears, breath coming so raggedly, Mrs. Snell probably thought him mad. Was he? In the middle of Louise's rant, the best way to answer had come clear to him, the masterstroke to end it all. And so he'd acted, convinced of his own rightness, utterly sure. Now the full realization of what he'd done was sinking in. He'd never discussed the question of adoption, not with Kate and certainly not with Henry. As for the heir to his personal fortune, how was Kate likely to react to him deciding such a thing unilaterally? On television?

*At least this answers the question of how I'll spend my retirement. In a box, six feet under.*

Harvey had the front door open before they reached the steps. "Forgive me, milord, I hope I did right by refusing them entry. They promised reprisals, and before I knew it, that van pulled up...."

"You performed admirably," Tony said, ushering Mrs. Snell inside first. "Harvey, you remember my administrative assistant?"

"Of course. But if I might ask, why are you home so soon? Has something happened? Did a neighbor call to inform you of the commotion?" the butler asked, giving Mrs. Snell an uneasy smile. He'd always been a touch wary of her at the office. Finding her at Wellegrave House, smack in the center of his territory, seemed to alarm him.

"Things are under control. In a state of flux, but under control." Tony clenched his hands into fists to conceal how they shook. "Would you excuse me if I don't put you in the picture till this evening? Or possibly tomorrow? The day thus far has been... less than ideal."

"Good heavens. That bad? Well, I've no wish to pry. But milord, if you you'll forgive me for saying so, you look rather— florid. Can I get you something? Green tea? Some fresh squeezed orange juice, perhaps?"

"No, thank you."

"Sir, forgive me. But this isn't some sort of health scare, is it?"

Tony bit back a smile. The poor man probably thought he'd been diagnosed with something dire, like the need for a quintuple bypass. He owed Harvey the truth, but there was a good chance the manservant would weep longer and harder than Mrs. Snell, and Tony couldn't face another round of consoling. It would have to wait until the morning.

"I'm fine. Hot under the collar, that's all. Mrs. Snell is embarking on a special project for me, one that will operate out of this house. I believe I'll take her through the ground floor myself, see what space we can free up."

Looking more than a touch worried about what Mrs. Snell's incursion into his domain might mean, Harvey withdrew back to the sanctuary of his kitchen. Tony, still beset by waves of adrenalin, stiffened his back, set his teeth, and led Mrs. Snell to the first likely spot, a disused guest room. He was attempting to open some rather stubborn brocade curtains when she said,

"This is not only excruciating, but unnecessary. You're too flustered to operate a pull-cord." She waved him aside and parted the curtains herself, letting in a flood of winter sun.

"I'm not flustered…."

"Yes, you are. Never mind, I'm perfectly capable of exploring the ground floor on my own. When I'm finished, perhaps you can introduce me to Henry. My offer to serve as nanny, at least until things are more settled, wasn't just for the cameras. And I think you'll find I'm rather better with children than my interactions with DS Bhar may have suggested. But that can wait until after you've spoken to the boy."

"I'm not ready to speak to him. I've no idea what to say," Tony said, still clenching and unclenching his fists.

"Well, you still possess epees and a piste, do you not? Suit up, and face him over crossed swords."

"Fencing? I just got in trouble for fighting," Henry groaned. He lay in bed atop the covers, flat on his back with a comic book unopened on his chest, apparently contemplating the unfairness of the universe. "Shouldn't I stay in my room and think on what I've done? Lie here and be punished? That seems right. I don't want to practice."

"The day you don't want to practice is precisely the day you most need to," Tony said. It was the sort of nonsensical thing his own boyhood instructor had told him, and to his surprise, it worked. Still looking downcast, Henry nevertheless trudged to his wardrobe, located his white trousers, white shirt, padded vest, gloves, and face mask, and carried them into the hall bathroom to change. He was a private child, not given to stripping down to his shorts in front of anyone save Kate. Such innate dignity was one of the qualities Tony most enjoyed about him.

"Fine. Dressed." Still morose, Henry emerged with face mask under one arm. "I know you're angry with me. Go ahead, let me have it. Unleash."

Tony refused to laugh, but sometimes the boy tempted him as much as Bhar. "I was told your mother visited you at the school. Another boy called her a name, and you responded by hitting him. Is that true?"

"Yes."

"This other boy, how old was he?"

"Seven."

"Taller than you?"

"No."

"So you attacked a younger, smaller boy for calling someone a name?"

Henry fiddled with his face mask.

"Did you slap him?"

"No. I punched him. Right cross, just like you showed me."

Tony sighed. "And what did I tell you when I showed you that?"

More fiddling.

"Henry?"

"Only use it on bigger, older boys," he muttered.

"As...."

"As a last resort."

"That's right. Only go for the knockout when you have no choice. In those rare moments when you or someone you care about is seriously threatened. A schoolmate calling your mum a clot doesn't strike me as serious."

"She is a clot," Henry burst out. "She shouldn't have been there! She embarrassed me, smoking by the fence until the teacher told her to put it out. Everybody knows you don't smoke in school. And she shouldn't have come here last night. She was never around when I wanted her. Now that things are good, she's back, and she'll ruin everything."

"No, she won't. And it's all right to feel a little sympathy for Maura," Tony said, as much to himself as to Henry. "She's your mum. She's sick and unhappy and wants to see you. That's not so hard to understand."

Henry caught his breath. "Kate's giving me back to her?"

"I didn't say—"

"I don't want to go back to her! That was a TV van out there, wasn't it? I saw the aerial. Who was she talking to?"

"No one. A gossip program of negligible influence."

Henry shot a glance at his laptop, which hadn't functioned since he spilled a glass of chocolate milk on its keyboard. "Can I use your computer? Just for a sec. I want to see what she said."

"The video won't be up yet. Come along. Lessons first, all else later." Tony ushered the boy down the hall and into Wellegrave House's gymnasium. A long, high-ceilinged room, its walls were mirrored, and its heart-of-pine floors were bare except for exercise equipment: free weights, a heavy bag, an elliptical machine, and the piste, a fourteen meter strip fitted to keep score electronically. From a wall rack, Tony selected two practice epees, both standard size; Henry had progressed sufficiently to put away his plastic child's version.

They took their places opposite one another within the strip. As instructor as well as combatant, it fell to Tony to issue the initial warning:

"*Pret.*"

Henry assumed the *en guard* stance.

"*Allez.*"

They began. As usual, Tony gave Henry the first lunge, parrying with minimal speed and power. On good days, the boy kept his form, lunging with back leg straight, front leg bent knee-over-ankle, thrusting his sword at a forty-five degree angle. In such cases, Tony withheld the obvious ripostes, only parrying and gently pressing forward, leaving himself open so Henry could score the occasional "touch." On bad days, Henry forgot his form, stepped off the piste with one or both feet, scored off-target touches, and occasionally fell over in his desperation to prevail. This was a very bad day.

"*Arrêt!*"

Tony put out a hand to Henry, helping the boy rise after another uncontrolled lunge led to yet another fall.

"Form! Form is paramount. From the moment you step onto the piste and assume the *en guard* stance, every move must be controlled. Precise. If you train yourself to perform correctly, thinking through each step no matter how much the effort slows you down, the day will come when you don't have to think any more. Muscle memory will take over, your speed will increase, and your mind will be free to strategize."

"I just want to attack," Henry cried. "If you'd let me fight my own way, I'd score!"

Tony removed his mask, raking fingers through his hair. He'd broken a sweat, but from frustration, not exertion. "You think so?"

"I know so."

"Very well." He switched off the piste's electronic sensors. "Step wherever you wish. Move however you want." Replacing his face mask, he resumed his position, crouching in the classic *en guard* stance.

Henry charged, driving straight ahead with his slender sword as if it were a battering ram. Tony remained motionless until the blade was *there*, in that precise opportune place. He flicked his fingers so the tip of his weapon ducked under Henry's, and the boy's epee went flying. Unable to stop, Henry crashed into him, but Tony was braced and prevented their fall.

"Care to try that again?"

He expected another outburst or tears of frustration. Instead, Henry stayed where he was, holding Tony tight.

"I'm sorry I hit that kid. I shouldn't have done it. I wanted to hit *her.*"

"Yes, well, we'll work out something with the school. There's sure to be discipline, and you'll just have to bear up. The main thing is, don't do it again."

"But she's taking me, isn't she?" Henry whispered, daring to look up at him. Tony pulled off the boy's steel-fronted mask, removing his as well.

"Henry. I should have brought this up to you before. Truth is, I should have brought it up to Kate, and for that I'm sorry. But the fact is… if you're not opposed… I think it's high time we adopted you."

The boy blinked behind half-fogged spectacle lenses. "Really?"

"Really."

"But Mum said she'll take Kate to court. That no magistrate will keep a son from his mother."

"That remains to be seen."

"I heard it all, everything she said before Kate hit her. Money can't buy a child… the courts will see this for what it is…."

"Yes, well, your mother and grandmother talk a good game. And for all I know, the courts won't look kindly on the adoption. Perhaps they'll think me too old or Kate's profession too dangerous, or consider the whole thing unfair to Maura, now that she's putting her life together. I have no idea. Just tell me this. Do you want to stay here?"

"Yes." Henry had never been more adamant.

"Then you will. If my solicitors can't win the battle, they can surely drag it out for years. Long enough for you to reach legal age."

"But she—"

"Henry." Tony looked the boy in the eye. "I'm promising you this. Maura won't regain sole custody of you, not if I have to empty my bank account to prevent it." At Henry's shocked look, he laughed. "What did you think money was for?"

By half-six, most of the household was sorted. Mrs. Snell had declined to stay for dinner. After locating two rooms that would serve as a temporary "command center," as she put it, for a private investigation service, she'd left, promising to return the next morning.

Tony, Harvey, and Henry ate dinner together; Ritchie carried a plate to his TV for an early showing of *The Lego Movie*. To keep Henry off the web and away from *Best Buzz* news for as long as possible, Tony granted the boy use of the Xbox and his favorite *Star Wars* game. That was surely poor guardianship for a child sent home for fighting, but he didn't know what else to do. He had to prevent Henry from viewing the segment until he could speak to Kate.

But half-seven came, and Kate still wasn't home. On day one of a murder investigation, that was hardly surprising, but he'd expected a call, a text, something. Resisting the temptation to call her, Tony went back up to the gymnasium. He was still too tense for a passive activity like reading, and as far as pondering Hardwick's murder, well, in point of fact, his opinion wasn't wanted. That left the elliptical machine, or perhaps a few rounds with the heavy bag.

He'd scarcely put on his gloves and started swinging when he heard Kate say from the doorway, "That's a lot of aggression. I can relate."

He turned. She'd changed from her work attire to a T-shirt and trackies. Her hair was loose and wild, her face set. He'd seen that look before, the jutting jaw and flared nostrils. And like a guilty suspect, he immediately sought to remedy the situation with words.

"Kate. There's something I'd like to speak to you about. I should have done it sooner, but—"

"Don't." She held up a hand. "Don't try to manage how I feel about this, Tony. Or I swear I'll have your guts for garters."

"You heard what happened?"

She made an exasperated noise. "Of course I heard. Look at this!" Closing the distance between them, she pulled out her mobile and scrolled through the call log. "While I was interviewing Sunny Wainwright and her sister, a call from Henry's school. A call from Maura. From Henry's teacher. From Maura again. From Mum. From Harvey. From a producer at *Best Buzz* news. From Mum again. From Maura again. And then the cherry on the cow pat—a text from Sharada Bhar with a link to this: 'Peer Ignites Class Warfare with Adoption Demand.'" Kate shook her head in disbelief. "You decide you want to adopt Henry and I hear about it from *Sharada Bhar*?"

"Your voice," he said. "You might want to keep it down. I distracted Henry with the Xbox, but he still could overhear."

"Let him. He deserves to know! Last night you had the nerve to ask if I cared what Henry wants. Then you do this, *this*, without even asking him if he wants it?"

"I did ask him. This very afternoon. He said he wants to stay with us. Of course," Tony added quickly to stave off another attack, "you're right, you're quite right, I behaved badly with that TV reporter. I wanted the matter settled, and I went too far, too fast. It was inexcusable, and I hope you'll forgive me."

She sighed. The long, exasperated sound pierced him deeper than any accusation.

"Kate. I know we haven't talked about children of our own,"

he said, venturing into waters they'd avoided for months. "Not since the miscarriage and the complications that followed. But at your last visit, the doctor made it clear that another pregnancy is a longshot. And given my time of life and the rigors of your career... maybe that's not so terrible?" He said that last word softly, hoping he hadn't misread her feelings.

"No," she said after a moment. "Henry and Ritchie are enough. This is enough. Nothing's missing."

"So you approve of the adoption? You agree it's the best way forward?"

Kate's eyes narrowed. "Don't you go sounding all calm and reasonable. You pulled the rug out from under me. Twice in one day! Even if I agree, even if I think it's a wonderful idea, you're not getting off the hook that easily."

There was nothing he could say to that, so he kept silent, maintaining a chokehold on his emotions—his default behavior when seas turned rough. He'd never spent the night in his study before. With any luck, the sofa would be comfortable.

"Now," Kate continued. "I've been assigned to Vic Jackson for the interim, if you didn't know, but I'll bet money you did. I had to sit and listen to him apologize about you-know-what, which made me want to castrate him with a fingernail clipper. A suspect attacked me. I subdued her. I had to watch her and her sister vomit all over their shoes. *Then* I spent the afternoon taking down the names and addresses of potential drug mules. There's over fifty! Hardwick's art business was mostly a front. I still don't know if Buck killed him, but I've uncovered a good reason why somebody else might have. I'm tired, and I'm angry, and I'm getting in the shower."

"Of course," Tony murmured.

"And you're coming with me."

"Of course." Trying not to show his relief, he followed her out of the gymnasium.

# CHAPTER 12

"Tony," Kate whispered. The bedroom was dark except for a single lamp. "Are you asleep?"

"No. Just keeping my eyes closed."

He looked remarkably relaxed, younger even, basking in that masculine satisfaction she took such proprietary pleasure in. This was it: as undefended as the castle got. She almost hated to attack. Almost.

"So this morning, after you showed us the letter, I began to wonder—what was your end game?"

His eyes opened. "Kate...."

"Really. I'm curious."

"I've told you, nothing was certain. Michael—AC Deaver—thought they were bluffing. The first threat to your career came days before our wedding. I saw no reason—"

"No, I understand all that." She pushed back the duvet, raising herself on one elbow. "I mean, what was your end game in marrying me? If you didn't want a partner, what were you looking for? A trophy? 'Silver fox seeks younger blonde to play house in the West End. No pets, personal details furnished on a strictly need-to-know basis.'"

He groaned. "What do you expect? Histrionics? Shall I get pissed and pummel a wall like Buck Wainwright? Beat my fists black and blue?"

"I could understand that. I could understand almost anything but you shutting me out. You revealed more on TV this afternoon than you've ever revealed to me."

He sat up. Propping himself against the headboard, he passed a hand over his face. "Kate. If I wanted a trophy wife, I could have had one years ago. I don't believe the definition of a partner requires me to subject anyone, least of all you, to me at my worst."

"I heard the vicar say something about for better or worse."

"That's not what the phrase means."

"What else would it mean? Tornados? Asteroids? I accept the fact you were single for a long time, so playing things close to the vest comes naturally." She ran a fingernail up his bare chest. "But before you and I have even one serious conversation about Henry's future, you tell *Best Buzz* you want to adopt him? *Best Buzz* and not me? And why would you even want to, anyway?"

"Because it's the right thing to do."

"Not good enough."

"He needs a stable home. His mother—"

"Not good enough."

He sighed. Just when she thought he would shut down, turn to stone again, he took a deep breath and met her eyes. "Because I love him."

Kate's throat tightened. She knew what she wanted to say, but emotion made the words sticky.

"Right," she managed at last. "Was that so difficult?"

"I feel better showing you the best I can be." He, too, seemed to be forming each syllable with effort. "I don't want you to think of me as overly emotional. Impulsive. Out of control."

She kissed his earlobe. "You were out of control a little while ago...."

"That's different."

"As for impulsive—you always have been. You think I don't know that?"

Tony seemed so startled, even offended, Kate sat up straight. "Oh, my God. You actually think I don't know that?"

The look on his face confirmed it. She tried not to laugh.

"Tony. The first time we met, you took my part against Vic without any idea whether I was right or wrong. That was impulsive. When my relationship with Dylan blew up and I didn't know what to do, you offered to marry me. We'd known each other a few days. *Days*. And all that bollocks about me never having seen you angry? Of course I have. You were angry the day I confronted Madge. You were furious with me, furious with Madge, and willing to die in my place. The best parts of you are overly emotional. Impulsive. Out of control.

"It's not that I don't respect who you pretend to be," she went on, kissing his lips. "Cold, precise. But I would never have married that man. I wouldn't even have shagged him. I fell in love with the real you—the one who takes risks and damn the consequences. The man who told his family to stuff it, who took a job they loathed because *he* wanted it. The man with a willful streak," she ended, recognizing something she'd never understood before, "that matches mine."

He cupped her face in both hands, saying nothing. Seeing how his eyes shone, she didn't press him.

"You know the sort of blokes I used to date," she continued after a moment. "Gorgeous but bone idle. Musicians who never played gigs. Political agitators who never left the house. I had this idea men were basket cases, that I should take home the prettiest disaster and try to keep him alive, like a moldy houseplant. Then one day I turned a corner and ran into you—a man. A real man. And you were the best thing that ever happened to me. But surely you know it's not in my nature to be shielded from all harm.

Whatever happens to you, whatever hurts you, I want my share. For better or worse."

"But… how do I…."

"Tell me how they forced you out. Every detail. And how it made you feel."

Kate held her breath. He was quiet for a very long time. And then, to her relief, he did.

Even by mid-morning, it was too cold for an outdoor summit, so Kate and Tony awaited their guests in the dining room. Cream tea was already on the table: two pots of Earl Grey, two pots of Darjeeling, a three-tiered plate of scones, clotted cream, strawberry jam, and crustless finger sandwiches stuffed with cucumber or ham and mustard. Tony had requested something informal, and Harvey, still prone to brief bouts of weeping after hearing the news, had responded with a spread that was last meal quality.

"Thank you," Mrs. Snell said when the butler insisted on pulling out her chair. "After so many years providing the morning repast, this is a welcome change," she added, pouring herself a cup of tea.

"Henry liked you very much." Kate tried to keep the surprise from her voice. She'd expected him to run away screaming, not engage Mrs. Snell in a long discussion about his new favorite dinosaur, the recently reinstated Brontosaurus. "Harvey's been so busy since Henry and Ritchie moved in. It's very generous of you to help out."

"If only until my private investigation service takes off," Tony said. "Whatever that might entail. A case a week? A case a month? I've no idea."

Refusing the head of the table, he'd taken a seat on the window side next to Kate. With the exception of their honeymoon, she'd never seen him at eleven in the morning without one of his trademark Italian suits. Today, however, he wore an Oxford button-down shirt and a dark blue sweater, no tie. And even during their honeymoon, he'd shied away from public displays of affection, but that, too, had changed overnight. Ignoring the scone and teacup before him, he held Kate's hand, giving it a squeeze from time to time. She thought he'd pull away when Bhar entered the dining room, but Tony didn't let go. He merely smiled when his former subordinate's gaze flicked to their linked hands.

"Morning, guv, Mrs. S." Paul looked harried, despite his natty suit and obligatory Acqui di Parma fumes. "I didn't expect all this. Your lip looks better, Kate. Um...." He lifted his hands as if to rake them through his hair, stopping just before he ruined a look that must have taken beaucoup product to achieve. "Hiya, Harvey. Sad about the guv, eh? I mean Lord... I mean, him. The fact is, before we begin...."

"Are you off your meds? Sit down," Kate barked.

"Yes, I appreciate the invitation, it's lovely to be here, but the fact is—"

"Deepal!" A woman called from the front parlor. "I won't be hidden out here! It's undignified!"

"... I brought my mum," Paul concluded. "When I told her I was popping by the guv's—I mean, Lord—I mean, his place, she wouldn't take no for an answer."

"You're sacked," Tony said.

"Too late. Mum," Paul said, turning to intercept Sharada in the doorway, "Of course you've met, um, er, *Tony*, and Kate. This is Mrs. Snell, who used to be his secretary, and that's Harvey, the manservant. Like Alfred to Batman."

"Deepal, I write romances. I know what a manservant is." Evading her son's attempt to shepherd her into the nearest chair, Sharada made directly for the man with the title. "Tony, I'm so worried about Buck I've barely slept. They won't let me visit him.

I've had to apply for permission! So I sat up last night, researching the art man and all his women. Every one of them married! I made a list of cuckolded husbands, that is to say, suspects...."

"Please, have a seat," Tony said with the easy authority that worked so many miracles, even when dealing with the strongest of personalities. "Pour some tea. Try some clotted cream. We're waiting on just one more, and then we'll discuss the case in an organized fashion."

"If we're discussing the case, I'm not meant to be here," Paul said, sitting down beside Mrs. Snell. She looked sideways at him, and he put on a smile that didn't quite make up for all the times he'd not-so-secretly called her "ghastly."

"Nice shawl you're wearing, Mrs. S. White with gold trim."

"Yes. Lady Hetheridge gave it to me this morning. A personal token of appreciation for my years of service."

"Oh." Paul shot Kate a look that suggested if she was going to give presents, she had a duty to warn him beforehand. "Well. In recognition of your service, I would like to give you... my undying gratitude?"

Mrs. Snell regarded him coolly. "Thank you."

"But again, as far as the case, maybe I should let Mum say her piece and then go," Paul continued, biting into a cucumber sandwich as if time were of the essence. "Being in disgrace stinks. Know what I did yesterday? While Action Kate was going about karate chopping suspects and uncovering Hardwick's ties to the drug trade? I was chatting up an old gal named Mrs. Lobelia Nibley-Tatters. No kidding," he said, pouring himself a cup of Earl Grey. "Thought it was Michael Palin in a housedress at first. Her neighbor, Arry, has been at war with her over—wait for it—the nocturnal activities of her cat Jinxy, who likes to pop round gardens where he's not welcome.

"Anyhow, during the course of arguing with Arry over her cat's right to jump the fence and serenade him at two in the morning, she noticed the sort of people Arry keeps company with. Took down license plates. Wrote descriptions in her diary. All in hopes of turning Arry over to the Council, getting him cautioned for obstructing parking spots or the like. She never cottoned on that Arry's a drug distributor, or that some of those men she's observed were traffickers higher up the food chain. Not till Scotland Yard came calling. Now she's not so hot to testify. Afraid it might put her cat in danger."

Kate grinned. "Think you can convince her to take the stand?"

"I have to, if I'm ever going to get back to the murder beat. And I also need to keep well away from anything touching on the Hardwick case. There's no way I'm deliberately provoking Jackson. I know old Vic's a bit of a mingebag, and he has those crazy eyes, like he's one taut rubber band from snapping. But he was decent to me yesterday, and—"

"DCI Jackson," Harvey announced from the doorway.

Paul shot Kate a second look, more wounded than the first. Then he took a scone from the plate, cut it in half, and silently began anointing it with clotted cream.

"Good morning, Vic. Thanks for coming. Have a seat." Tony indicated the head of the table.

Jackson went to his place with shoulders hunched and head down. He looked like a man who'd crashed a wedding, or been caught stealing from the collection plate. As he sat down, Harvey said,

"Sir, I seem to recall you enjoy Bloody Marys. If you'd like, I can—"

Tony silenced his butler with a look. Catching it, Kate suddenly understood. Vic's changed demeanor, his liquor trolley stocked only with non-alcoholic beverages, the way he smelled of mouthwash these days, instead of a pint. It all made sense.

"No Bloody Marys, thank you." Jackson looked around the table warily. "A cuppa is fine. Sorry I interrupted. You were at 'one taut rubber band from snapping?'" he asked Paul.

Mouth full of scone, Paul widened his eyes and shook his head, as if genuinely at a loss.

Jackson cleared his throat. "I appreciate being asked over." Picking up a teapot, he poured himself a cup very slowly, as if mistrusting himself to perform the operation with so many people watching. "As for your presence, Bhar, if I think it's dangerous or counterproductive, I'll send you packing. Otherwise, you can stay. But later, if AC Deaver or a nosy parker like Saunderson asks, you'll forget you were here, won't you?"

"Yes, sir," Paul managed around the remnants of his mouthful.

No one else spoke. Kate glanced at Tony, who filled his own cup, still saying nothing. Gradually it became clear that Jackson not only occupied the head of the table. He was meant to lead the meeting.

"Right." Jackson cleared his throat again. "So. This afternoon, DS Hetheridge will interview Miss Georgette Sevrin. I've looked over the file provided by PC Fannon, Tony. It made for interesting reading. She's a career malingerer." Hauling out his battered leather notebook, he flipped to the relevant page and read,

"Aged fifteen. Miss Sevrin brought suit against the headmistress of her school for negligence. Slipped on a floor in her dormitory, said the danger wasn't properly signed. Obtained a settlement.

"Aged nineteen. Nearly drowned on holiday in Polperro. Brought suit against the beach commission for lack of lifeguards. Won a settlement.

"Aged twenty-nine. Suffered temporary blindness due to chemical exposure on the job. Brought suit, then dropped it, apparently after failing to secure a doctor's testimony. Score one for the ophthalmologists of the NHS.

"Aged thirty-five. Married a French millionaire. Soon developed a psychiatric disturbance she attributed to her husband's mental cruelty. Sued for divorce and won a settlement of over two million pounds. I reckon it took her awhile to burn through the money, because things went quiet.

"Aged forty-two, it starts again. A slippery floor in Harrods. A chemical burn on her arm from a perfume squirter in Harvey Nicholls. Finally, nine months ago, she was a passenger in a car driven by her former brother-in-law, Granville Hardwick. He swerved to avoid a pedestrian and crashed into a Routemaster. He was unharmed; she spent a week in hospital and came out mental. Now she has an open suit against the City of Westminster, which operates the bus in question, for negligence, and the NHS, for mistreatment while hospitalized. Looking to collect ten million."

"Was the art man involved in the scam? Did he expect a cut?" Sharada asked. She seemed to consider herself part of the investigation, and to Kate's amusement, Jackson went along with it.

"There's no evidence of that, beyond the fact he allowed her to stay at his place. But there may have been another reason. You know Hardwick's one and only marriage was to her sister, right? Monette Sevrin?"

Kate took out her mobile. It was time to start taking notes.

"Well," Jackson continued, "PC Fannon must have been hot to impress you, Tony, because he dug up the specifics of Hardwick's divorce from Monette. She named him an adulterer and her sister Georgette as the other woman."

"Interesting," Tony said.

"It does make one wonder what sort of relationship Miss Sevrin and Mr. Hardwick maintained," Mrs. Snell said. "For her to remain in his house, feigning illness, while he romanced a parade of younger women. Either they matured from lovers to co-conspirators, or she was using the possibility of a big settlement to stay in his life."

Kate goggled at the former administrative assistant. She'd never heard Mrs. Snell comment on a case.

"You read up on Hardwick, Mrs. S?" Paul sounded as astonished as Kate felt.

"I could hardly help it. Last night's papers and news reports were devoted to him. And even if they hadn't been, I would have gone looking. I'm committed now, aren't I?" She sipped her tea.

"What about Buck?" Sharada asked. "Have you proven him innocent yet? There must be CCTV camera footage. Eyewitnesses in the neighborhood...."

Jackson made a disgruntled noise but covered it over with more throat-clearing. "You're Mrs. Bhar?"

"Who else would I be?"

"Er, well, Mrs. Bhar, the camera footage is still being gathered, but what we have from East Asia House—that white eyesore Hardwick built—is useless. The last thing it recorded is from three weeks ago. Someone, probably a neighbor, coated the lens with black spray paint. Most likely a member of that protest group, the Society to Reverse Euston Brutality, intending to give Hardwick a piece of his mind and not wanting it caught on tape. Whatever was said, it must not have bothered Hardwick too much. He didn't lodge a police complaint. Didn't even have the camera repaired."

"Given his activity as a drug middleman, shipping contraband along with art, could the visit be related to that?" Kate asked.

Jackson shook his head. "I've spent years dealing with the drug trade. At that level—the level that comes knocking at your door—they're young, twitchy, shaved heads, neck tattoos. This was just a little bloke with a comb-over and loafers, fifty if he was a day. I'll email you the image," he added. "I'll bet he's one of your neighbors."

"So nothing to free Buck?" Sharada was turning plaintive.

"Mum. You promised," Paul warned.

"Well, the Holiday Inn footage corroborates his story," Jackson flipped to another section in his notebook, then fished reading glasses out of his breast pocket in order to read his own handwriting. "Here it is. Buck exited the premises at 2:05. Returned at 5:27. Exited again at 6:45. Each time, he wore a cowboy coat—leather, ankle-length—that hid his clothes. His tab at the hotel pub, as well as time-stamped use of his room key, line up with his taped testimony. But none of it precludes him from killing Hardwick around the official time of death, which has been set at 4:30."

"What about the maid he bribed to wash his clothes?" Kate asked.

"He picked a good one. She won't say a word. Insists it never happened," Jackson said. "We seized everything in his room and sent in forensic techs to check for trace evidence, but so far, nothing."

"Oh, Buck," Sharada moaned. "Why didn't you come to me? I would have washed away the art man's blood for you."

"Mum!"

"I'm a loyal woman. I won't apologize," she said stoutly. "And like Mrs. Snell, I've been reading up, doing my best to solve this case." From within the depth of her handbag, she withdrew a sheaf of papers, all printed from various websites, and placed it on the table triumphantly. "I give you—the wandering wives!"

Paul choked on his tea. Jackson looked like he was about to erupt, and Mrs. Snell became very occupied in spreading jam on her scone. Kate was searching for a something diplomatic to say when Tony picked up the printouts. Then he, too, fished out his reading glasses for a more careful examination.

"This is wandering wife number one?"

"Yes. Fiona Leeds, wife of Barney Leeds," Sharada said eagerly.

He read on. "It says she left her husband when he punched out his coach. I remember that. And according to this story, she dated Hardwick for the better part of last year."

"Yes! And look at this interview she did last week." Sharada dug out an article originally published in the *Daily Mail*. "It's supposed to be about her book tour. But all she could talk about was cheating men and lying men and men in general, how women are better off without them. I think she was angry at her husband *and* the art man."

Tony placed a picture of Barney Leeds in the center of the table for everyone to see. A big man with a perpetually angry face, he'd cleaned himself up for a red carpet photo op. To Kate, the effect was rather like putting a shaved gorilla in Prada—the designer clothes looked worse by association, and the gorilla didn't like it much, either.

"Has she returned to her husband?" Tony asked.

"No. And he's known to be violent," Sharada said happily. "Maybe he's the killer. Then there's this one," she added, fishing out a picture of a mousy looking woman with limp hair and sad eyes. "Patsy East. Another wandering wife. Her husband's Declan East. The bloke who's always going on about how Starbucks is ruining civilization."

"I know him," Paul said. "He thinks Britain is going the way of the Roman Empire, and men getting manicures is proof of it."

"She looks a bit outside Hardwick's usual type," Kate said. "Are we sure Patsy was dating him? They weren't just friends?"

"They were seen together quite often to just be friends," Sharada said. "I have a picture somewhere of her in sequins. Sequins! Must have taken that dress out of mothballs. But it looks like Patsy was the last woman to date Hardwick before he met Sunny. Maybe Patsy didn't like being replaced, eh? Maybe she turned up at his house and bashed him in the head."

"Supposition can be fun," Kate said, trying to inject a bit of sanity before Jackson exploded. He'd gone a quarter hour without that taut rubber band snapping; she wanted to help him continue the streak. "But did you find any hint of an actual motive, like a rant on social media?"

"There's this," Tony said, holding up a Declan East column less than a month old. It was called "Infidelity: How Its Widespread Tolerance Cheapens Us All." "I've skimmed his writing.

The man seems to take virtually every facet of daily life as a personal insult. No surprise he didn't take kindly to his wife's extracurricular activities with Hardwick."

"Hang on." Jackson reached for the printout, studying East's portrait beside the op-ed piece. "I know that face." Withdrawing his mobile, he went through some lengthy maneuvers with apps and passwords, obtained what he sought, and placed the phone on the table for all to see.

It was a picture, obviously a security still, of a gloomy-looking man with a comb-over and loafers. He frowned up at the camera, spray paint can in hand.

"Well, if it isn't Declan East," Kate said.

"I told you the cuckolds should be suspects." Sharada smiled. "There's a person of interest!"

"Not only that. He's one of our neighbors," Tony told Kate. "I've seen that face, now and again, for twenty years or more. He must live on Euston Place, though I'm not sure which house."

"One last wandering wife." Sharada riffled through some pages, squinting. Then she stopped, located her bejeweled reading specs, and tried again. Kate and Paul exchanged amused glances. They were now the only people in the room who didn't require magnification to read, unless one counted Harvey standing in the corner, and his half-glasses were on his head.

"Here it is." Sharada passed the correct page to Tony. "Tabitha Quarrels, wife of Jimmy Quarrels. I used to watch his cooking show, until he browbeat that poor single mum for doing meatloaf in the final round. Someone should wash his mouth out with soap."

Tony placed the couple's picture in the center of the table, and Kate studied the celebrity chef. Like his more famous counterpart, Gordon Ramsey, Jimmy Quarrels often looked fraught. On his cooking shows, he always verged on a tantrum, even in the first five minutes. Perhaps there was something deeply satisfying about taking such offense at the shortcomings of others. It made him a victim, and a comfortably superior victim at that.

Quarrels' wife, a leggy redhead name Tabitha, was pictured beside Granville Hardwick. Posed at a gallery opening, they stood near an aggressively incomprehensible statue called *Peace*. To Kate, it looked a bit like a Dalek.

"Tabitha Quarrels seems familiar. I've seen her down the street, haven't I?" Kate asked. "Screeching at the postal carrier over a dented package?"

"Yes, she's another one of our neighbors," Tony said. "Resides at No. 22."

"Oh? So you managed to notice where that pair of legs lives but not Declan East?"

He winked at her, then turned to Sharada. "Well done. I agree Mr. East is a person of interest. Given the public behavior of Barney Leeds and Jimmy Quarrels, they may be of interest, too. None of this exonerates Buck, but it does suggest legitimate avenues of investigation. If," he added with a deferential nod toward the head of the table, "DCI Jackson concurs."

"I do." Jackson sounded a bit surprised by his own declaration. Eyes on his teacup, he said, "DS Hetheridge and I discussed canvassing Euston Place yesterday. An evaluation of that protest group, the REB, is wanted, too. I could do it myself, but something about my manner puts off the poshies. DS Bhar can't be involved, and DS Hetheridge is slated to spend the afternoon with Miss Sevrin, AKA Miss Bloody Carpet Slippers. So it's probably best for me to enlist the help of a local. Someone trusted, who's lived here a long time." He looked up at Tony at last. "Are you willing? To talk to your neighbors, I mean?"

"Of course. I'll even return an invitation I've ignored since Christmas, or longer," Tony said. "From the organizer of the REB herself. Tabitha Quarrels."

# CHAPTER 13

P aul, who had endured the cream tea with equal parts trepidation (regarding Jackson) and mortification (regarding his mother) breathed a sigh of relief when the chief departed. Then Mrs. Snell excused herself, citing new duties elsewhere within Wellegrave House. Soon, Tony joined her, and Sharada announced her intention of powdering her nose, which Paul recognized as code for snooping in the loo. Her departure left him alone with Kate at last.

"Whose idea was it to invite Jackson?"

"Tony's. And it seems to have worked well."

"Weird how Harvey knew to offer him a Bloody Mary. Think Vic's been a guest here before?"

"I'm sure of it. Tony socialized with them all for years," Kate said. "Christmas parties, dinner parties, drinks down the pub. He never mentioned it to us because, as his subordinates, we didn't need to know."

"I always thought Jackson hated him."

"Me, too. But maybe hate's too strong a word. I think Vic was, and probably is, envious. Definitely more than a little intimidated. You saw how his neck sort of gradually disappeared as he poured tea?" She chuckled. "But now that Tony's been forced out, I guess even Vic feels secure enough to be generous."

"Asking for help with the local interviews, though…."

"I think it's brilliant. And you know Vic, he always used to complain about the powers that be. Using Tony unofficially, despite their decision, sends a message up the line, a little…." She made a rude hand gesture.

"Yeah. Vic does enjoy that sort of thing. Still, not to beat a dead one, but Kate. I thought *you* hated him. After… well…."

She shrugged. "I don't have to like him to work with him. He keeps it zipped, we'll see. By the way, your mum did all right, didn't she? When she pulled out her research, I was ready to sink under the table, but a lot of what she ferreted out has merit."

"Please don't tell her that. Unless it means she'll stop writing the sexy books and start doing mysteries." Paul seemed to rally at the notion. "Yeah. Good, clean mysteries. No descriptions of anything rippled, rigid, or covered with hair."

"But she's brilliant at that stuff! I realize she's moved on from obsessing about Tony to actually dating Buck. But I was re-reading *The Lordly Detective*, and you know what? There are parts that are surprisingly accu—"

"Don't tell me that. Bad enough she makes me read everything she writes. No son should be forced to know his mum's fantasies. Protection from that should be a basic human right." Paul's tea had gone cold, but he drank it anyway. "Speaking of the lordly one. How is he?"

"Made of steel."

"Kate. I'm serious."

"So am I. That's what he'd want me to tell you," she said, smiling. "So that's what I'll say. We've become a united front."

"You always were."

"Er, well, it got a little rocky once or twice. But now we—"

"Who's a united front?" Sharada interrupted. "You and your husband? Regarding the adoption of your poor little nephew?"

Sweeping back into the dining room, Sharada insinuated herself into what had been a private conversation. "Kate, dear, I hope you didn't mind me sending you that news story. When you didn't text me back, I was afraid I'd committed a *faux pas*." She snatched the half-eaten scone off her son's plate, popping it into her mouth. "Tony looked so dashing on TV. You weren't surprised, were you? I confess, I wondered if you were surprised. Since Deepal tells me everything you say and do, and Deepal never mentioned anything about an adoption in the works...."

"Really? Everything I say and do?" Kate asked, dangerously sweet.

Paul gave a nervous laugh.

"And I'm sure it goes without saying, I was very shocked when your husband announced his retirement. You would think he could have stayed on the job until Buck—" Sharada cut herself off. "No, no. It's only right he should choose to be with his family. Naturally, I was very stern with Deepal for giving me no hint of what was to come. But I was happy to see Tony looking so relaxed this morning. And holding your hand." She beamed at Kate. "As far as the adoption...."

"It's long overdue," Kate said. "Sorry I didn't reply to the link you sent. Things were a little hectic. Sometimes I hate the press. I hope the class warfare angle doesn't play as well in Family Court as it does in the media."

"Should you need legal counsel, I can give you recommendations." Gathering up her loose printouts, Sharada consigned them to the depths of her handbag. "We have an embarrassment of riches in our family. Four barristers—"

"And thirteen solicitors," Paul finished for her. "You and Aunt Gopi and Aunt Dhanvi never get tired of trotting that out, do you? Even if Sri quit practicing to raise her family and Fahd never passed the bar."

"What?" Kate looked puzzled.

"Pay no attention," Paul said. "I'll bet the g—your husband already has the best counsel money can buy."

"No. It's only—I've heard that phrase before," Kate said. "A constable mentioned it the night Buck was arrested."

"Gopi and Dhanvi went round the Yard, poking their noses in, as usual. I'm sure they said it."

"Yes, but somewhere else, too. Paul—your father. What's his name?"

"Haresh."

"Does he have a dog? An Alsatian called Mani?"

"You spoke to Haresh?" Sharada cried. "When? Why?"

"Outside the crime scene the night Hardwick died. Right up by the barriers. I had to warn him off with threat of arrest."

"What? My dad? Are you sure?" Paul couldn't remember the last time he'd spoken to his father. A year ago, perhaps, or maybe two.

"You tell me. The man said that line about barristers and solicitors," Kate told him. "He was walking a very friendly dog called Mani. And he said the great Lord Hetheridge was about to get what he deserved."

"I don't like this about Dad," Paul told Sharada as they exited Wellegrave House. Despite the January chill, it was a sunny afternoon and plenty of people were out, enjoying a bit of fresh air. "Dad lives in Shoreditch. What was he doing in Mayfair?"

"Who knows? Your father does what your father does. Papa was a rolling stone. I'm just so disappointed more hasn't been done to help Buck," said Sharada, mind slipping into its one and only track, right on schedule. "And you, why did you have to sell the Astra?"

"I couldn't afford it. Too many fees."

"I wish you still had it. I'm not taking the Tube this time of day. I refuse to fight like an animal just to sit down. You'll have to hail a taxi."

"Fine. There's usually a stand around the next turning. But Mum," Paul said. "Dad wasn't just taking a walking tour of Mayfair after dark. He had Mani with him. That's a long way to take a dog. What was he doing so far from his house?"

"You mean that slut's house." Although Haresh had left her for his mistress years ago, Sharada still never referred to her romantic rival by name. "Maybe the slut wised up, sent him packing. Maybe a few years with Haresh taught her not to pick through another woman's rubbish."

Paul thought about that. For a long time, he'd assumed Sharada tended an eternal flame for Haresh. That she still hoped and prayed for a reconciliation that no one in the extended family, including him, Gopi, or Dhanvi, ever thought would come to pass. But that semi-nonsensical line about stealing garbage shed new light on the matter.

"All right, let's say there's a good reason he just happened to be walking Mani in Mayfair. Even so, isn't it strange he was outside East Asia House just after Hardwick's body was discovered? And that crack about Lord Hetheridge getting what he deserved?"

"Haresh knows Tony was the inspiration for my character, Lord Kensingbard," Sharada said. "He accused me of having an affair with him."

"What?" Paul stopped walking, leaving the pedestrian on his heels no choice but to plow into him.

"Oi!"

"Sorry," Paul muttered. "Mum, stop. Come back here. Dad accused you of having an affair? When?"

"Last month," Sharada said. "Deepal, it doesn't matter. Sometimes your father gets an idea in his head. The stupider the idea, the longer it takes for it to work its way out the other end."

"So I'm guessing Dad read *The Lordly Detective*?"

"Yes, finally. Who knows why? Heaven knows he never cared about anything that mattered to me before. Then he rang me up and accused me of all sorts of mischief. I was tempted to confirm it all."

"Mum!"

"I said tempted, Deepal. I hung up and blocked his number."

Paul blew out his breath. "This can't be a coincidence, Mum. He was outside Hardwick's house."

"And I was inside, remember? Maybe your father was following me."

"What?"

She shrugged. "He's done stranger things. But hurry, we have to find that taxi stand," she said, frowning at the sun as if it had no business being in its current position. "The book signing starts at two o'clock."

"What book signing?"

"Fiona Leeds's book signing at Harrods. Wandering wife number one wrote a memoir. She's been blitzing Facebook and Twitter with promos for weeks, and now she's making personal appearances. What better way to question her than to ambush her in public?"

This was too much. Paul took Sharada by the shoulders, forcing another mid-pavement stop. This time two pedestrians bumped into him, and a woman with a mobile glued to her ear gave him the death-look. He ignored them, focusing on his mother.

"All right, Mum, here's the truth. You're not a detective. You're not on Buck's case. You're not on any case. I *am* a detective, but I'm not allowed to participate in the Hardwick investigation. So we can't go to Harrods. And we certainly can't scream, 'Did you kill your ex-boyfriend?' at Fiona Leeds during her book signing."

"Oh, Deepal. You're so literal sometimes," Sharada said with the breeziness that made him want to shake her till she rattled. "I know I'm not a detective. I'm an author who wants to support a colleague's signing. And since I'm not investigating, there's no reason you can't be with me. If you hear something significant, you can pass it on to Kate. And Buck will be one step closer to freedom."

This was more sensible than Paul had expected. He couldn't think of a denial.

"Well?" Sharada prompted.

"All right. As it happens, I'm fresh out of ideas for how to convince Mrs. Nibley-Tatters to testify against Arry. Maybe concentrating on something else for an hour will help. Mum, you called Fiona a colleague. Do you actually know her?" Since embarking on her career as a self-published romance novelist, Sharada had met dozens, even hundreds, of authors online. She had argued with, unfriended, and blocked a great deal of them, but still.

"Of course I know her. I follow her on Twitter."

"Does she follow you back?"

"No, but last week she retweeted my retweet. We're like this." Sharada held up crossed fingers. "Now, we'll be late if we don't find that taxi stand. Can we get on?"

Harrods of London was made up of seven stories, four and a half acres, and—in Paul's expert opinion—some of the most beautiful sales clerks in the western world. Most never gave him more than a polite smile, and that was only after he showed them his credit card. Still, during the rare times he visited, he tended to linger in zones where he had no business, such as lingerie, pretending to be in the market for things he couldn't afford, such as G-strings by Agent Provocateur. Today, the clerks were as lovely as ever. But with Sharada frogmarching him past displays, the likelihood of him chatting one up was plummeting to zero.

They entered Harrods five minutes before the signing was

due to begin. Thinking it would looked suspiciously overeager to appear right on time—how many people were likely to care passionately about a footballer's ex on a bright Saturday afternoon?—Paul floated the notion of visiting Wine, Spirits, & Cigars. Not because he could afford anything sold in that department but to gather talking points for his current squeezes, Emmeline and Kyla. Emmeline, always brand conscious, loved a frothy discussion of fads and trends. And for the more serious-minded Kyla, Paul could turn the dialogue on its ear, tutting about high street prices. Either way, it would be brilliant, as long as his mouth didn't run away with him. Sometimes he liked the sound of his own voice so much, he forgot which woman he was speaking to.

"No, Deepal, we shall be on time," Sharada warned, steering him toward the escalators. "I refuse to wait behind a mob just because you have a fatal attraction to vice."

"Vice?" He stepped on the escalator, staring at its giant Egyptian-style decorations, in which colossal pharaohs were rendered in glowing plastic. So much gold, purple, and green was overwhelming. It was one part Art Deco, one part Burger King, and one part gay pride. "And why are we going up? Aren't books down?"

"Books are up," Sharada insisted. "I was here two years ago. As for the vices sold in that other section, the name says it all: wine, spirits, and cigars. Three things my only son should avoid."

"I gave up the ciggies. As far as a drink, come on."

The escalator spit them out into what was plainly women's fashion. Sharada surged forward, undeterred.

"Come on? What does that mean, come on?" she asked. "Are you being seduced by peer pressure? Giving in because the other boys do it?"

"I'm not a—" He stopped. It was no good reminding her that he was long past thirty, not unless he wanted a refresher on how his birth had made her suffer. "The point is, I don't drink like Buck, and you never say a word to him."

"Buck is cutting down."

"Buck is always one or two in the bag. The night Hardwick died, he was well and truly pissed."

She made a dismissive gesture.

"Seriously, Mum, I think he's an alcoholic."

"Red brassieres?" She frowned at a mannequin. "Why are there red brassieres in the book section?"

"Because I told you, this isn't the book section. Mum. Listen," he said, stopping her from charging into an area she was sure to consider highly inappropriate, at least for his eyes. "Are you actually okay with that? A boyfriend with a drinking problem?"

"Buck can manage his own affairs. The most important thing now is to prove he's innocent."

"It's just... after dad. I don't want you to get hurt again."

He expected her to get teary or perhaps wrap him in an embarrassing embrace. Instead, she wagged a finger at him. "Deepal, I am a grown woman. I don't need your meddling. I should be meddling with you! You think I don't know you're seeing two girls at once? It's outrageous. I didn't bring you up to—"

"Look, there's a sign. Books downstairs," he lied, jumping back on the escalator. To his relief, she followed.

Harrods bookshop was located in the middle of several departments Paul found more interesting—fine gift, travel goods, bed linens, even an ice cream parlor. It wasn't that he disliked books, he just had no interest in tell-alls or C-list celebrity memoirs. And Fiona Leeds's autobiography, *More Than a Footballer's Wife*, seemed like a cross between the two.

The book's dust jacket featured her in a velvet evening gown; small pictures on the back showed her skiing, snorkeling, and taking the stage for Miss Universe's bikini round. But the shop's towering promotional posters only showed her alongside Barney Leeds: at their wedding, at a World Cup match, on the red carpet. Clearly, despite the book's title, reminding readers of her connection to the man who'd punched out his coach was a major part of the book's marketing scheme.

Fiona sat behind the signing desk. She looked dignified, as least compared to herself in the beauty pageant photo. Her long hair, twisted in a bun, was accented with chopsticks; she wore a turtleneck, black slacks, and no jewelry. She'd also acquired a pair of rectangular black spectacles, the big, aggressively bookish sort. Paul wondered if they were borrowed.

An older woman in a yellow dress sailed up to greet them. She didn't wear a Harrods name tag, which suggested she'd accompanied Fiona; her publicist, perhaps.

"Yes, here early, very wise," she said, as if Paul and Sharada weren't ten minutes late. "Get your copies and hurry up to the table. Such a splendid opportunity! You'll get to spend a moment with Fiona and ask questions before the crowds surge in."

Paul glanced around. No crowds threatened, though he did see several people browsing in Stationary. A pack slavered around the Godiva Chocolatier cases. And a rather unimpressed-looking man held an open copy of Fiona's book, frowning as he read. It was an inauspicious start.

"I'm not buying one of those," Paul muttered to Sharada.

"Yes, you are. Take it to the table. Question her."

There was nothing else for it. Selecting one from the top of a five-foot stack, Paul opened the book, glimpsed the retail price, and immediately regretted it. With any luck, Emmeline would appreciate such a gift and reward him accordingly. Otherwise, he was spending a bundle just to humor his mother.

He approached the table. Fiona's eyes flicked up; otherwise, she affected not to notice his arrival. Her head was bent studiously over a book, lips moving slightly as her eyes moved down the page. Only when she looked up, smiled, and shut the book did he realize it was *More Than a Footballer's Wife* she'd been reading so intently.

"That good, huh?" he said, giving her his most winning smile.

"Hmnh?"

"Your book? It's that good, eh?"

She squinted at him. "What do you mean?"

"Never mind. Little joke. Too small to be seen!" Even behind those perhaps unnecessary glasses, Fiona Leeds was intimidatingly beautiful, and he was starting to babble. Sometimes he went off a cliff when his icebreaker fell flat.

"Let me sign that for you." She reached for his copy of the book.

"It's so nice to meet you," he continued, clutching it with both hands to slow down the interaction. "Can I ask a question? Is old Barney as mental as he seems?"

"He has anger management issues," she said, sitting up straight as the publicist gave her the eye. Apparently Fiona had been drilled on how to answer this sort of query and was eager to show off. "I've asked him to seek therapy. Chapter Seven provides all the details."

"Yeah, it's only—punching out a coach. You don't see that every day. Does he just go round attacking anyone who looks at him cross-eyed? I mean, with a wife like you, it must have been tough. Every time you stopped traffic, did he run into the street and beat his chest?"

"Oh, he was mad with jealousy," Fiona agreed, flashing dazzling veneered teeth. "Always telling me what I could wear and who I could talk to. I felt like a prisoner in my own life. That's what drove me into the arms of a sophisticated older man. Chapter Twelve: the affair with Mr. Name Withheld."

"Right. Granville Hardwick, wasn't it?"

The publicist cleared her throat. Fiona was so surprised, she whipped off her smart gal glasses, probably to see Paul better. "Who told you that?"

"Oh, I have friends who live on Euston Place. Lots of gossip after the murder. Shocking, wasn't it?"

"So shocking! I mean, when all was said and done, I hated the little bugger. But they wouldn't let me put that in the book."

The publicist said, "Fiona! Darling! There's another lady waiting, and I do believe this gentleman's about to commit."

The unimpressed-looking man seemed offended by the hint. Snapping the book closed, he replaced it on one of the towering stacks and moved toward the chocolatier.

"Dating Gran was fun at first," Fiona continued, "but all he wanted was arm candy. He didn't care about my mind—my soul—any more than Barney did. And at least when I left Barney, he had the decency to punch a hole in the wall. Gran just smiled and said 'Sayonara.' Can you believe that? We spent months together, and all I got was a goodbye in Spanish?"

Not surprisingly, the publicist moved to intercept. Just as Paul braced himself to be ejected from Harrods bookshop, something crashed behind him. He turned to find Sharada standing beside a five-foot stack, now collapsed. She was the very picture of confused regret.

"I have no idea how… Oh, please, let me help you," she told the publicist, who looked angry enough to tear a page from Barney Leeds's book. "I'll gather them and you can restack them. Will that do?"

"My mum. She's mental," Paul told Fiona conversationally. "Anyway, I know for a fact that everyone on Euston Place hated Granville Hardwick. Even organized a protest group against that barmy white house. Police may never find out who killed him, sorting through so many leads."

"Especially since they arrested the wrong person."

Paul blinked at Fiona. "Wrong person? Why do you say that?"

"Because they led a man out in handcuffs. But I saw a woman leaving the house."

# CHAPTER 14

Paul looked around to see who might be listening. A few shoppers had been drawn by the crash of falling books, but otherwise, folks seemed to be giving the signing zone a wide berth. No one was nearby except his mother, who shot him an excited look, and the publicist, who seemed utterly focused on the stack she was rebuilding.

"You saw something?" he said, trying to sound like a bloke hypnotized by Fiona's pretty face, not a cop salivating over a lead.

"Of course I did. I keep an eye open," Fiona said a touch defensively. "Since Barney left, I don't have a man around to protect me. And London's never been less safe. Men with knifes, serial killers, a mugger on every corner. Pull your wheelie-bin to the curb and you're dead!"

This didn't quite describe the Mayfair Paul knew, particularly not Tony's street, but he had the feeling Fiona almost believed it. Perhaps ratcheting up her own fears about shadowy evildoers gave her a good reason to gaze out the window toward her ex-lover's house.

"Gran always had lots of people in and out. Delivery men, artists, that nutter ex-sister-in-law," she continued. "Visible from space, she is, with the crazy hair and the housedresses. When I came home Thursday night, it was twilight. I looked over at Gran's and saw a man going inside. Tall fellow. The one they arrested."

Paul nodded. Would his mum choose this moment to shriek Buck's name or rush over, demanding explication? He dared a sidelong look. Sharada was still rebuilding the stack alongside the publicist and a sullen clerk who'd apparently been pressed into service.

"Later I checked back and saw daft old Georgette heading toward Declan's. No hat, no coat, and it was freezing outside. She climbed his garden wall right before my eyes. And not long after that, there were blue lights everywhere."

"Miss Sevrin climbed into Declan East's garden? You're sure?"

"Told you. I could see that hair from orbit. I'll bet she killed Gran. Snapped or something. After all, she ran away, and the tall man stayed."

"But if it looked like she was fleeing the scene, why didn't you tell anyone? You could have crossed the street and told an officer —" Paul stopped, remembering he wasn't the bad cop, the good cop, or even a cop at all, as far as Fiona knew. "I mean, call a tip line or something?"

"I've been busy." She cast a resentful look at her publicist, who was putting the final book atop the restored stack. "Seriously, I've been a cocktail waitress. I did a little exotic dancing. I've never had to sell myself as hard as in the writer biz!"

"I'm sure it must be terrible," Paul said, passing over his copy for her signature. "But Georgette? Any idea why she'd want Hardwick dead? He was letting her stay with him, after all, and they'd been close for a long time."

"Yeah, but she wanted closer, didn't she? When Gran and I dated, she was a nightmare. Always interrupting, walking in at the wrong time, making demands on his attention. When I started seeing Gran, I was afraid Barney would catch wind, storm over, and rip his lungs out. I had no idea the real stalker lived in the house." Her pen, gorgeously crafted and suitable for signing a royal decree, hovered over the book's flyleaf. "Who do I make it out to?"

"Um... Emmeline Wardle. That's E, m, m...." He spelled the rest. "So your ex, Barney, never got up to his old tricks? Never threated Hardwick or tried to settle the score?"

"Nope. Too busy with his coked-out friends and their skanky party girls. He left for Manchester a month ago and may never come back. There!" She'd signed "Fiona" with a heart over the *i*. "Enjoy!"

∼

"Investigating is fun," Sharada burbled happily as they traded Harrods warm interior for Brompton Road's bracing cold. "Exciting!"

"Yes, well, expensive fun," Paul huffed. Not only had he been obligated to pay for his copy of *More Than a Footballer's Wife*, Sharada had insisted on getting one, too, then wandered off to the chocolate cases, leaving him to settle up with the expectant clerk. "And remember, if anyone asks, we were not investigating. We were supporting your quote-unquote colleague."

He'd already texted everything to Kate. She could use her Met connections to double-check Barney Leeds's whereabouts on the night of the murder. If he was in Manchester, that eliminated one suspect.

"That woman with the wild hair and the staring eyes, she's the culprit, you'll see," Sharada said. "My Buck will be free any day now."

"I don't know. I think Fiona might actually need those specs. Need them adjusted, at any rate. What she claims to have seen makes no sense."

"Why shouldn't Georgette run from the scene of the crime?"

"Because she didn't leave, remember? She was there all along. Buck called you. You called me. I turned up at East Asia House, and five minutes later, she popped out of the wardrobe."

"Oh." Sharada led them to a sheltered place beside one of the famous Harrods window displays, where they could stand and talk without arousing the ire of busy pedestrians. "What about this? Suppose she fled, got rid of the murder weapon, and came back?"

"The weapon was left behind. The statuette, remember?"

"Maybe her clothes were bloody, and she needed a friend's help to conceal them."

"She still had bloodstains on her housedress and carpet slippers when Tony interviewed her." He pinched the bridge of his nose. Why was he working the Hardwick case, which was forbidden, and ignoring the task his new chief had set for him?

"All right, Mum. This has been a wonderful day out. A little hard on the bank account, but lovely. Now I have to do the thing that allows me to pay for it. Go to Mrs. Nibley-Tatters' house and convince her to testify."

"Lucky for you, I have ideas about that, too." Sharada waved at a passing cab. "Taxi!"

Mrs. Lobelia Nibley-Tatters lived in Fitzrovia, in what was once called a rather promising address, back when the Duke of Wellington was called a rather promising young man. Alas, the sun had set on those days, and Mrs. Nibley-Tatters's house had aged badly. Her fence was missing a section. The gate was gone from its hinges, and her porch swing was off its chains. The roof had been patched many times, and the woodwork along the windows was rotten. But all that was merely cosmetic; the real trouble was the junk.

Dirty, discarded children's toys surrounded the porch. They'd been there so long, wild shrubbery had grown up around them. Broken clay pots decorated the front steps. As for the front door, it was impassable, owing to a collection of rain-soaked shipping boxes, all open, all overflowing with garbage. On Paul's first visit, he'd attempted to ingratiate himself with Mrs. Nibley-Tatters by offering to haul the rubbish away. She'd reacted with alarm, informing him the clutter was placed there deliberately, as a home invasion deterrent.

"Deepal." Sharada, whose housekeeping approached obsessive levels, stared at the mess. "Is this where the drug dealers lived?"

"No. Arry's house is there." He indicated a modest but pin-neat cottage that looked for all the world like a math tutor's home, not a den of iniquity. "Follow me around back."

If the front porch was unpromising, the back garden was post-apocalyptic. There were more cracked flower pots, many bearing the skeletal remains of unlucky plants. Also an old steamer trunk, its leather sides warped and rotted, full of over-stuffed rubbish bags. And everywhere there were piles of rusted and broken tools—rakes, hoes, shears, shovels—interspersed with out-and-out junk, like takeaway boxes, dented soda cans, and decomposing coffee cups.

"Deepal! What's that?" Sharada cried, pointing at a pile that rustled.

"Rats. Feral cats. Foxes, maybe. Foxes are the new dingoes. Steal your baby," he said heartlessly, enjoying her discomfort. He'd been counting on the sight of Mrs. Nibley-Tatters's house to frighten his mum into minding her own business.

"She's covered the windows in tinfoil," Sharada said, stepping carefully around a bucket of rusty screws and nails. "Why? Because she's afraid of Arry's friends?"

"Probably because she's afraid of Environmental Health. They've taken action against her because of the garden. If they see what's inside, they may remove her altogether," Paul said, approaching the back door even more carefully than Sharada. On his first visit, he'd stepped on a concealed garden rake, hit himself in the face with the handle, and gouged a hole in his secondhand Gucci horsebit loafers.

"No soliciting!" Mrs. Nibley-Tatters cried from behind the back door, which stood a few inches ajar.

"It's me! DS Paul Bhar." Holding out his warrant card, he advanced up the steps despite the toy cars, hubcaps, and rusty hand trowels that tried to repel him.

"Who's that lady? No social workers, Paul. I said no social workers!"

"Oh. Er, no, she's—"

"Witness protection," Sharada supplied, puffing out her chest, as if she not only arranged for bodyguards, but functioned as one, too. "Here to assure your safety."

"Why are you carrying a Harrods shopping bag?"

Sharada seemed to have forgotten she was holding it. "Appearances. Can't be too obvious."

"As far as protection," Mrs. Nibley-Tatters said, "it's not mine that matters." Although she was slender, even she had to work to extrude herself through the narrow space between door and jamb. Having once sweet-talked his way into the house, Paul knew why: inside lurked veritable mountains of clutter, reaching the ceiling in some spots.

"It's my cat Jinxy's safety," the septuagenarian continued. Despite her sprigged dress and long white hair, she did resemble a member of Monty Python in drag. "Arry took against poor Jinxy from day one. Cross when he got in his garden. Grumbling when he took a squat in his hedge. Now Arry will have his revenge, even from the inside."

"Well, Arry's not 'inside' so much as on remand," Paul said. "I'm sure he's shaken up, given the number of years he's facing, and not too concerned with grudges against cats at the moment. But to ensure his conviction, and the safety of this entire community, including you and, er, Jinxy, Scotland Yard needs you to commit to—"

"You're not listening," the old woman said. "I'm telling you I can't testify. Jinxy went missing last night. Unless I make peace with Arry, I'll never see her again!"

"Missing?" Paul glanced around the back garden, which could have concealed any number of cats. "But you said Jinxy liked to roam. That's how all your trouble with Arry started."

"It's true, Jinxy's a tom. He can't be tied down," Mrs. Nibley-Tatters said. "But he turns up twice daily at feeding time, and we have tea every afternoon. Today—nothing. Look at his food dish. It's untouched. He's been taken. Only a specialist can get him back now."

"Um, right. How about this? Let's sort out the details about the testimony, shall we? Then perhaps I can get someone from the correct municipal service to come round with an animal van, perhaps some nets, and—"

"Nets? Jinxy's not a wild dog. I don't think you know what he means to me," she insisted, voice quavering. "DCI Jackson did. He spoke nicely to me. Never climbed on his high horse, never rushed me. I should call him and complain about you. Jinxy's all I have in this world. I won't think of testifying until he's safe, and you can promise me he'll stay that way."

"Ma'am?" Sharada pointed to the rustling pile that had frightened her earlier. "That black cat. Is that Jinxy?"

Mrs. Nibley-Tatters squinted. "My specs... need my specs...."

"Jinxy!" Sharada called.

Something fat, black, and rumpled exited the rubbish heap, leaping onto the stone wall that enclosed Arry's back garden. It was the biggest, most malevolent looking cat Paul had ever seen.

"Jinxy, is that you?" Mrs. Nibley-Tatters cried, still fumbling in her apron for her spectacles.

"Jinxy!" Paul hurried down the steps. Eyes on the cat, he stepped in a pile of tangled clothesline and went down flailing.

"No, Jinxy, don't run," Sharada pleaded.

"I didn't see him." Mrs. Nibley-Tatters had her specs on at last. "Are you sure it was him?"

"Get him back," Sharada ordered Paul as he struggled to his feet. "Go! Hurry! I'll stay with her."

Groaning, Paul ran for the garden as Jinxy disappeared into a mass of evergreens.

*Five minutes,* he told himself. *I'll give this wild cat chase five minutes. Then it's done, and the old woman will just have to see sense, with or without the wretched beast.*

∿

Three hours later, Paul flung himself onto a Tube train bound for home. Forcing aside two pensioners, he stole the car's last seat out from under a very big, very weary-looking construction worker. Although the man in the highly reflective yellow vest appeared strong enough to twist him into a pretzel, Paul ignored the man's glare, refusing to give up his seat. After the night he'd had, a severe beating hundreds of feet beneath London did not frighten him.

*Over the fence. In the bushes. Up a fire escape. On a roof. Off a roof. Down the street....*

If at any point the bloody cat had simply run for it, or burrowed into a small space and refused to come out, Paul would have given up. Even if it meant going back to Mrs. Nibley-Tatters empty-handed. Even if it meant returning to DCI Jackson and admitting he couldn't complete one straightforward, murder-free assignment, despite his promise to sort it out. But Jinxy, hideous and green-eyed, seemed to understand all that, and therefore played a different game.

He never ran fast enough for Paul to lose sight of him, nor climbed higher than a detective sergeant in an overpriced suit could follow. More than once he stopped, raised a leg, and went to work cleaning his nether regions while Paul advanced. Seemingly tired of the pursuit, Jinxy had placidly licked his fur, letting Paul get close enough to smell him. Then the big black creature had looked directly at him, as if to transmit some sort of feline curse, and bounded away again.

Paul, reasonably fit and reasonably well-versed in the streets of London, even without GPS or a map, became so focused on the chase, he allowed himself to be lured far from Fitzrovia. At some point he'd turned a corner, blundered into a busy high street, and realized two things: he'd lost track of Jinxy and lost track of himself, too.

His mobile had gone dead during the chase. Forced to ask directions of a street vendor, Paul headed back to Fitzrovia in a state of defeat. Maybe the chase would inspire Jinxy to return home on his own. If so, maybe Mrs. Nibley-Tatters would give him credit for that, if Sharada hadn't said or done something offensive in the intervening time.

It was gathering dark when he approached the old lady's house. Despite the blocked front door and tinfoil covered windows, a sliver of light should have been visible from within. But the place looked dark, deserted. Paul was making for the back entrance when a deep growl startled him.

The black dog moved slowly, head down, growling. Tonight he wore a collar, and his lead trailed behind him.

"Hey, mate, remember me?" Paul lifted both hands in an instinctive show of friendliness. "The guv's been sacked. I'm probably next. Your work's done here. Go haunt someone else."

"Kaiser! Nein!" A tall man approached, his bright blond hair shining under the streetlamps. Paul would have known that handsome, hateful face anywhere. It was Sir Duncan Godington.

"DC Bhar! Good evening. Sorry about my dog. He's developed a bit of a fixation on you, hasn't he?"

"It's DS Bhar," Paul said. "And I should have known you'd be involved. Have you been following me?"

"Oh, you sound a touch paranoid, Paul." Sir Duncan showed his teeth in that trademark grin, the one some called shark-like and others called cannibalistic. "Do you consider me your nemesis? If so, I'll have to do better. I never consider you at all. But what's that you told Kaiser?" he asked eagerly. "Something about Hetheridge getting the sack?"

"I, er... no. I meant someone else at the Yard. Um...."

Kaiser growled. Picking up the lead, Sir Duncan issued a command in German. The dog fell silent, though his gaze remained hostile.

"Don't lie. You do it poorly. What happened to the chief superintendent?"

"He retired." Paul spoke with all the confidence he could muster, trying not to think of how much he feared this man but only of Tony. "I'm happy for him. Don't take it too hard. You'll love my new boss. He's a huge fan of your work."

"I doubt anyone at Scotland Yard will ever interest me quite as much as Anthony Hetheridge. Or the lovely Kate. Or you, Detective Sergeant Bhar. Keep an eye out. And if you've come back looking for your mum ... she and the old lady got into a cab a half-hour ago."

And so Paul had been forced to turn his back on Sir Duncan, never a cheerful proposition, as well as the black dog, Kaiser, and walk away as fast as his aching feet could carry him. During his last high-profile murder case, Sir Duncan had approached him in public, issuing a few silken, playful threats. Now, it seemed, the never-convicted murderer had traded his verbal threats for something more physical. Had he intended to let Kaiser tear his throat out? Or was it just another game, the sort of predator-prey interplay Sir Duncan so enjoyed?

That was a sobering thought. It made courting death on the Tube by snatching a bigger man's seat seem like child's play.

By the time Paul reached his house, the moon and stars were out. Mrs. Nibley-Tatters's home might have been dark as a crypt, but at his own, light spilled from every window. That was unusual, but he liked it better than darkness. He'd just started up the steps when another bark interrupted. But this one was both playful and familiar.

"Mani!"

The friendly Alsatian stretched her lead to reach him, tongue lolling, tail wagging. Behind her, Haresh Bhar walked more slowly. He wore his usual expression, a look of faint suspicion.

"Hello, Deepal."

"Dad. What are you doing out here?"

"What does it look like?"

"Um, well, stalking, actually. Given that you live miles from here."

"I don't. I'm renting a room not far away, thank you."

"Why? Did Neer throw you out?"

"Deepal. Remember who you are talking to."

Paul shuffled his feet. His father's disdain always had a way of making him feel eight years old again, in trouble for cheek.

"Fine," he told Haresh. "It's a free country. Any particular reason you chose to walk Mani past Mum's house? Planning to knock on the door and say hello?"

Haresh made one of his inscrutable noises, somewhere between a grunt and a sigh. "Perhaps. Is the American still in jail?"

"Not for long." He had no way of knowing that. He just wanted to see how his father would react.

"He's a drunk," Haresh said angrily. "And a killer. What sort of job are you doing, you and that man you work for, letting these people go? Bad enough the mistakes you made with Godington. My son freed a serial killer. I should be dead of shame."

"I didn't—" Paul took a deep breath. "Never mind. Know what? Mum said you finally read her book. The fictionalized, I assure you, entirely fictionalized novel based on Lord Hetheridge. You don't really think she had an affair with him, do you? She never looked at another man till you left her. And left her high and dry, I might add. If she hadn't written those books, we'd have lost the house by now."

"Don't lecture me about my business. I've seen how she carried on with that American. I know she's sleeping with him."

Mani, sensing the tension, barked anxiously. Paul, who'd missed the dog, knelt beside her, scratching between her ears and murmuring reassurances. When he rose, he was composed enough to reply without raising his voice. He'd been brought up to be a respectful son; to behave otherwise went against the grain. But his recent encounter with Sir Duncan had caused certain aspects of the Hardwick case fall into place, making it impossible to stay silent.

"Dad. I don't know what happened between you and Neer. I don't know what you think is still possible for you and Mum. But I know you were outside Hardwick's house the night his body was discovered, and I think I know why. You've been watching Buck for some time now, haven't you? You even talked to him, outside the Yellow Earl. He was drunk. Probably ranting about Hardwick. Did you encourage Buck to confront him? Have it out?"

"Certainly not."

"But you followed him, didn't you? To see what would happen?"

"I was going that way. Deepal, don't interrogate me. I have nothing to do with—"

"Dad, this is important. What time in the afternoon did Buck leave East Asia House?"

"I don't remember."

"But you saw him go."

"Yes."

"Did he seem upset?"

"Of course. The man with the green hair was shouting at him from his front step, saying he'd have the police on him."

Paul let out his breath in relief. "So Hardwick *was* alive when Buck left. The blood on Buck's clothes must have been his, from his own hands. But later Kate saw you outside the police barriers. Why did you go back?"

"I was here, walking Mani. I thought perhaps I'd call on your mother," Haresh said coolly, as if stalking first Buck, then Sharada, was perfectly rational behavior. "Sharada came out but didn't see me. She met a taxi at the curb, and I heard her give the address. East Asia House. I wanted to know what she was doing. She's my wife. I have a right to know. Maybe she was carrying on with the green-haired man, too!"

Paul groaned. "So when you realized a murder happened inside, you just loitered about, enjoying the show? Bragging to Kate about all the lawyers in our family? Saying Lord Hetheridge will get what he deserved?"

"He will," Haresh said, so furious Mani barked again. "He had no business doing those things with a married woman. With my wife!"

Paul didn't know whether to groan again or laugh in his father's face. Perhaps it was a testament to his mum's skill as a writer that at least one reader had bought the Lord Kensingbard story, lock, stock, and barrel.

"Dad. You're a material witness. You can corroborate Buck's version of events and testify that Hardwick was alive when Buck left the house. You have to come with me to the Yard and give your statement."

"I won't. I'll say nothing. And if you contradict me, Deepal, I'll say you're lying to help her and the man she's sleeping with. No one will believe you. Your word is worthless."

Paul stared at Haresh. He wasn't hurt, or even surprised. His father had always been a stern man, prickly about his dignity, and given to threats. But this was more than Paul could swallow.

"You know what, Dad? Fine. Keep doing what you're doing. Follow people, eavesdrop, drag poor Mani all over London. Scotland Yard will prove Buck innocent. Whether you do your duty as a citizen or not, we'll make it right. And tomorrow I'll convince Mum to call up one of those fourteen solicitors and divorce you, once and for all. We'll be better off without you. You're a—a—*an unpleasant person!*" It wasn't much, but it was the worst thing a respectful son could hurl at his father on short notice.

Haresh never had a chance to answer. Sharada's door opened, spilling more light into the street. Two squat figures, both with towering hairstyles and flowing pink caftans, stood silhouetted in the doorway. Then they were down the steps and upon Haresh like a plague of locusts.

"What are you doing here?"

"Do you think we can't see you through those windows?"

"Sharada doesn't need you!"

"Why turn up unwanted after all these years?"

"Where's your fancy lady now? Washing your stink out of her satin brothel?"

Hurriedly, Paul escaped inside. When Aunt Gopi and Aunt Dhanvi stepped onto the battlefield with voices shrill and fingers pointing, it was impossible to stop them or even slow them down. A wise man got out of the way.

"Mum!" he called, closing the door behind him. "I looked for you at Mrs. Nibley-Tatters' house, but someone said you'd gone. I tried to catch Jinxy, but…."

He stopped. A fat, black, rumpled creature occupied the sofa cushion usually reserved for him. As he watched, it uncurled with exquisite leisure, lifted its head, and stared at him with malevolent green eyes.

"Deepal! Here's Mrs. Nibley-Tatters. Lobelia to her friends," Sharada said, entering the living room with the old woman in tow. "We talked and talked the whole time you were gone. Just when I thought I should call the police, Jinxy came home. Strolled up to us, sweet as you like. By then, Lobelia and I were agreed. The best way to keep the poor dear safe was for him—and Lobelia—to come home with me. Just until Arry's put away, of course."

"Er. Lovely. Lovely. Um, Mum? Can I just...." He indicated the hall, giving Lobelia Nibley-Tatters what he hoped was a friendly wave before pulling Sharada out of earshot.

"Just till he's put away? You do realize that could be weeks. Months!"

"Deepal, she was quite set. No cooperation unless someone took her fear for the cat seriously," Sharada whispered. "And you saw how she lived, poor thing. No space left in that house to even have tea! I told her come, meet my sisters, hear all about us. Three barristers, fourteen solicitors, and a Scotland Yard detective in the family. She feels quite secure with me."

"What about that witness protection rubbish?"

"I said it was a little white lie. Research for a novel. She understood completely. Likes romances, our Lobelia. And Gopi and Dhanvi made her feel very safe. Who is that they're telling off, down in the street?"

"Dad. You were right, he's been following you."

"Ah. Well. They'll soon have him sorted." She made a dismissive gesture. "I really must divorce him. I know it's shocking. There's never been a divorce in our family. But things have to change, don't they?"

"Mum. I'm proud of you."

She beamed at him. "And now that Lobelia's agreed to testify, your new chief will be proud of you. He'll have you back on a murder case in no time."

"Yes, well, maybe we'd better give it a few days. What if Jinxy doesn't like it here? Or if someone looks cross-eyed at Mrs. Nibley-Tatters, and she gets cold feet again?"

"That won't happen. Gopi and Dhanvi agreed to stay for the duration. Anyone would feel secure with them around. Dhanvi will take your bed, Gopi will share mine, and Lobelia and Jinxy will be on the sofa."

"Mum. That's fine, except… where will I sleep?"

"Deepal. We all have to make sacrifices. This one is for your career." She sighed. "I really wish you hadn't sold the Astra."

# CHAPTER 15

When Paul and Sharada departed for Harrods, Kate headed to Scotland Yard. She needed to know if there were any new forensic details on the Hardwick case and to prepare for her interview with Georgette Sevrin. She could have asked DCI Jackson for a ride, but that was much too chummy; sharing cream tea was a sufficient breakthrough for one day. Or she could have asked Harvey to drive her in the Bentley, but he was too busy with dishes and laundry. Finally, she could have driven her husband's silver Lexus, but since their marriage she'd given up driving altogether. Life in London was better suited to walking or public transport. So the Tube it was.

She hadn't walked far from her own gates when something caught her eye. A woman was snapping photographs of East Asia House.

There was no law against it, of course. Murder houses were attention magnets, sometimes years after the deed was done. And this woman, middle-aged and wearing what appeared to be a new quilted parka, was taking photographs respectfully. She shot only from the street or pavement, never stepping into the front garden or getting close to the windows. Still, Kate decided to cross Euston Place for a better look. Something about the woman's lank hair seemed familiar.

"Hiya," Kate said. "You're Patsy East, aren't you?"

Being addressed by name in a friendly manner was apparently tantamount to a threat, at least in Patsy East's book. She flinched so hard, she dropped her camera. Fortunately, the rig, which looked expensive, was attached to her via neck strap, and simply smacked her in the chest.

"Sorry!" Kate said. Like most Londoners, she'd once hated the necessity of marching up to strangers and introducing herself, but the Met's training had beat such reluctance out of her. "I'm Kate Hetheridge. Tony's wife. You know—Wellegrave House? Sorry I haven't been round to meet the neighbors yet. But you're a start, eh?"

Patsy nodded too much, like a cornered person willing to agree to anything for a chance to escape.

"Taking pictures, eh? That's brilliant," Kate continued, determined to get the mousy little woman to say something. Had Sharada been correct to label her a wandering wife? She really wasn't Hardwick's type. Too short, too plain, too obviously introverted. Maybe those society photos with her and Hardwick—drinking champagne, wearing a sequined dress—signified something else.

"You're with Scotland Yard," Patsy said so quietly Kate had to strain to hear. "It's all right to take pictures, isn't it? Not against the law?"

"Not against the law," Kate agreed, a touch overly jubilant to her own ears. Something about speaking to a person as colorless and restrained as Patsy made her want to overcompensate. "Are you a professional?"

Patsy looked blank.

"A professional photographer, I mean."

"Oh! No. I'm not a professional anything. Declan wouldn't like that. Expects me at home."

"Sad about Mr. Hardwick," Kate continued, and cursed herself when she saw suspicion flare in Patsy's eyes. She added hastily, "But of course I can't talk about the investigation. I do think if you want pics of East Asia House, now's the time. What with that REB group working so hard to get rid of it."

"Yes. Declan's very involved. Says it will be gone soon," Patsy said. "That's why I'm taking pictures. A little something to remember it by. I'd better go." Without another word, Patsy turned and fled, leaving Kate standing with an unsaid "goodbye" on her lips.

*And that,* she thought, *is why I should have left all the neighborhood interviews to Tony. Me as future head of the Toff Squad? Please.*

"Oi! Gulls," she called, surprised to find the uniformed constable in Scotland Yard's third floor bullpen. "Don't you know it's Saturday?"

"Hello, DS Hetheridge." PC Gulls wasn't her usual chipper self. "Had a date last night. Worst two hours of my life. Decided to come in today and see if I could do something right, since I can't pick a decent bloke to save my life." More carefully, she asked, "So, how are you? Since... you know."

"You mean my husband? Oh, well, 'keep calm and carrion' sums it up. That's life at the Met. I—" She stopped, realizing Gulls had asked a sincere question and took her flippant words as a sincere answer. "No, don't look like that. I just have my riot gear on. It's habit, Gulls, trick of the trade. The truth is, he's fine. We're both fine."

Gulls still looked distressed. The young officer's respect for Tony was genuine, Kate realized. Buck-toothed Derek Saunderson and his ilk notwithstanding, there were many at Scotland Yard who felt nearly as betrayed by the turn of events as she did.

"I should follow your example. About the riot gear, I mean," Gulls said, pushing back from her workstation's computer and stretching. "I come over as too earnest. Everyone says so. When I heard what happened to the Chief, I almost cried."

"I did cry," Kate admitted, after a quick look around to make sure no other officers, particularly males, could hear. "But behind closed doors. The men around here gossip more than women ever do. Especially if they see a chink in the armor."

"I just wish I'd been able to sit in with him on an interview. I could have learned so much," Gulls said. "And I was so chuffed because he promised. I considered it done, only a matter of time, because he never makes assurances lightly. Definitely never promises, not unless he means it. I suppose he had no idea what the next morning would bring."

Kate bit her lip. She was beginning to like Gulls. The young woman's friendliness and gentle nature was refreshing, now that Kate had dropped her defenses long enough to appreciate it. And that tempted her to share something, or at least hint. But no. Being privy to Tony's secrets meant keeping them. Now that Kate had finally broken through to him, she wouldn't risk their rapport, not for anything.

"Say, Gulls. I don't want to burden you," she said in that tone that signaled an opportunity for unpaid, possibly unacknowledged work that might lead nowhere or to bigger opportunities in the future. "But if you're serious about getting your mind off that lousy date…."

"I am!" Gulls sat up straight. "Is it for the Hardwick case? Please! Burden me."

"Yeah. It's about the murder weapon." Withdrawing her mobile, Kate consulted her notes, a mishmash of words and sentence fragments the uninitiated would assume encoded. "A tabletop reproduction of a famous sculpture by Giambologna:

*Hercules Beating the Centaur Nessus.* It was marble, very accurate, but the sort of thing real art lovers consider in bad taste. Since Hardwick dealt in originals, it seems like he would have hated it... except it was in his house, and someone killed him with it. FME Garrett thought maybe it came from a home shopping network. I'd like you to check into its origin. Someone from the lab should be able to get you a photo of the base and any maker's marks."

"Because where Hardwick bought it might be significant?" Gulls asked, then shook her head as if disgusted by her own slow wits. "Or do you think it was a gift? A gift he might have not have accepted with good grace?"

"Yeah. It hit me on the ride over—sure, the statuette made a convenient weapon. But what was it doing in Hardwick's gallery in the first place? Most murders are committed over love or money," Kate said. "Everyone knows that. And Buck and Sunny cornered the market on those motives. First Hardwick took Buck's wife, then he took Buck's money. But ridicule can be a motive, too. Ingratitude. Snobbery. A gift that wasn't appreciated? It's worth looking into."

Georgette Sevrin had been detained for questioning in a secure wing of St. Thomas hospital. The Met frequently placed vulnerable witnesses there, citing round-the-clock care and topnotch mental health resources. But it also had barred windows, electronic locks, and strict regulations against unsupervised egress. In short, the wing was well equipped to keep Georgette safe and comfortable if she needed psychiatric help, yet continuously monitored if her disturbance was all an act.

After showing her credentials, accepting a temporary badge, and being lectured on rules and procedures, Kate was finally permitted to meet Georgette in a small conference room. It offered nothing but beanbag chairs and a coffee table bolted to the floor. No loose objects, cabinets to hide in, or way out, except for a single door with a nurse on the other side. High on the wall, a camera with a blinking red light recorded everything, the better to provide interview footage to Scotland Yard.

"Hello, Miss Sevrin. How are you today?" Kate asked.

Georgette didn't answer. She looked markedly different than she had on the night of the murder. Then, she'd worn thick spectacles to rival Mrs. Snell's. With her graying hair uncombed and wild, she'd appeared perfectly unhinged in her mugshot, gazing into the camera with terrifying intensity. Today, the specs were gone, and her hair was shorn in a buzz cut to rival the one favored by Kate's only society friend, Lady Margaret Knolls. Instead of a *Mad Men*-era housedress, Georgette wore cotton pajamas, too finely made to be hospital-issued, and matching blue socks.

"You look nice," Kate ventured, sitting down. "I hope my sudden appearance hasn't frightened you. I'm from Scotland Yard, but I assure you, I only want to ask a few questions. If at any time you feel confused, we can—"

"I have a migraine coming on," Georgette interrupted matter-of-factly. "Spare me the preamble. Ask what you want and go away."

"Er, well, I see. It's only... the night of Granville Hardwick's murder, you were noticeably, um, confused. I think you said you were trying to reach Narnia via the wardrobe? In light of that—"

"Listen, Miss whatever you are. You didn't introduce yourself. Don't they teach basic courtesy at the Met anymore?" Georgette asked in that mercilessly acute tone. "Let me explain how this works. I have lucid moments. Familiar with that term? *L,U,C,I,D*," she spelled. "It means there are times when I can understand what I hear and respond with clarity. Like today. When I'm being unlawfully detained against my will in an abominable place that considers green gelatin a food and not a plaything. It makes my head hurt. You make my head hurt. But they tell me I can't leave until I answer your questions. So fire away."

Kate absorbed that. How would Tony proceed? For that matter, how would sweet, sympathetic PC Gulls proceed? *I'm not him. I'm not her. Time to roll the dice.*

"This is the downside of faking it, eh? Being treated like you're actually a nutter?" Kate shrugged. "My sister's schizophrenic. Better lately, but she doesn't much like the drugs her doctors prescribe. No matter how much they help, she always wants to quit them. A little booze, a little meth—old school self-medicating."

"Words cannot express," Georgette said, "how little I care about your sister, Detective....?"

"Hetheridge," Kate said. "And I'm not surprised you don't want to hear about Maura. I know you've been doing the Sally Slip and Molly Moan routine most of your life. People who get hurt or sick for real are your competitors, eh? And you love the attention, don't you? That's what it's all about."

Georgette's nostrils flared. She sat up as straight as her squishy beanbag permitted. "It's about money, you stupid bloody cow. Money I'm owed for real injuries caused by careless people who should have done their jobs properly." She raked Kate up and down with her sharp gaze. "Then again, you don't look too familiar with money. I know your sort. The kind with a bedsit, a pile of unpaid bills, and a husband on the dole."

"You see right through me," Kate said, suppressing a smile. "So well, in fact, those specs must have been part of the act. Plus a fright wig, right? To make you look round the bend?"

"When I'm not lucid, Detective," Georgette said, shooting the camera a lingering glance, "that's *L,U,C,I,D*, your new vocabulary word, I prefer the wig and glasses. They offer me comfort. The accident left me so confused, you see. It destroyed my hope of finding employment or another husband."

"Right. Speaking of husbands... what's the story with you and

Granville Hardwick? He was married to your sister Monette. Yet all these years later, she divorced him and made a new life for herself while you stayed by his side. It's not much of a leap to think maybe you were in love with him. I'm not sure what he had, but he must have had something, judging from all the women under his spell."

Kate had hoped this more daring jab would further inflame Georgette, but instead, she regained her composure. Then again, a career liar with her years of experience had surely faced hostile interrogators before.

"Detective Hetheridge, you should know, my lucid phases don't last forever," she said warningly. "You want something to take to your superiors. I want out of this prison. Ask me about the murder."

"All right. Last Thursday. Were you inside East Asia House all day and all night?" It was the question Paul had suggested she ask, based on what Fiona Leeds had seen—a woman with wild hair, big specs, and a housedress climbing over Declan East's fence.

"Yes. I hardly go out and never alone," Georgette said firmly. "Since the crash, I've lost all independence."

"Who visited East Asia House that day?"

"Buck. Sunny's husband. She used to natter constantly about how she resented him. Didn't stop her from squandering his money, though."

"What time did he arrive?"

"I don't know."

"What time did he leave?"

"Haven't the foggiest."

"When did he come back?"

"No idea. How I wish I could help you," Georgette said coldly.

"Help me with this. When did you go downstairs and walk through Hardwick's blood?"

Georgette touched her throat in pretended shock, like a

dowager clutching her pearls. "I don't believe I ever did. Come to think of it, the night it happened, a man from Scotland Yard talked to me. His name was Hetheridge, too. My goodness." She smiled. "That was the baron, wasn't it? And you're the gold digger he married. Congratulations. I married for money once, too. And it was far harder work than anything else I've done to pay the bills."

"You knew about me from the moment I walked in, didn't you?"

She nodded.

"Well," Kate said, "it just so happens, I knew about you. Before I came to St. Thomas, I telephoned your sister Monette. She told me she's never been happier since she divorced Hardwick. Since she left London to get away from you two. You know what else she said? That you fell in love with Granville Hardwick when the three of you were at university. That even though he loved your sister, you wanted him so much, you made yourself the third wheel. Always unwanted. Always following them about like a hopeful puppy. So desperate to win his attention."

Georgette's smile disappeared.

"Monette said you tried to be prettier, but that didn't work. Hardwick always had an eye for beautiful women, and you couldn't hold a candle to your sister. You tried to be smarter, but Hardwick didn't care. He already thought he was the cleverest bloke in the room. The only thing you had, the only thing that could make him look your way, was the capacity to be hurt. To moan, to cry, to make people feel sorry for you," Kate said, enjoying the growing horror in Georgette's eyes. "He finally pitied you so much, he strayed from Monette, didn't he? But you couldn't keep him. In the end, I'm surprised you didn't saw off a limb or gouge out an eye, just to hold his interest a little longer."

"You're abusing me!" Georgette cried, looking at the camera. "This is abuse!"

"You were bracingly frank with me, and I accepted it because

207

I'm a big girl," Kate said calmly. "Now it's my turn. I think this crash scheme was your all-or-nothing play to regain the love of your life. I think you endured the whole routine, the glasses, the hair, the feigned dependency, so you could be with him as much as possible. And when that didn't work, when being the most pitiful, desperate, helpless woman on earth didn't do it, you snapped. Dashed his brains out. Slipped in his blood. Rubbed out the footprint, ran upstairs and hid in the wardrobe."

"You have no proof—"

"I have plenty of proof," Kate said, enjoying the moment perhaps a little too much. "The lab came back with preliminary fingerprints today. Yours are all over the murder weapon. Buck left three prints on it. You left thirteen. There's motive, opportunity, forensic evidence—"

"I lived there!" Georgette retorted. "Of course I touched it. It was a gift, some stupid gift. I don't know who gave it to him. Probably Sunny Wainwright! Gran and I joked about it, pretended to re-gift it to each other, passing it back and forth like the ugly piece of rubbish it was. I touched it, yes, but I didn't use it to kill Gran. And heaven knows I didn't love him anymore."

"You did love him. You killed him, panicked, and ran. There's no use denying it. It's all captured on your neighbors' CCTV cameras," Kate lied, thinking she was onto something and eager to find out if she was right. "Then you came to your senses, returned to your bedroom, rifled a few drawers, and climbed into the wardrobe. You were frightened and guilty. The nutter routine was your only hope."

"Rifled a few drawers?" Georgette repeated. "I knew it! Someone *was* in my room."

"What?"

"Listen. It's true I found Gran dead. I stepped in his blood and rubbed out the print. That's all! I went back upstairs to hide. For all I knew, the killer was still in the house. I looked around and realized someone had been up there. A drawer was open. I hid in the wardrobe to protect myself. I never had time to discover what was taken."

Kate shook her head. "This won't work. If you were home all day, how did you miss seeing or hearing Buck's killer? You must have done it yourself. As for your bedroom, it was analyzed down to the atomic level. Buck didn't leave a trace up there. No one else did, either, apart from a few unknowns, and I'm sure Hardwick must have employed cleaners. This doesn't look good for you, Miss Sevrin."

"I didn't kill him. And whoever you have on camera isn't me!" Georgette shrieked. For the first time, in extremis, her words had the ring of truth. "Now get out. I won't say another word without my solicitor."

# CHAPTER 16

"Sir Duncan? Really?" Kate squashed her mobile against her ear to hear Paul better. It was loud inside the Yellow Earl, and as it was barely seven o'clock on a weekend, the pub was sure to grow louder as the night wore on. "I guess I owe you an apology. I thought the dog was a figment of your imagination."

"'Harebrained psychodrama.' Those were your exact words. Anyway, I'd worry less about saying sorry and more about when and how he's going to kill me. Then again." Paul sighed. "Maybe death is better. I have no car, no home, no hope."

"Er, true. But you'll have the goodwill and approval of our Chief, when he hears you won the old lady over."

"Yeah. Vic's goodwill. Lucky me," Paul muttered. "So what about Mrs. Tumnus? Did she fling herself back to Narnia when you said she was spotted climbing a fence?"

"No, she denied it. Vehemently. I even bluffed, said we had proof. She still insisted it wasn't her." Kate took a sip of ale. "Given her history with Hardwick, though, plus her prints on the murder weapon and her tracks in the blood, the circumstantial case against her is good. As good as the one against Buck, or better."

On one the pub's many televisions, the underdog team scored, prompting a round of cheers and applause. After the noise died down, Kate asked, "Do you really think your dad will refuse to alibi Buck? Even if Jackson leans on him?"

"Especially if Jackson leans on him. My father is…." Paul huffed into the phone. "I have no words to describe him. Just that sound." He did it again. "I mean, he leaves my mum, carries on with another woman for years, *then* gets angry when he doesn't find her still waiting at home? Can you believe the nerve?"

"I can, actually. Garden-variety cheater. Thinks the rules only apply to women. Maybe she traded up with Buck. At least he strikes me as faithful."

"I don't know. He has issues, too. But what's all that noise? You and Tony on a date somewhere?"

"I wish. I'm waiting for the Chief. We're meeting to discuss the case."

"Where?"

"The Yellow Earl. The barman who worked Thursday afternoon will come on shift soon. If he remembers serving Buck, that will lock down Buck's timeline. Maybe even alibi him. So even if your dad won't cooperate, Buck will still be freed."

"I have nowhere to go and nothing to do. Want me to come by? Provide backup?"

"Why?"

"Um, Kate. It's you. And Jackson. In a pub."

"I know. But I suppose I have to give him a chance eventually. Now's as good a time as any. Besides, I picked a two-seater in the middle of the room. Dead center. No chance he can—oh. There he is," she said, catching sight of her new guv's familiar rumpled form. "Better let you go. But seriously, Paul, where are you sleeping tonight?"

"Right now, it's a tossup between the bathtub and a hotel. My credit card's almost maxed, but I might have enough for one night."

"No. Tony and I will put you up. We have plenty of room."

"Wellegrave House? I don't know. I always feel like I don't belong there. Like I might stain something. Or break something."

"Never fear. If it can be broken or stained, Henry and Ritchie have beat you to it. We've lost two rugs, three lamps, and quite a lot of downstairs plumbing."

"How's Tony handling it?"

"Suspiciously well. I'm beginning to think he was never best pleased, being surrounded by museum pieces, and seeing it demolished suits him fine. Now Harvey... Harvey may snap if Mrs. Snell doesn't whip the boys into shape. Anyway, don't be intimidated. Our place has guest rooms, clean linen, and nightly showings of *The Lego Movie*. How can you say no?"

After a few awkward attempts to do just that, Paul finally said yes. By the time he rang off, Jackson was hovering by the table, a glass of fizzy pop in hand.

"Hiya, Chief. Have a seat. What're you drinking?"

"Pepsi." He settled himself on the opposite stool, looking every bit as uncomfortable as she felt. She instinctively tried to set him at ease.

"The bitter's two-for-one tonight. I have another one coming to me. If you want to drink it, I'll go back to the bar and—" She stopped, remembering. "I mean, er, sorry. Pepsi's good."

His eyes narrowed. "Who have you been talking to?"

"No one."

"Someone tell you I'm off the sauce?"

"No. I just noticed you cleared out your drinks trolley. And turned down a Bloody Mary this morning. I don't mean to pry. It's a detective thing." Feeling guilty, she added, "I probably shouldn't have snagged us a table. Or ordered this," she added, glancing at her pint of lovely golden ale, still more than half full.

"Well, you're right. I am off the sauce, but never mind looking out for me." His voice was edged with bitterness. "Can't step out my house without seeing a pub, a corner market, a Guinness advert. Even if I stay inside, every program on the telly is sponsored by a bottle of this or that. And every character on every program has to enjoy his little drinky before hurrying off to save the world."

She'd never thought of it that way. Was that why Maura couldn't seem to give up the booze, no matter what her doctors said? Louise was enjoying herself, that much was obvious, but Maura seemed as miserable drunk as she did sober.

"Crikey, Hetheridge, don't look like that." Jackson sighed. "There are places I can go. Meetings I can attend. The whole, 'I'm Vic and I'm an alcoholic' thing. It works. When I let it work. So drink up. And please, make this worthwhile. Tell me your interview with Georgette Sevrin wasn't a waste of time."

Kate described the encounter, muddling the facts to make it seem like she, not Paul, had dropped by Harrods to question Fiona Leeds. At her description of a fleeing woman, Jackson perked up.

"I asked Saunderson to go over the footage requisitioned from the CCTV cameras of Hardwick's neighbors. Saw the results just before I left the Yard. Buck Wainwright was captured briefly on several. Nothing useful there. But a young man dropped by East Asia House around eight. Drove a lorry, had on something like a uniform, but looked dodgy to me. Shaved head. Multiple piercings. I'll bet he was calling about Hardwick's drug distribution scheme. Then there's the lady in the lavender coat and scarf who entered East Asia House's back garden and never came out."

"Fiona Leeds said she saw Georgette leaving...."

"We have pictures of that, too. A woman, medium height, scarf over her hair, lavender coat, punching in the code to Hardwick's back fence around six o'clock. The neighbor's cameras are roof-positioned, so the angle is bad, but we see her enter. She never comes out. Ever. Half hour later, Georgette Sevrin exits. Wild hair, big glasses, housedress. Climbed the fence to Declan East's back garden and never appeared on camera again. Not

until she emerged from the wardrobe inside Hardwick's house."
He took a sip of cola. "It's like a magic trick. A bloody annoying
magic trick."

"All right," Kate said. "Let's pick this apart. Hardwick was into
more than art. He was using his gallery's order fulfillment system
to ship drugs for a third party. Maisie refused to play along and
said she was threatened. You think Hardwick courted death on
that front?"

"It's possible. I've chased these types for years. Most of them
kill someone in their own network from time to time, just to be
taken seriously," Jackson said. "But the fact this third party knew
Maisie flushed the gear and pressed several times for repayment
says something. The really tough customers only ask once. Then
they make an example out of you. And the lorry driver? He may
have come round to threaten Hardwick, but he didn't kill him.
Hardwick was alive a few hours later to open the door for Buck."

"Okay. Next item. A woman in a lavender coat entered, but
didn't exit. A woman who took steps to conceal her identity with
the scarf...."

"It was cold out."

"True. Still, whoever she was, she knew the code. Sunny
tweeted some odd stuff the day of the murder."

"This woman's too short to be Sunny. Too short to be any of
Hardwick's women, if you ask me. Liked legs, our Granville."

"Finally, Georgette appears to leave," Kate said slowly, trying
to envision it, "but never comes back. She's cruel and mocking
and a certified liar. But I almost believed her when she said
someone was in her bedroom, rifling her chest of drawers. And
there *were* unknowns in the fingerprint analysis."

"There always are, unless you're a total hermit," Jackson said.
"There are unknowns on every surface, including the murder
weapon. They just don't tie into any person of interest."

"Those shots of Georgette. Were they also from a roof
camera? Did you identify her by face, or just by hair and glasses?"

"You think it wasn't her?"

"Well, you said she wore a housedress but no coat. And it *was* cold that night. I wore my best coat to the scene, and so did everyone else. Leaving aside the issue of how Georgette got back in the house, why would she leave without a coat?"

Jackson seemed to consider that. Kate, who already had a theory, waited. In the past, he'd maintained an excellent arrest ratio by coming down with both feet on the first likely suspect, detective work be damned. Now that he was off the sauce, as he put it, would he still be so quick to plow through cases without examining all the evidence? Or would he stop and actually ponder an unanswered question or two?

"So you think the woman in the scarf may have killed Hardwick?" she asked Jackson. "Then she went up to Georgette's room, took some of her things, and exited in disguise?"

"Maybe."

"That's fine, but if Georgette Sevrin was home, as she claims, why didn't she notice? I realize she likes to play nutter, but she has the lucid routine when things get hot. Why not lucidly mention who actually did it?"

"I'm not sure yet," Kate said. "But let's say the woman in the lavender coat killed Hardwick. If she wasn't one of his girlfriends, she was definitely a neighbor. Someone who'd had an opportunity to learn the gate code.

"Anyway," Kate continued, warming to her theory. "This girlfriend or neighbor quarrels with Hardwick. Bashes him with the statuette and gets blood all over her coat. If the murder wasn't premeditated, maybe she panics. Thinks about all those TV crime shows, the forensic traces she might have left behind, the neighborhood cameras. Decides she can't leave as herself and risk being seen. So she exits dressed as Georgette."

"Leaving the lavender coat behind, either tucked in East Asia House or one of its rubbish bins." Jackson looked impressed. "Not bad. Not sure if I buy it, but not bad. Tomorrow I'll go back over every inch of the place with my own team. The CSIs are good, but in a house that size, there's plenty to overlook. If a bloody coat is hidden inside, I'll find it. So now—this mystery lady who climbed over Declan East's garden wall. Didn't Bhar's mum list Mrs. East as a wandering wife?"

"Yes," Kate said, chuckling. "It's amazing what some time with Google and absolute, unswerving devotion to a man can accomplish. If Sharada ever turns stalker, Buck's finished. I've met Patsy East. Kind of a shrinking violet. But she seems to have had an affair with Hardwick. Certainly her husband, Declan, wrote at least one column taking all Britain to task for condoning adultery."

"I've read his stuff. Angry man," Jackson said. "Never satisfied. I'm tempted to knock on his door and hear his unvarnished opinion of his poor dead neighbor. But Tony's meeting with the REB tomorrow, and the Easts should be among them. Best leave it to him."

"That reminds me. About Tony…."

Jackson's eyes narrowed again. "More gossip?"

"Not really. I just—"

"Look, you can think what you want, Hetheridge, but I never wanted Tony out. Maybe we weren't the best of friends, but he overlooked a lot from me. So anything you heard, anything about decisions that came from the MoJ or wherever…." He glared at her, gripping his cola glass with both hands. "Sod it. Never mind. Maybe you never had a relative who made you want to leave the country. I do."

"Actually, I have one or two," Kate said. "And to be honest, I was only trying to thank you. You came to Wellegrave House for tea. Showed mercy to Paul and his mum. Even invited Tony to continue in the investigation as a private citizen. That was big of you."

If Jackson had looked uncomfortable before, now he seemed positively mortified. "Oh. Well. Er, it was all for me, really, asking

Tony to handle the neighbors. He doesn't need my help. He's Lord Hetheridge. He'd beat cancer with a pack of cigarettes."

"Maybe." Kate smiled. "But thanks anyway. Chief."

"Right. Um, look, there's the barman," Jackson said, either catching sight of the witness or pretending to. Standing up, he brushed the dandruff off his shoulders and straightened his sport coat, which he'd probably bought off the rack when Prince Harry was a baby. "I realize tomorrow's Sunday, but I'll expect you in no later than noon, is that clear?"

"Crystal."

"Good. And good work on the theory. Go home," he ordered over his shoulder, and walked away.

By the time Kate reached home, it was almost nine. She was taking off her coat in Wellegrave House's foyer when her mobile rang.

"Hello, ma'am!" PC Gulls sang, cheerful as ever. "Hope this isn't too late. I've spent all day on your assignment, and ooh, it was a tough one. Funny how many people don't work Saturdays and dodge calls on the weekend, even from Scotland Yard."

"I always say straight out it's a murder investigation. That gets people's juices flowing," Kate said. "The less they have to do with it, the more keen they are. But you're right, it's late. Have something for me on the statuette?" She feared Gulls, in her zeal, might have actually called her after hours to report negative progress.

"Yes. It was quite a long and twisted road, ma'am. First I had to track down the maker's mark. It's for the St. George & the Dragon Replica Company, which was founded three years ago and went out of business soon after. After it failed, its holdings were liquidated, so it took some little white lies on my part to determine—"

"Gulls."

"Ma'am?"

"I'm sure you did an amazing job. I'll probably never fully appreciate everything you went through to track down that piece. But if you did track it down, could you skip to the grand finale? I'd really like to see my husband before dawn."

"Of course! So, *Hercules Beating the Centaur Nessus* was limited to one thousand copies. A home shopping club sold most of them, and I'll be getting those names and addresses by next week. Always like to be thorough, ma'am," Gulls said happily. "But twenty-five copies were bought by a magazine called *Our Beloved Heritage*. It's one of those aren't-we-English things, all about restoring fox hunting and abolishing immigration and getting back to our roots, which I think is code for something unpleasant. Anyway, those twenty-five copies were given as gifts to the magazine's regular contributors." Gulls couldn't suppress her rising excitement. "And one of those contributors, who submits an opinion piece for every issue, lives in your neighborhood."

"Declan East," Kate said.

"Yes!" Gulls emitted what was, for her, a rather wicked laugh. "The statuettes are all numbered. Unfortunately, the magazine didn't keep track of which piece went to which recipient. So even though we know it was statuette 371 of 1000 that killed Granville Hardwick, we don't have a document affirming statuette 371 is the one Declan East received. Still, it can't be a coincidence, can it?"

"I don't think so. Well done, Gulls. I won't forget this," Kate said, and rang off.

In Ritchie's room, she discovered Paul and Henry sitting in on the millionth re-watching of *The Lego Movie*. Henry was reading a book. Ritchie was on the floor, constructing something new from his beloved plastic bricks. Paul, however, seemed captivated by the film, laughing at all the right spots.

"Did Harvey find you a room?" Kate asked.

"Yes. Thank you. And have you seen this? It's brilliant!"

"Stick around. Before long, you'll be hearing the theme song in your sleep."

Leaving him to it, Kate went upstairs to find Tony sitting up in bed, reading specs on, duvet pulled up to his waist, frowning at his iPad. He was shirtless, which she considered a good start. So she locked the bedroom door against any possible incursions from Henry or Ritchie.

"You don't look happy," she said, stepping out of her heels. "It's not because I invited Paul for the night, is it?"

"Of course not. I did wonder if it was your idea of revenge. I decide we should adopt Henry; you decide we should adopt Paul. But no, if I seem frustrated, it's just a bit of aggro over this," Tony said, indicating the device on his lap. "Mrs. Snell believes that, retired detective or no, in order to obtain my PI license, I'll have to attend at least one weekend course. Not online. In person. Possibly with a sticky name tag affixed to my lapel. I've been checking behind her, and she's correct, as usual."

"What's the topic? How to submit information requests in triplicate, then start over again when the government loses them?" Kate asked, draping her blazer over a chair.

"No. This. 'Achieving Best Evidence in Criminal Proceedings: Guidance on Interviewing Victims and Witnesses, and Guidance on using Special Measures,' by the Ministry of Justice."

"Tony. You could teach that."

"I have taught it. Offered to rewrite it, as a matter of fact." Putting the iPad aside, he removed his reading glasses, the better to watch her undress. "Never mind. Carry on."

Smiling, she removed her skirt, then began unbuttoning her blouse. "So you're actually committed to the private investigation service? You think things will go that way and not…." Trailing off, she unhooked her bra, enjoying his unwavering gaze.

He didn't answer.

"Tony?" she said, wriggling out of her knickers.

"Hmnh? Sorry, you distracted me. As for the future, I suppose it's fifty-fifty. You know me, I like to keep my options open, and I'm certainly not ready to retire in earnest. So I'll get that license, whether I actually use it or not." He patted the space on the bed beside him. "Come closer. Tell me about the case."

"The case?" She feigned disbelief. "But we have a rule. No work in bed."

"That was before. When I was your commanding officer. Now I'm merely a citizen. And very interested to know what my wife has uncovered."

"I don't think discussing it would be very professional of me."

"Shall I convince you?"

"Please."

# CHAPTER 17

The home of Jimmy Quarrels and his wife, Tabitha, was arguably the most palatial on Euston Place, and certainly the oldest, predating Wellegrave House by fifty years. Tony, accustomed to the reality of homes which had passed their bicentennial, wasn't surprised to find that within No. 22's Georgian exterior, only the front parlor was maintained as a period showplace. Beyond that chamber, with its neoclassical furniture, antique rugs, and Moorish mirrors, the house opened up, walls falling away and picture windows appearing, brightening an expansive living room and an oversized, airy kitchen.

"We're so lucky we had that faulty wiring," Tabitha said. The REB had settled in the living room, and she was going from seat to seat, serving mojitos garnished with blueberries. "Plus I have friends on the planning committee. It's so much easier when the demolition occurs due to fire. I keep telling them I'm just enduring all this open space. That soon I'll dig up some reclaimed timber and brick, locate an approved builder, and get this place back to its original floorplan. And I will, in a decade or two," she added, winking at Tony. "Remember that, if you decide to gut your place and start over. Sure you won't have a mojito?"

"Perhaps later."

"I think what Lord Hetheridge is too polite to say is, men won't touch a drink with floating fruit," Declan East announced from his seat near the colossal television. Of middle height, narrow-shouldered and fiftyish, he looked even gloomier in person, his comb-over down to a few thick strands plastered to the otherwise hairless zone.

"James Bond drinks martinis, and martinis have olives," Fiona Leeds said. "Olives are a fruit."

"Who told you that? Your ghostwriter?" Declan shook his head. "For what it's worth, James Bond drinks vespers. No olive, just a bit of lemon peel. Though I suppose before long he'll order a Toffee Appletini. Tabby, I hope you realize you're contributing to the pervasive feminization of Britain."

"Declan. Don't show off just because Tony finally graced us with his presence." Tabitha said, winking at Tony. "We're so pleased you could come. The REB is a small group, but determined. We were on the brink of forcing Granville out of the neighborhood when he died. And now that he's gone, we'll have the White Elephant knocked down and replaced with something acceptable in a matter of months."

Tony nodded, working to maintain an expression of benign interest. The group was small, only twelve people; apparently, interest in gathering to excoriate Granville Hardwick behind his back had fallen off after the murder. The traditional adage "Nothing but good of the dead" still held sway, at least in Mayfair. But the neighbors who'd turned up were longtime residents, and all knew Tony by reputation. They seemed genuinely happy to see him, as if a Peer's interest might speed their efforts to rid the neighborhood of East Asia House once and for all.

"Besides," Tabitha continued. "Jimmy made these drinks, and no one would call him girly. A poll last week said he was the most feared man on TV." She handed a mojito to Patsy East, who to

Tony resembled a female version of her husband—same height, same narrow shoulders, and equally gloomy, from her limp dark hair to the downturned corners of her mouth.

"Oh, well, of course, TV," Declan sneered. "Nothing more instrumental in the fall of western civilization than the public's obsession with TV."

"Jimmy came back?" Patsy East asked Tabitha. She had a soft, breathy way of speaking, as if she'd trained herself to communicate as unobtrusively as possible. "That's wonderful."

Tabitha nodded. "We're together again. Stronger than ever. The best marriages have their ups and downs, Patsy love, and come out better for it."

*So two of Sharada's wandering wives have reconciled with their husbands, either before Hardwick died or just after.* Tony studied Tabitha, every inch the gracious hostess, and Patsy, who looked quietly miserable. *Is that guilt? Or just the wages of being married to Declan East?*

"So, Lord Hetheridge. Or Tony, if you insist," Declan said. "Though I see nothing wrong with addressing a man by the title God gave him. What do you make of the hatchet job Tabby did on this house?"

"Quite nice. Practical for entertaining. And for her husband to pursue his cooking, I suppose."

"Erm. I can't agree. Beige walls and fitted carpets make me want to vomit. All rather soulless, if you ask me. Of course, it's indoors, and the Society to Reverse Euston Brutality was formed to fight public outrages, not private ones. Still." Declan seemed determined to engage Tony, to find some point of agreement between them. "I've heard your home hasn't changed in any meaningful sense, inside or out, for more than fifty years. That's what I call traditionalism."

"That's what I call sloth," Tony said lightly. "And now that I've seen what a bit of fire can do, perhaps I'll encourage my house guest to play with matches. I only wish I'd seen it sooner. And I would have, if I hadn't waited so long to accept your group's kind invitation."

That brought smiles all around. This was the sort of social obligation he loathed, that he voluntarily endured for only two reasons—charity, or murder. But it was nice to know he could still win people over with easy manners and a touch of self-deprecation. Most people, at least. Not Declan.

"You disappoint me." The man stared at Tony as if suddenly recognizing the tell-tale signs of a counterfeit. "Why did you come here, really? I was told you retired from Scotland Yard. Is that true? Are you actually investigating Hardwick's murder?"

"Dee… please." Patsy sounded nervous.

"I did retire," Tony said pleasantly. "I just got married. I'm planning to adopt my wife's nephew, and I'm embarking on a new chapter of my life. As for the Hardwick murder, my understanding is the police arrested a man at the scene. He confessed. Case closed."

Declan looked at the floor, pursed his lips, and said nothing.

Before long, Jimmy Quarrels himself appeared, in jeans and a chef's white shirt, to thank everyone for coming and announce the lunch menu, which was sea bass and seared vegetables. He seemed in a splendid mood, happy to linger and chat, but after five minutes, Tabitha tired of her husband answering questions about recipes and cooking show contestants.

"Jimmy! Are you mental?" she demanded, interrupting him in mid-sentence. "You haven't even begun the prep. If you don't hurry and start cooking soon, our guests will die of starvation while you're still dicing the onions."

"Er, um, of course, of course," he muttered, running a hand through his hair.

"Get to it. Chop-chop! And not too much rosemary. Last time you ruined it with too much rosemary."

Giving his guests a sheepish wave, the celebrity chef retreated to his kitchen.

"I used to be his *sous* chef," she told the group, sinking gracefully into an armchair and taking a sip of her drink. "He needed a firm hand in those days. Still does. Now let's get down to business. Tony, a bit of background. Someone suggested making the REB more than just a protest group. That's negative and might strike the Council as hostile. So we're about to *rebrand* ourselves"—Tabitha smiled, very proud of that word—"as the Society to Restore Euston's Beauty. We'll position ourselves as a network of historic and nearly historic homes that beautify London. Therefore, when we complain of the White Elephant in our midst, we'll be taken more seriously. Besides." She took another sip of her mojito. "Becoming recognized as a group with preservation goals could benefit us in lots of ways. Grants from the government. Tax breaks. I mean, we've earned it, right? Let's keep it. Now look at this."

A laptop was positioned in the center of the coffee table. Opening it, Tabitha began clicking keys, continuing, "I hired someone from Jimmy's show to make us a website. Right now it's just an example, privately hosted. A little manifesto about who we are, what we stand for, pictures, slideshows. Photos of Fiona and her book, Declan and his columns, and me and Jimmy cooking together. People love a bit of TV magic! And naturally, all our homes are shown to their best advantage. Anyone viewing the site can't help but see how this isn't just about keeping our property values up. It's about beautifying the city."

Seated as he was beside Tabitha, who seemed to be playing directly to him, Tony watched politely as she clicked from house to house, letting everyone in the group see how their home was represented. When Declan's came on the screen, he sat up.

"No. No. 'Best advantage,' you say? Who did you hire to take these pictures, one of Jimmy's reject contestants? Look at that!"

He pointed at the screen. "Why shoot the house so that our trouble with the bloody construction crew is visible?"

Tony studied the picture. Most of the front garden was flawless. But the gate to the walled back garden was surrounded by wheelbarrows, stacked bricks, and a pile of lumber.

"Fine, I'll swap it out. We have dozens of images to choose from," Tabitha said, her patience with Declan clearly growing thin. "But now that you mention it, it's just as well you and the workers had your dispute before that new electric gate went in. We all need to think carefully about modifications to our property that will be visible from the street. Patsy told me your old gate was circa 1870. The best thing you could do for our movement is get those workers to clear out the debris and restore the gate to its place, at least till the REB gets what it wants."

"Bugger the REB."

"Dee," Patsy said again. Her husband rounded on her.

"Oh, I get it. You took that picture, didn't you? Lovely. Untold hundreds flushed away on photography lessons, and you can't even frame a snapshot without making a fool of yourself."

"I did them yesterday," Patsy said. "I was late submitting them, so a few didn't turn out perfect. But the interior shots are lovely."

"I doubt it," Declan said savagely. "All right, Tabby, what are you waiting for? Show us Patsy's snaps of the toilet bowl and the mudroom floor. That's sure to impress the Peer in our midst."

"Declan, be reasonable. They're perfectly fine," Tabitha said. "See? Front parlor. Front living room. Looks like a page from a magazine."

Tony took it in as Declan stared at the picture of his living room, clearly searching for an excuse to further berate his wife. Most of the Easts' décor was antique, but the room's wallpaper and light fixtures were modern. Framed photographic art hung on the walls.

"Zoom in," Declan said.

Tabitha did. Now greater detail was visible—one of Declan's journalism awards gathering dust on the piano, a stray glove on the sofa, smeared fingerprints standing out on the coffee table. Any space sheltering human beings would have such imperfections. And if the compositions on the walls were examples of Patsy's work, her strengths ran to simple subjects, hugely magnified. Tony saw an orchid petal, ripples on a pond, the stem of a leaf, and something more abstract: four puffs of red, each a dark spot surrounded by a halo of droplets.

"Why do we even have a maid? Couldn't you have asked her to tidy up before you blundered in, camera in hand, to capture it all for eternity?" Declan asked Patsy. His shrillness in anger, his small hands and narrow shoulders, reminded Tony of Kate's conundrum: the woman in a scarf and lavender coat who had entered Hardwick's house just before the murder, yet never came out.

*Did Declan disguise himself as his wife to get into East Asia House? And disguise himself as Georgette Sevrin to get home again?*

It was past six o'clock when Tony extricated himself from the REB. He'd tasted the sea bass, complimented the dessert, taken the obligatory sip of post-prandial sherry, and finally been set free after three-and-a-half excruciating hours. With any luck, what he'd observed would help Kate resolve the Hardwick case, and render the sacrifice of his time worthwhile. Thoughts focused on Declan and Patsy East, he crossed to his side of Euston Place. He'd just started toward Wellegrave House when a dog growled behind him.

"Kaiser! Nein!" a familiar voice said. "Don't mind him, Chief. He's just excited to see you."

Tony turned. Sir Duncan Godington stood before him. Tall,

blond, and handsome enough to turn heads even in London, Sir Duncan looked as stylish as ever in a black overcoat and cashmere scarf. He held the lead of a black dog that strained against his grip, as if disliking Tony on sight.

"Hello, Sir Duncan. What are you doing here?"

Sir Duncan made a wounded noise. "Not very polite, are you? Then again, I suppose you feel a bit beat up these days. I was shocked, *shocked*, to hear the news." His blue eyes snapped with amusement. "The invincible, always-on-the-job Chief Superintendent Hetheridge, giving up his career to be a house husband? Stepfather to an in-law's brat?"

Tony said nothing.

"I can't believe you'd ever voluntarily choose such a thing. Tell me the truth. Did they sack you for marrying Kate? Has the Metropolitan Police Service become so open and transparent, it actually x-rayed the oldest boy in the old boy network?"

"So it seems."

"Ah, but you're keeping a stiff upper lip about it. Good for you," Sir Duncan said, issuing another command in German when Kaiser's attention shifted to a poodle across the street. "Keeping up appearances is so important. And you know," he went on, feeling in his pocket and withdrawing a dog treat, "it used to be, a man retired at fifty-five. Died at fifty-eight. That's why they gave him the gold pocket watch. So he could keep track of every miserable moment, unwanted, put out to pasture, until the Grim Reaper arrived. How old are you now? Sixty-five? Seventy?"

Tony smiled.

"Never mind. And who knows, perhaps it won't all be soft food and Zimmer frames. Perhaps you'll get a bit of excitement before the end," Sir Duncan went on, feeding Kaiser the treat. "You'd be surprised how many times I've run into Paul Bhar lately. Encounters like that are so much more fun in the real world, as opposed to the interrogation room. I feel a bit bullied in there. But out here, under the sky, in the fresh air, there are so many more... possibilities. People lead real lives out here. Let down their hair. Let down their guard. At all sorts of places, like Waitrose ... Boots ... the Tube...."

"Careful," Tony said.

"Oh, but I'm always careful." Sir Duncan didn't break eye contact. "And don't go losing sleep over Paul. It's true, I've been playing with him, tracking him with Kaiser. But it's all too easy. He falls apart at the smallest push."

"You'd do better with me." Tony felt exactly as he did on the piste, epee in hand, facing a well-matched but overconfident opponent. Holding his form, he allowed time to slow, waiting for the moment the blade would be *there*, and one flick of his fingers could sweep it away.

"You?" Sir Duncan shook his head. "You'd accept your fate without a sound. Take it like a man. Very boring. But *Kate*...."

"Listen to me now. And listen closely," Tony said. "When I was at Scotland Yard, I owed that institution certain things. Qualities like integrity. Honor. Decency. Not any longer. I don't have to wait for you to commit a crime, Sir Duncan. If you threaten my wife, if you give me the slightest indication she's in danger, I'll kill you."

Sir Duncan's smile widened, but Tony knew it was pure theater. He saw the true response in the other man's eyes.

"Why, Lord Hetheridge. Making idle threats here, in the middle of the street." He turned to smile at Fiona Leeds as she passed, also on her way home from the meeting. "This man just threatened to kill me!"

"Really? That's awkward!" Giggling, she kept on her way.

Tony ignored the attempt at distraction. "I have an advantage over you, you know."

"What? Senility? The inability to discuss murder obliquely, like a gentleman, instead of making ham-handed threats?"

"I'm not a serial killer. I'll take no vile pleasure in the act.

Therefore, I won't be compelled to do it myself," Tony continued quietly. "When you kill, Sir Duncan, you're driven to commit the act personally. You need to hear your victims' pleas. Spill their blood. Watch the light go out of their eyes. That sort of thing is difficult to pull off without getting caught, no matter how clever you are.

"But me? I'm a retired policeman. I've looked into the abyss. And let me assure you, the abyss looks back. I know precisely how to arrange for someone with a gun or a knife to end your worthless life. I can pay the sort of man who'll not only do it, he'll let himself be caught red-handed so the Met never looks my way. Someone who'll serve twenty to life in Wandsworth just so my money can send his kids to uni. All I need do is make a phone call. One phone call, and you'll be dead in a matter of hours."

Sir Duncan studied Tony for what felt like eons. Then his smile returned, though his eyes were hooded. "Well said."

Tony waited, pulse beating in his ears.

"Lovely talking to you." Sir Duncan pivoted, guiding Kaiser in the opposite direction. Over his shoulder, he called, "And Kate was never in danger, you must know that. I adore her. *Ciao*!"

Tony returned to Wellegrave House only a few minutes before Kate arrived from Scotland Yard. He was in his study, pouring himself a large scotch, when she found him.

"Oh! What's the occasion?" She laughed. "Was an afternoon with our neighbors that brutal?"

"As I walked home, I ran into Sir Duncan."

She groaned. "This is getting out of hand. What did you say to him?"

"I threatened to kill him."

Kate seemed to absorb that. "Were you bluffing?"

"No."

"Then you'd better tell me."

"Yes. One other thing, though, before it escapes me." He closed the study door. "The night Hardwick died. You took pictures at the crime scene, didn't you?"

Kate nodded.

He put out his hand for her mobile. "Let me see them."

# CHAPTER 18

Kate put on her best professional smile when Patsy East opened her front door. As it was eleven o'clock at night, she wasn't surprised to find the woman in robe and carpet slippers.

"Good evening, Mrs. East. My name is Detective Sergeant Hetheridge." She held up her warrant card. "And this is my commander, Detective Chief Inspector Jackson."

"Oh. What's this? Is it about Granville Hardwick?" Patsy asked in a low voice, glancing over her shoulder. "You'll want to come back tomorrow. My husband's about to go to bed. He won't like being disturbed so late."

"Do you know what hour this is?" Declan's shrewish voice issued from the electronic call box beside the doorbell. Following the wire, Kate looked up into a corner mounted CCTV camera, from which Declan surely viewed her. "Patsy, I've told you not to open the door after seven o'clock. See who's calling on the security monitors. That's what they're for. Now shut the door in their faces. And as for you, Lady Hetheridge," Declan continued through the call box, "you should be ashamed of yourself, intruding on tax-paying citizens. Tomorrow I'll place a formal complaint to your superiors. I'll be citing your husband, too, who clearly abused his neighbors' trust under false pretenses."

Jackson made an angry noise. Kate shot him a warning look. She'd told him on the way to the Easts' that in the end, it always seemed to come down to this: a doorstep and a rude reception. If he wanted to take charge of the Toff Squad, even temporarily, his first task would be learning to take highhanded insults on the chin.

"Declan East, we're here to arrest you for the murder of Granville Hardwick," Kate announced into the camera. "If you think we've come in error, invite us inside and make your case. Otherwise, we'll pull you into the street and make a right royal show for all of Euston Place."

"Arrest Declan?" Patsy clutched her robe to her throat. "No, that can't be right. Someone else was arrested. Another man. Your husband told us he confessed."

"Haven't you ever heard of a false confession?" Jackson asked. "He was drunk. Confused. But forensic evidence and eyewitness testimony pointed us here."

"Patsy, shut the door in their face," Declan ordered via the call box.

"Arrest Declan?" Patsy repeated dully. She stepped aside to let Kate and Jackson over the threshold.

They followed her through the formal front parlor and into the living room. Seconds later, Declan marched in, bristling with anger. He wore a red silk smoking jacket over striped pajamas. On the breast of the jacket was a big, black D.

"I demand to know what evidence justifies this intrusion. And please be specific. London will be reading about it in tomorrow's newspapers."

"Shall we sit down?" Kate asked.

"No, we shall not. Go on. Present your evidence. Astonish me," he sneered.

Patsy backed out of the room, creeping toward the hall. Jackson moved to intercept her.

"Sorry, Mrs. East, this concerns you, too," Kate said. "You knew Granville Hardwick quite well, didn't you? In fact, you were having an affair with him."

"Yes," she said, eyeing Jackson warily. "But that was weeks ago. After it ended, my husband was generous enough to forgive me."

Kate turned to Declan. "Did your wife's affair end naturally? Or did you put a stop to it? We have footage of you on Hardwick's porch, sabotaging his security camera with a can of spray paint. Why? Were you about to say something outrageous? Threaten to murder him?"

"If I did, do you think I'd tell you? I believe in something called privacy," Declan said. "What I said and did is none of your business. And since Mr. Hardwick never reported the matter to the police, he clearly felt safe and secure thereafter."

"True," Kate said, smiling sweetly at Declan just to watch him tremble with rage. "And from what we gather, Mrs. East was a brief stepping stone between Hardwick's affairs with Fiona Leeds and Sunny Wainwright. No offense, Mrs. East, but you're a bit outside Hardwick's usual type. Only one of his ex-lovers reminds me of you, and her name is Georgette Sevrin."

"Proof! I said proof!" Declan cried. "So my wife is weak. Pathetic. She's still my wife, and I know my duty, heaven help us both."

"Georgette's good at playing weak and pathetic," Kate continued. "And you know what? It worked on Hardwick, at least for a time. He felt sorry for her. Is that how your affair with him started, Mrs. East? He was your neighbor. Did he see what you dealt with, day in and day out," Kate's eyes flicked to Declan, "and decide you needed a bit of fun?"

"Probably," Patsy mumbled, looking at the floor.

"But you loved him, didn't you?" Jackson asked. "Wanted to

make a go of it, I'll bet, and who can blame you? Maybe you had a few things in common. He was an art dealer. You're a shutterbug. Is this yours?" He pointed at the framed photo of a magnified orchid petal.

"Yes."

"Give him any of your photos as gifts?"

"No. Couldn't be sure he'd like it," Patsy said. "Didn't want him to laugh. He could be good to me, but Granville had a mean streak. Just like every other man in my life."

"God knows you drive us to it." Declan sounded bitter.

"As for the murder weapon," Kate continued. "It was a statuette. A replica of a sculpture by Giambologna called *Hercules Beating the Centaur Nessus*. We happen to know you own such a piece, Mr. East. Given to you by one of your publishers in recognition for your writing. Can you show us where it is?"

"Got rid of it." Declan lifted his chin. "Passed it on to the church for a jumble."

"Have a receipt?"

He made a contemptuous sound. "So that's your evidence? I once owned something similar to the murder weapon, and now that I can't prove I gave it away, I'm done? Ridiculous! Where's the forensic evidence he mentioned? Fingerprints? Hair strands? You don't have any, do you? You have nothing, nothing but a story *Bright Star* wouldn't take seriously."

"You're right, it started with a scenario," Kate said, wishing the man would become incensed enough to take a swing at her. Few things would have given her more pleasure in that moment than flattening Declan's pug nose. "In that scenario, Hardwick is seeing Sunny Wainwright, but he's not quite done with Mrs. East. Either that, or Mrs. East isn't quite done with him. Maybe she's stopping by that house you hate so much. Sending him letters. Bringing him gifts. That statuette, maybe? To some people, it would have seemed like the epitome of bad taste. To others, it would have looked perfect—a piece of serious art for a serious art lover.

"Then last Thursday," Kate told Declan, "Buck Wainwright sees Hardwick around three in the afternoon. He's pissed, loud, making a scene. At least one witness observes Buck leaving East Asia House, and Hardwick shouting at him from the front step. You see it, too, so you go over. Words are exchanged, tempers flare, and *bam*! Hardwick gets bashed over the head. You come home and rejoice when Buck returns to the scene, still more drunk than sober, and gets himself nicked for the murder you committed."

"I told you, utterly ridiculous. What about that nutter he lived with? Georgette?" Declan countered. "She never leaves the house. Wouldn't she have seen or heard all this?"

"As a matter of fact, she wouldn't have," Jackson said. "Her character, Georgette the Nutter, stays home all day, but the real Miss Sevrin goes where she pleases. That's the point behind the wig, the big glasses, and those poplin housedresses. When she looks like herself—short hair, no specs, nice clothes—she's an entirely different person. One who has no intention of remaining under house arrest while she waits for her ship to come in. Yesterday, when we rechecked all the neighborhood camera footage, we confirmed the real Georgette is out most days from noon till dark. And when my forensic team reexamined East Asia House, they found a window unlocked. Her fingerprints are all over it, inside and out. It's how she comes and goes when she's not in character."

"So Georgette wasn't home when Buck turned up," Kate said. "Or when the murder happened. She probably climbed back in through her window just minutes before Buck returned. She found Hardwick dead and panicked when Buck entered. So she put on her costume and got in the wardrobe. But she noticed some of her things were gone. She didn't have time to take inventory, but I think she was missing a wig, some specs, and a housedress. And when DCI Jackson's crew searches this house, they'll find those items hidden away, won't they?"

"You're babbling," Declan insisted. "I would never!"

Kate nodded. "You know what? I believe you. It *is* starting to sound like rubbish. Because in our scenario, you would have worn your wife's scarf and lavender coat to go to Hardwick's house, and you would have worn Georgette's wig and housedress to get home again. And a man so in love with his fantasy masculine ideal wouldn't do that, would he? You'd let yourself be arrested for murder before you'd spend five minutes in a dress."

Declan stared at Kate. Then slowly, with loathing, he looked at his wife. "What have you done?"

"He laughed at me," Patsy said, clutching the neck of her robe even tighter.

"Hardwick, you mean," Jackson said. "Why did he laugh? Because you used his row with Buck as an excuse to come over, see if he was all right? Or because you wouldn't accept he'd moved on to Sunny?"

"Both. He said he was tired of me calling. Writing. Trying to catch his eye on the street. He said I should bugger off and take that monstrosity with me. That's what he called the statuette. A monstrosity," Patsy quavered. "He said I wouldn't know art if it bit me on the arse. So I picked it up, and I hit him with it. Just once. But with everything I had."

"I don't believe it," Declan said.

"Blood was all over my coat," Patsy continued, still in that whispery voice, not looking at her husband. "I took it off and stuffed it up a chimney."

"We know. My boys found it this afternoon," Jackson said. "The blood matches Hardwick's. The hairs on the collar will match yours. And some of those unknown fingerprints on the murder weapon will be yours, no doubt."

"I had to get home," Patsy went on in that dull voice, still staring into space. "I knew about Georgette, how she played dress up, so I took some of her things. Couldn't risk the front door, not with Declan's security system, and our gate is blocked. Climbed over the fence and slipped in through the back."

"One more thing. At the crime scene," Kate said. "After you hid your coat and disguised yourself as Georgette. You took a memento, didn't you?"

"Yes. A picture of the blood spatter. Mobiles take such lovely images now. High quality, good as a proper camera. So I brought it home. Blew it up. Printed it off and hung it, just there." She pointed at the image Tony had recognized, the one Kate had snapped on the night of the murder, of four huge spots marring Hardwick's wall. Together, they were like a bouquet rendered in blood.

"My God." Declan was turning white. "Why did you do that?"

"Because it's the most beautiful thing I've ever seen." Patsy turned to her husband at last. "When you made me break it off with Granville, you asked me why I went to him. And I couldn't tell you. I didn't have the courage. Now I do," she said, voice rising. "Because you talk about being a man, and write about being a man, but you can't *be* a man, can you? He could. That's all He could."

Declan was speechless. After a few moments, he seemed to remember Kate and Jackson were still in the room. "I—I don't know what you mean."

"Yes, you do," Patsy said. "And if I had it do over again, I'd kill you, not him. That's where I went wrong. Both my men laughed at me. I just killed the wrong one for it." Crossing to where the framed photo of Hardwick's blood spatter hung, she removed it from the living room wall, clutching it to her chest. "I'm ready to go, detectives. And I'm taking this with me."

"You can handle the processing. It's your collar, really," Jackson told Kate as Patsy East was led to a waiting panda car.

"I was thinking I'd let you do the honors and go get Buck. I mean, it's late, and I could leave him in lockup till morning. But that doesn't seem fair, since he never belonged there in the first place," Kate said.

"No, I'll get him out. There's something I want to talk to him about."

She looked at Jackson curiously. "Buck? Why? I didn't think you ever spoke to him."

"I haven't. But I watched his interview. All that stuff about booking a flight to England while in a blackout. Touching down and looking for a pub. Sobering up not sure what he'd done, up to and including murder. We have something in common."

"Oh. Sure." Kate thought about her sister Maura, who reacted violently whenever anyone criticized her drinking. "Are you sure now's the best time?"

He laughed. "Don't worry, Hetheridge. I won't give him the hard sell. That never works, anyway. I'm just going to explain my credentials, so to speak, in the booze arena. And tell him what somebody once told me."

"What's that?"

"You don't have to live this way if you don't want to."

# EPILOGUE

S ix weeks after Patsy's arrest and Buck's release, Kate had fallen into a new routine at the Yard. Breakfast at home with Tony, Ritchie, and Henry, then a morning conference with Paul over coffee, usually in Pret A Manger. Neither of them had much desire to return to the canteen ever again.

As Scotland Yard's move from Broadway to Victoria Embankment loomed, many people were getting a touch sentimental about the old building. DCI Jackson's new assistant, Joy, was not among them.

"It's my only hope of getting him to release the hoard and start over," she told Kate and Paul that morning as they entered Jackson's office. "He starts sweating, and I do mean physically perspiring, when I suggest he throw out one little piece of paper."

"Believe me, I know," Paul said. "Mrs. Nibley-Tatters has carted in loads of junk. She's trying to do to Mum's house what she did to her own, hoard it up to the ceiling. If Mum doesn't find a way to get rid of her soon, I may never be able to move back in."

"Do you want to?" Kate asked. She had the impression Paul enjoyed the freedom and independence of his tiny bedsit, no matter how much he complained. "Besides, you owe that woman. Her testimony got you here. Not chasing cats but back on a murder case."

"True. Let's all give thanks for murder," Paul agreed, following her into Jackson's office.

Today was, apparently, a two-boxes-of-doughnuts kind of morning. Jackson had both types, powdered and filled, on his desk. He was eating his favorite, the powdered sort; Derek Saunderson was eating a jam one. He looked thrilled to be included on the murder team and energized by the presence of Assistant Commissioner Michael Deaver.

"If it isn't Frick and Frack," Jackson said as Kate and Paul entered. "Late again."

"Sorry, Chief."

"DS Hetheridge. DS Bhar," Deaver said in his heavy, fatalistic way. No one could ever guess from his demeanor if future events boded good or ill; his bearing could make a royal wedding seem like a funeral.

"AC Deaver," Kate and Paul said more or less together.

"You visited the crime scene yesterday?" Deaver asked.

"Yes, sir," Kate said. "DCI Jackson had a look as well."

"The dead woman. She's well-known."

Kate and Paul nodded.

"There is some concern," Deaver continued, "that the victim's family may not cooperate with Scotland Yard. That they may be more interested in maintaining their image than pursuing justice."

"Given what those bluebloods are worth—" Saunderson began. Jackson glared at him, and he silenced himself with another bite of doughnut.

"Therefore, I believe it's best to hire a consultant. This man is not beholden to Scotland Yard, but he has my full confidence. Grant him unimpeded access to your investigation." Deaver rose.

"Listen to his suggestions. Think carefully before disregarding them. I'll be watching this unit," he added, ostensibly to Jackson, but looking at Saunderson. "And I won't be the only one. That is all."

Saunderson groaned as soon as the office's outer door closed, signaling that the assistant commander was out of earshot. "Well, isn't that lovely? We have a babysitter, boys. And girl," he added, casting an eye toward Kate. "Someone to change your nappies. I guess that means top brass isn't sure you and Paulie are quite ready for prime time."

"I don't know," Jackson said, casting a lecherous eye on yet another powdered doughnut. "You weren't around when we arrested Mrs. East. That husband of hers was no treat. And he wasn't even real quality, just a wannabe with a big mouth. This will be a bigger hurdle, and I won't say no to a bit of help."

"Yeah, but what does 'unimpeded access' mean?" Saunderson continued. "I don't like the sound of that. Does it mean a desk? An office? The power to order me into work on a Sunday after-noon? All the rights and privileges, so to speak, yet no obligation to anyone up the food chain?"

"That sums it up nicely," said a familiar voice. Kate turned to see her husband standing in the doorway, as she'd known he soon would be.

"Hiya, Tony," Jackson said. "Doughnut?"

"Perhaps later." Taking the seat AC Deaver had so recently abandoned, Tony Hetheridge looked around the room, focusing on Paul.

"DS Bhar, I'd like you to start. Put me in the picture as to the victim and the circumstances under which her body was discovered."

"Excuse me, but I'm the senior officer," Saunderson said, buck teeth jutting. "If anyone's to start, Chief Super—"

"None of that. I'm not the Chief any longer."

"Then what do we call you?"

Tony smiled, and Kate felt a welling of love and pride. When he played this role, he played it perfectly; nobody did it better.

"Why, you can call me what you've always called me, DS Saunderson. 'My lord.' Or if you prefer, Lord Hetheridge."

## *THE END*

# FROM THE AUTHOR

Thank you so much for reading. And for waiting a bit longer than usual for this installment of my *Lord & Lady Hetheridge* series. It took me extra time to get it just right. If you enjoyed this book, please consider writing a brief review. It doesn't have to be long, and in this digital age, it serves as the crucial word-of-mouth that gets books read.

If you haven't tried my wartime series, the Dr Benjamin Bones Mysteries, take a look. There are two installments so far, plus a couple of novellas. As for the Hetheridges, never fear: I have every intention of continuing to write about them as long as I draw breath. So yes, you'll see them again soon in book #5, *Blue Blooded*.

Last but not least, if you like my work, please consider joining my mailing list. I promise never to give away or sell your email address, but only use it to alert you when I have a new release.

Cheers!
Emma Jameson

# MORE BOOKS BY EMMA JAMESON

Ice Blue (Lord & Lady Hetheridge #1)
Blue Murder (Lord & Lady Hetheridge #2)
Something Blue (Lord & Lady Hetheridge #3)
Deadly Trio: Three English Mysteries (Ice Blue, Blue Murder, Something Blue)
Marriage Can Be Murder (Dr. Benjamin Bones #1)
Divorce Can Be Deadly (Dr. Benjamin Bones #2)
Dr. Bones and the Christmas Wish (Magic of Cornwall #1)

# ACKNOWLEDGMENTS

The author would like to thank her expert early reader, Kate Aaron, for her help with countless small details. It is a truth universally acknowledged that no matter how many books you read on England, or how many times you turn to Google, there's no substitute for a conversation with a native. On a few occasions, I may have fictionalized or blurred a few truths for the sake of the story. In such places, the errors belong to me alone.

The author would also like to thank the following early readers: Shéa MacLeod, Alisa Tangredi, Tara West, and Mary Ellen Wofford. Thanks also to Theo Fenraven and Jenx Byron. I'm so grateful to you all!

Made in the USA
Monee, IL
24 January 2020